AN HOUR-GLASS TO ETERNITY

The two men who came to the island after
three days in an open boat claimed to have lost
their yacht on a coral reef; but this was untrue
and the ordeal of exposure had been deliberately
planned. They were men with a secret purpose,
and because they knew suspicious eyes would be
watching them they had to act their parts with
meticulous care. One entered into his rôle with
an amorous zest that worried his companion,
though in fact it would have been impossible for
either to avoid becoming involved in the lives of
the other members of this small Pacific community, where something evil was stirring below
the surface and so many tensions seeking an
outlet.

AN HOUR-GLASS
TO ETERNITY

MICHAEL HASTINGS

MACDONALD : LONDON

First published in 1959 by
Macdonald & Co., (Publishers) Ltd.
16 Maddox Street, W.1
Made and Printed in Great Britain by
Purnell and Sons, Ltd.
Paulton (Somerset) and London

For
MARGERY AND RICKY
of
Jack o' Lantern
Where the theme for this
story began to flicker

CONTENTS

PART ONE

PART TWO

PART ONE

THE FRINGE OF ORDEAL

It was our third day in the boat, and it threatened to be like yesterday and the day before. We'd rigged a rough sail and it hung as lifeless as a dead crow on a cornfield gallows. The sun was sheer hell, torturing the skin and drawing out sweat and more sweat.

I'd given up trying to work out whether progress was an illusion. The waves raised the dinghy listlessly and it slid wearily into the next watery valley; but the horizon never changed. It was an opaque, bluish ring which was a compromise between sea and sky. The only alteration was at night, when it darkened and closed in on us, merely to expand again with the dawn. We remained in the centre of an uncrossable circle, or so it seemed.

I looked at Keefe. He was taking a turn at steering, though very little was needed. He had the tiller held between his arm and his body and he was counting the cigarettes left in a packet. Unhurriedly, he extracted one and lit it. Then he glanced at me.

"You?" he invited.

I shook my head. "Mouth's too damned dry. And we're getting low on water. Many more hours of this and we're in for some real suffering. You certainly do things the hard way."

He smiled. "It's essential for everything to appear genuine," he reminded me.

"You needn't worry. In spite of your tan your skin's peeling and there are dull red patches, your eyes are sun-glare strained, and you've got a dirty black stubble over the lower half of your face. Anyone will believe you've lived in your clothes for at least a week. In brief, you look a lousy tramp." I passed a hand over my chin and it was worse than stroking coarse sandpaper. "You don't have to tell me—I look the same myself, except that the stubble's not so dark. But if only we'd started to grow beards while we were on board the *Stonechat* and had gone in for a bit of artistic faking, Lewis could have dropped us within a day's sail of the island. . . ."

Keefe shook his head. "This is too serious for taking chances. The *Stonechat* might have been sighted by the copra schooner. Then there's a character named Hooley who has a boat of sorts. Also, Milson owns a natty cabin cruiser. Quite apart from those risks, we couldn't have faked the strained appearance of two chaps who've come through a bit of an ordeal."

"We'll have a full-blown ordeal," I said gloomily, "if this calm persists and the water runs out."

"We'll manage," he said. He sounded very confident. "If the worst comes, we might try a bit of fishing. You cut a deep gash, wait a little—and then drink."

"A fish like that one?" I pointed to a dark triangle which created a miniature wake and then vanished. I'd been watching its regular appearances for about half an hour.

"Old man shark," Keefe said. "I don't agree with the widespread belief that he's a coward. It's intelligence to wait until your victim's too weak to resist. Does he worry you?"

"No. But I'd prefer the sea without him in it."

"Could amuse ourselves by trying to shoot him; but it would be bad tactics. It's astonishing how quickly a dead or wounded shark attracts his fellows. A certainty we'd finish up with two or more fins to watch. Anyway, it doesn't matter. We'll have the last laugh—he's wasting his time."

"I hope so."

"No need to worry," he said.

I'd yet to know Keefe. We'd only been together a matter of weeks. That covered the period of my unobtrusive arrival in Singapore, our first meeting in Charles Lewis's luxury bungalow at Katong, and our surreptitious departure in the *Stonechat* for a voyage which had terminated in the acute discomfort of this small boat. Long enough to have weighed up some men, but not Keefe. I hadn't, for example, taken the measure of his self-confidence, his apparent assurance that everything would work out as we wanted. On the one hand there was his record, so much as I knew, and there was his reasoning, hard and compact. But set against these I suspected a glint of mockery in his dark, restless eyes. And there was at times a touch of flamboyance which made me feel he was trying to live up to a romanticisation of himself.

I couldn't be certain though. Perhaps the fault lay with me, that I'd expected someone very different. I'd pictured him as Colonel Sutherland had presented him. That was back in London. The colonel, lean and ascetic, more like a literary don than a military man, had said: "You couldn't, I assure you, be going into this with a better man than Keefe. His reputation might be described as—er—formidable. He was —er—remarkably young for some of the special missions he was called upon to undertake during the war. There were —er—considerable misgivings on that count at first; he wouldn't have been considered but for the fact that we were so desperately short of the right material. Then as he consistently succeeded it became—er—inevitable to detail him for the seemingly impossible." He'd given his bleak smile and added: "So with the two of you on the job, Randall, I'm very sanguine about the outcome."

Colonel Sutherland was rarely lavish in his tributes, and to have doubts after this one smacked of heresy. But here I was, in a small boat with Keefe at the start of the undertaking, and I had my doubts. Keefe was very sure that everything would go according to plan; but I couldn't stifle a suspicion that he was just selling me the idea. I even wondered if he could be selling it to himself.

I sat baking in the merciless sun, watching him as he finished his cigarette. He smiled at me, and even the black stubble failed to detract from a sudden glimpse of youthfulness.

"I've heard that this chap Milson's made a lot of improvements. Gone all out on amenities. I hope he's included showers—and I'm not thinking of a big tin with holes in it." He laughed. "Getting soft."

"I could use one right now," I said. "I'd like to book it for about an hour. Talking of Milson, you've not got around yet to telling me what you know of him." I was putting it tactfully; he'd been evasive.

He didn't answer immediately. I sensed he was considering a problem, and when he spoke this was confirmed.

"My fault, Randall. Sorry." He had the sort of smile which compelled you, even against your judgment, to warm towards him. "I've been holding out on you rather. An instinct born of the war; no more to it than that. The less a chap knew, the less he could tell under persuasion. You see, I played a lone hand whenever possible. Anyone who assisted me did so in a very minor capacity and it was only common-sense caution to tell just what was essential and no more. You'll have to forgive me—working in partnership's a new experience."

"I understand," I said.

"Good man! Thanks. Well—Milson. You know he's in copra. Working for a company. The day of the individual planter's about over. He's on Main Island, the largest of the group, but actually supervises all the plantations. There's a schooner, captained by an ex-merchant-navy type named Lodge. She brings the copra in from the other islands. The company charters a steamer which calls at Main Island only, a more efficient method than trying to load a cargo from eight or nine small places with no facilities."

"And Milson himself? Are we taking these gruelling precautions because it always pays to be careful? Or is he a doubtful?"

Keefe considered for a minute. Then he said: "It's better for him to be convinced we're exactly what we appear to be, because that will give us a measure of cover. If we're all right with Milson nobody's going to question us much. So far as our information goes he's sound enough, but he's not the man to take into our confidence. He's no actor; moreover, he worries. He'd get stomach ulcers. A pity, because a man in his position could be very useful to us. For the rest, he's near enough to fifty to be anxious about holding down his job. And he's got wife trouble."

"She's with him on Main Island?"

"Currently—or so rumour has it. No knowing how long it will last. Periodically they make an attempt to keep the marriage going. For the sake of a daughter, I believe. That part of the report on him was sketchy, based on gossip, and queried."

"I don't see that it affects us much, anyway," I said. "If they're concerned about appearances they won't squabble while we're around."

Keefe gave a slow smile. "It's not quite that kind of trouble, apparently. The poor devil's very much in love with her and seems to be always ready to forgive and forget. She's said to be attractive and still craving for the real thing in passion. She's bored with him and the plantations."

I didn't like the sound of it. "That could mean we're going to find her something of a nuisance. If she's bored she's going to see two newcomers as something like a gift from the gods. The last thing we want is an amorously predatory woman trailing after us."

He smiled again. "Don't worry. We'll cope with it. Besides, there's always time for a bit of play."

I didn't like the sound of that either. Keefe wasn't at his most presentable now, of course; but even unshaven and in crumpled, grubby clothes he'd plenty in the way of looks. He was tall, broad in the shoulder, still narrow in the hips although he probably weighed a stone more than when he'd been at his best. His hair was very black and naturally crinkly. His dark eyes had a strange vitality. It wasn't hard to imagine a woman finding him overwhelmingly attractive. I hoped there wouldn't be that sort of complication. But I didn't say anything of this. Instead, I asked about Lodge.

"He's likely to be the danger, surely? If we're going to pose as two chaps with a thirst for adventure, who've tried to sail from Colombo to God-knows-where in the Pacific, we're going to invite plenty of questions. I know we've memorised the general story, right to the point when we struck the coral reef; but how's it going to stand up to probings from an interested expert?"

"No need to worry," said Keefe. "You'll understand when you see Lodge."

"Which suggests you've met him. Isn't that a risk?"

He shook his head. "It was a long time ago and I didn't have any talk with him. He was beyond intelligent conversation, sinking into alcoholic gloom."

"A soak," I said. "Surprising he's trusted with a schooner."

"I think that was an exceptional occasion. He drinks, of course, but not to the extent of risking his job. If Milson chucks him out he's finished. But it's the chip on his shoulder which will prevent him from subjecting us to searching questions. He's obsessed with his own ill-fortune. He's got no interest in anyone else or their troubles. A brooder."

"Sounds safe enough," I agreed. Secretly I wished that

Milson's wife could catch some of the lack of interest from him. It would make the future easier.

I shifted my position slightly. Much longer in the dinghy and I'd be developing sores.

Keefe said: "We might have some water. I've talked myself dry."

"The supply's dangerously low," I reminded him.

"We'll make landfall to-day," he promised. As usual he sounded confident and unworried.

Keefe was right. Shortly after noon I was at the tiller, keeping to the course he'd indicated. He was sleeping, lying so that he was in the maximum of shade, which was barely worth the effort of finding. It wasn't a sighting of land so much as becoming aware of it. There was a darker patch in the haze rim. At first I assumed it was some trick of the light. When it persisted, I imagined there was a low cloud and began to hope it might bring us a welcome shower. Drying out afterwards would be unpleasant, but how worth while if the stickiness had been washed from my body for even a short time.

Then the supposed cloud hardened at the top, its lower part remaining hazy. I used the binoculars and the black line was too substantial to be any form of cloud. I awakened Keefe, shaking his shoulder gently.

He was alert immediately, taking the binoculars from me as I pointed. He watched for a minute or so, then lowered them and smiled at me. It was a comment in itself.

"Twin peaks with a saddle between them and an isolated one to the south," he said. "Main Island."

"There's still plenty of sea to cross," I replied. "But don't think I'm carping. I take my hat off to your navigation."

"Done quite a bit of it at one time and another," he said casually. "But I won't deny there's often been an element of luck."

15

It seemed the luck was going to favour us again, for the sail suddenly produced a few feeble flaps like the first wing stirrings of a bird recovering from exhaustion. There was very little breeze, though, and it died away completely within the hour. By this time, even to the naked eye, there was unmistakably land ahead; not only the summit line of the island we'd first sighted, but others, seemingly lower, perhaps more distant. With the aid of the binoculars we could make out that the mountain peaks were comparatively bare and harshly ragged, the lower slopes having a dense coverage. The haze rim was well behind the island, but the shore line still appeared mist-blanketed.

"We'll be seeing them any time now," Keefe said. "As that means there's just a chance we'll be spotted, it'll be as well to ditch the extras."

It was a waste; but it wouldn't be compatible with our story to turn up well-provisioned, suggesting we'd had all the time in the world to load up the boat. We had a large net-like bag, and into this Keefe crammed the bulk of our food. He swung it over the side and the depths swallowed it at once. I wondered about the shark. I'd not seen his pointed fin for some time but he might still be following us. If so, he'd find the stuff we'd jettisoned mighty indigestible as the greater part of it was tinned.

Keefe had a small canvas bag, holding the various papers with which we'd been supplied. Those relating to the yawl that was supposed to have foundered on a coral reef were completely fictitious. Our own could best be described as part-genuine. The passports were recent, the photographs and personal details correct. It had been decided that we could safely use our rightful names. I hadn't been anywhere in South-East Asia or the Pacific before and Keefe, while he had operated on the mainland, had always done so under an assumed or a code name. The passport entries covering our separate and date-spaced journeys to Ceylon were false.

When Keefe had checked the papers he replaced them in the canvas bag. With them he put our automatics and clips of ammunition and on top of these he crammed the various personal items.

"This mustn't leave our possession," he said. "The way to avoid any slip-up is for one of us to take responsibility. Shall I?"

"Suits me," I told him.

He nodded. Then he looked critically at the limp sail and from that to the distant island.

"We still have to do it the hard way, as you describe it. If we're to get ashore before dark there must be more rowing sessions. The sooner the better, I suggest. Then we can take a few well-earned rests, rather than be forced into keeping it up without respite. Agree?"

"Couldn't agree more."

At first the exercise was welcome. I'd stiffened up during the past hours. But after a while the oars seemed to increase in weight and the consistency of the sea seemed to thicken. I was glad when Keefe announced a break. We shipped the oars and he went to the stern to take a spell at the tiller. I looked towards the island. It was disappointingly remote.

I said: "I think having a visible target is actually more disheartening. It emphasises how little we've achieved. When we rowed with nothing in sight it was possible to feel we'd covered quite a distance. But after this last lot it looks as though we've only progressed a few yards."

"We've done better than that," he encouraged. "Wisest thing is not to look so often. Sooner or later you'll have a pleasant surprise."

"My money's on later," I said.

And, indeed, it was much later when the island became clear enough for us to see the formidable volcanic summits, the bunched masses of vegetation covering the greater part of the slopes, and the narrow fringe of gleaming beach broken only by a huddle of roofs. Through the binoculars it was possible to distinguish a jetty and long, low storage sheds. There was a white building on higher ground beyond them, tucked away in the palms. And more distant, not standing out so clearly against the foliage, were the roofs of native houses.

I handed the glasses to Keefe.

"No schooner there," I said. "So Captain Lodge is presumably cruising round the islands. Just as well, perhaps, not to meet up with him immediately."

Keefe didn't speak for a minute or two. When he lowered the binoculars he was frowning.

"I can't see anything that looks like a cabin cruiser, either, though perhaps the distance is too great. I think I can make out some native canoes drawn up on a beach. There's no sign of Hooley's craft, which was a pearling lugger at one time, I believe."

"And is Hooley an ex-pearler?" I asked.

Keefe grinned. "Not guilty of holding out on you this time. There doesn't seem to be much known about Hooley except that his sort were common enough in the islands at one time. Most of them have died or been sent packing. Hooley may be useful to us, though. How useful we'll have to decide when we see him."

"Assuming we can find him."

"He'll find us, I expect. Probably try to attach himself like a leech."

"Which is going to offset any usefulness. He's unlikely to let us have the lugger excluding his services."

Keefe said quietly: "Under pressure of circumstances he can always be eliminated."

I stared at him. "You mean——"

"About time we took another turn at the oars," he said, smiling again.

And so the subject of Hooley was postponed.

I lost count of the number of spells we had at the oars.

Long before we reached the island we could hear the steady monotonous crashing of the waves on the reef. The sun began to dip and there was a perceptible relief from its full torment, but there was physical weariness which increased relentlessly. My protesting body sent pain messages vibrating through the nerve cells and I began to wish fervently that somebody on the island would see us. I watched hopefully for canoes, but none appeared. . . .

We were sighted eventually; but not until we'd nearly made the entrance to the small harbour. The sun was already touching down and the light was going fast. There were excited voices and the jetty became crowded with jostling, fuzzy-haired, dark-skinned figures. The chattering grew noisier as we pulled those last few exhausted strokes. Then, as we finally came alongside the jetty, we suddenly had an abundance of eager help which came near to sinking the boat beneath us and tearing the bedraggled clothes from our bodies.

Somehow, hauled and tugged and pushed, I found myself standing on the firm planking, with Keefe only a little distance from me. I called to him, but couldn't make myself heard over the tumult of voices. Neither could I reach him because of the human turbulence about us. It began to seem that we'd be stuck like this until all the excitement and curiosity had expended itself; but, unexpectedly, the crowd broke up in front of us and I was able to see a white man approaching. As the commotion died down I could hear his acidly impatient voice: "Stand back there! And stop kicking up such an infernal racket!"

Whether they had sufficient English to understand the words I don't know; but the meaning of his vigorous arm movements was unmistakable. The natives drew back on either side, making human walls into which a few straggling youngsters wriggled and disappeared.

There was still sufficient light to see that our rescuer had greying hair and a rather long, thin face. His neatly clipped grey moustache, his perfectly pressed white drill, made me very conscious of my own rough appearance.

He was a little breathless, either from excitement or from having hurried. He panted: "I'm Milson. Only just heard about you—or I'd have been along sooner. Where the devil have you come from?"

Keefe said: "Our yawl foundered on a coral reef three days ago."

"Three days! My God! You must be all in! It's no distance to my bungalow. Can you make it unaided?"

"We'll manage," Keefe said.

"That's fine." Milson sounded relieved. He pounced on one of the staring natives and gave swift instructions in a language I didn't understand. Then he turned to us again: "That's taken care of your boat."

We started along the jetty. My legs felt stiff and land had become a distinctly unfamiliar element. I found myself balancing in anticipation of the ground behaving as the boat had done. It wore off pretty quickly though. I glanced at Keefe and saw that one of the natives was trying to take the precious canvas bag from him. He held tightly to it and shook his head.

Milson noticed and said: "You can trust him. He's one of my men. Quite reliable."

"The yacht's papers and our own documents," Keefe explained. "I'd better hang on to them."

Milson shrugged his narrow shoulders. "As you wish." He spoke sharply to the native, who drew back.

We passed the storage sheds, which seemed to be the source of a rancid smell tainting the still, warm air. Drying copra, I assumed.

"So you've been three days in an open boat." Milson sounded impressed. "Glad I wasn't sharing the experience with you."

"It wasn't too grim," Keefe said. "Our water lasted until we sighted land. This, by the way, is Paul Randall. I'm John Keefe."

"Delighted to make your acquaintance," Milson said, the formal words sounding oddly old-fashioned. "Visitors are an event here. Judith—my wife—will be overjoyed. Annoyed at not having greeted you right away; but the news wasn't brought to the bungalow. I was told on my way from the office. I expect she'll have heard by now. News travels fast here." He paused and then said: "You weren't intending to visit this island?" And answered the question himself by adding: "Of course not. I should have been informed."

Keefe said: "Randall and I got bitten by the adventure bug. So many people have sailed half across the world at least, that Colombo to the South Seas didn't appear particularly formidable."

"Colombo!" Milson sounded awed.

Keefe laughed. "We're not completely disgraced. As a matter of fact we were managing quite well until we hit a reef which I'm prepared to swear was not marked on the chart."

"That's true of a number of them, especially those off the normal routes. You should hear Lodge on the subject."

"Lodge?" Keefe sounded mildly interested.

"He's skipper of our copra schooner. If you'd turned up a day earlier, like as not he'd have sighted you and shortened your ordeal. He left yesterday on a routine cruise, collecting from the smaller plantations on some of the other islands." He stopped and pointed. We'd passed the sheds and were on a path which led up a gentle, cleared slope to a large white bungalow, partially screened by tall, bushy shrubs. "That's my place. And I think I can see my wife. Yes—she's coming down the verandah steps."

There were two women, and as I was wondering about the second Milson said: "Oh, and my daughter's with her."

I glimpsed Keefe's momentary frown and thought I understood. Milson's daughter was likely to present more of a

21

problem than his wife. She might be very persistent about accompanying us when we started looking round the islands.

"So your daughter lives out here with you," Keefe said. It was half question.

"Not permanently. England being so far away, she's been educated in Australia. I've a married brother who emigrated there and who's now an accountant in Sydney. Pat's spent most of her school holidays with them. Now that—and college—is over she's staying with us for a while. Her future's rather a problem. My wife feels herself to have been deprived of a daughter over-long—in spite of frequent visits to Australia." He gave a short, exasperated grunt and might have said more, but evidently he judged there wouldn't be time.

The two women were very near us now. He called: "Unexpected visitors, darling."

"Unexpected and very welcome," Judith Milson replied. Then we were introduced and making apologies for our disreputable appearance and receiving sympathy. And I was trying to sort out my first impressions. Milson's wife must have been around forty, but didn't look her age and it wasn't just that the failing light was kind to her. Her figure may have owed something to carefully chosen foundation garments, but her slenderness seemed natural. It was no more than slenderness, she wasn't thin. Her arms were bare and were beautifully shaped. She was two or three inches shorter than her daughter. Her hair was dark, very dark. Her face was lively. She had splendid eyes, the whites clear and contrasting with the dark lashes and the dark, slightly arched brows above. Her husband at her side appeared dull and colourless.

Pat Milson resembled her mother to some extent but was taller, and her hair, seen under the lights in the bungalow, was less dark and had coppery glints. The curves of her body were a little richer. Her manner was quite different, though. True, these were first impressions, but it seemed to me she was more reserved, more cautious, as though suspending any decision on us.

Milson said: "You'll be glad of some decently prepared food."

"I'd be grateful for a shower and a chance of sprucing myself up first," I said. "I feel indescribably dirty."

"We're rather proud of our shower," Judith Milson said eagerly. "Not up to first-class hotel standards, but pretty good for the islands. At least, these islands." There was the faintest tinge of bitterness, the dash of angostura. But she continued: "Oliver can fix you up with some clothes." She turned to her husband. "Get Kim Lee on the job, darling."

Kim Lee, it transpired, was the company's store-keeper. Fortunately for us there was plenty of trading done as well as supplying plantation requirements. Kim Lee was a short, thick-set Chinaman, dressed with band-box neatness. The most noticeable items of his attire were his patent leather shoes and his gaudy silk tie. We learned later that he had a peculiar passion for ties, and it was rumoured he possessed so many he could wear a different one on each day of the year. It was true enough we never saw him in the same tie twice.

He bowed to us, peered solemnly through the thick lenses of his glasses, then smiled and murmured: "Can do." Either we were very lucky or he had an amazingly good eye for measurements, for the white drill and the shirts he produced were a reasonably good fit.

Milson fussed round us, placing all that we needed at our disposal. We became a little weary of him after a time and were glad when he said: "Very well, I'll leave you to it. Join us as soon as you're ready, but don't hurry unduly."

We didn't. The shower was something to be remembered. I felt as though my pores were absorbing all the moisture of which they'd been deprived. My tiredness and stiffness left me. When I emerged, towelling myself vigorously, Keefe was just finishing his shave. He turned his head as I laughed.

"What's funny?"

23

"Nothing much; but it just struck me how very ordinary our arrival was. The conversational part, I mean. I don't know what the natives were saying, of course, but between Milson and ourselves there was no evidence of excitement. We could have come a rather tedious journey by bus."

He chuckled. "The Stanley and Livingstone tradition! We don't easily escape our natural reserve, eh?" He turned back to the mirror, removed a bit more beard, and said: "What do you make of Milson?"

"I appreciate why he's not being taken into our confidence. Just as I think I can understand things not going smoothly between him and his wife. Put them together and he immediately appears remarkably dull."

"Dull and faithful," Keefe agreed. "Strange how often you can bracket those two. Suggests there's something adrift somewhere in the moralistic structure." He paused, razor poised. "I wonder what would have been the outcome if Woman had dispensed the moral code. Lilith instead of Moses as the law-giver. Not, mark you, that the conventional woman . . ." He broke off and began to hum softly.

"The conventional woman?" I prompted.

He didn't take it up. Instead, he said: "I didn't expect to find Milson's daughter here."

"She might create difficulties," I said. "She's reserved at the moment; but I can foresee some problems in diplomacy if she wants to take a cruise round the islands with us."

Keefe removed the last of the stubble. Then he turned and smiled. "May have to use shock tactics. Take her with us, but not so far she can't swim back to Mother."

I wasn't altogether certain he meant it lightly, so I said: "You can count me out of that sort of game."

He laughed. "Scared that if Mother heard about it she'd insist on coming for the next trip?"

"More to the point, I feel our mission and women don't mix. We'll have enough on our plate without piling up additional complications."

24

He didn't answer that. He finished at the wash-basin and said: "All clear for you."

I'd shaved and was dressed, giving my tie a final jerk, when I heard voices outside. I glanced immediately at Keefe. He understood and followed me to the slatted window. We stayed one at each side so that no shadows should be thrown. We listened.

The speakers were men and I recognised Milson's voice. He was annoyed and wasn't keeping it as low as he might have done. He'd probably forgotten we were in the guest room, though he'd made enough fuss about hoping that we wouldn't mind sharing because having his daughter at home had cut down the spare accommodation.

"I don't care a damn what you think," he was saying. "I'm not having you up here, Hooley. I've made that clear before."

"You've made it bloody clear." The voice was aggressive and had a thickness suggesting alcohol. "And it didn't matter a red cent to me. I don't want your lousy company. I keep away from you, you keep away from me—and that's fine. But these two chaps arrivin' makes a difference. I'm not standin' you goin' all high hat and drawin' bloody class lines along the beach. How we run things in private is one thing. But this is another. I'm entitled to my place as a white man. I'm not goin' to be written off as an outsider from the first word. I'm warnin' you, Milson, I mean to see these two chaps."

Milson said sharply: "I'm not taking warnings from you. If you'd been down on the jetty you could have met them. But you're not meeting them at my place. And that's final. You can see them to-morrow."

"After you've bloody well had every chance of tellin' 'em a pack of lies about me. Puttin' 'em against me before they've set eyes on me! Think I'm takin' that?"

"It's unlikely your name will even be mentioned. You're not a topic of conversation in my home, Hooley. Another thing, you're not deceiving me with your talk about social distinctions. You've heard—or guessed—enough about these two fellows to fancy you've an opportunity for chartering your lugger. That's all you want."

"What I want's my business," was the sulky, resentful reply.

"And you're not doing *your* business in *my* bungalow," Milson snapped. "That's final. Now are you going quietly or do I order my servants to throw you out?"

"Set Chink bastards on me, would you?"

Milson didn't answer.

There was a long pause, during which I imagined the clash of wills. Evidently Milson emerged the victor, because Hooley growled: "Very well. We'll have it the way you want it. But bear this in mind, Mr. Bloody Milson—you're not king of this goddam island. If you think you can push me around you've got some nasty surprises coming to you. One way and another you can run into plenty of trouble. Just chew over that."

Again Milson didn't answer. Keefe and I remained at the window a minute or so longer, but we heard no more. Then, as we moved away and crossed the room, Keefe said quietly: "I don't like it. It's a complication we could well do without." He was almost scowling.

"No hint of this in the reports you received?"

"Nothing," he confirmed. "I'd reckoned on making use of Hooley's lugger."

"No reason why we shouldn't. I agree, though, it's going to be a bit awkward, especially if Milson is stubborn about not having Hooley inside his bungalow. But there's one way we're likely to gain."

"What's that?"

"It's unlikely that Milson will allow his daughter to step aboard Hooley's lugger. So maybe we shan't be troubled that way."

"If Milson has any control over his daughter," Keefe murmured.

"He stood up to Hooley quite firmly."

"True. Is he as strong on the domestic front, though?"

"That's one I can't answer yet."

"I'll be very surprised if he has much say in things." Keefe paused at the mirror, regarded himself critically and added: "We'll probably have a better idea before the night's out. I don't think I'm far wrong, though."

Secretly I agreed with him, but I didn't say so.

Milson was alone in the main room of the bungalow when we joined him. It was a large room, serving as lounge and dining-room, with beaded curtains for partitioning as required. They were half-drawn at the moment. The furnishing was luxurious for this part of the world, contemporary in style, conveying the impression of having been transplanted from the colour pages of one of the more expensive magazines devoted to home-making. Milson was at a cocktail cabinet. He turned with a smile. There were no signs of ruffled aftermath from his encounter with Hooley.

"Always mix drinks myself," he said. "It's a habit from when I was first here and had only native boys. I found them unsatisfactory. Did most of my own cooking, as a matter of fact."

"Your wife wasn't with you?" I said.

"It wasn't much of a place for a woman. Judith didn't join me until this bungalow was ready, and by that time I'd acquired a Chinese staff."

"It's an attractive home," I said.

"You like it?" For a moment he looked pleased. "Selected most of the stuff myself. Judith put the finishing touches." He'd prepared gin slings and passed the glasses to us. "You'll appreciate something long and cool."

"This will be a memorable drink," Keefe said gaily.

Pat Milson joined us. Her father handed a glass to her. With a touch of irritation he demanded: "What's become of your mother?"

27

"Went to her room after asking me to do a spot of supervision in the kitchen. Shall I give her a call?"

He looked frowningly at his watch. "No. She knows the time. Can't expect us to wait for her." He didn't speak like a man supposed to be very much in love with his wife. I said: "We don't mind waiting. Don't on our account——"

"We'll drink," he said, "to your safe landing."

"Here's thanking you for your hospitable reception," Keefe said.

"Only too delighted to have visitors. We see very few. There's the doctor. For some reason the authorities put his small hospital on the far side of the island. Comes across fairly regularly. Then there's Swale, on Okama."

Pat Milson raised her eyebrows, looked upwards, and took a deep breath.

"Swale's not too bad, Pat," her father protested. To us he explained: "He's a missionary."

"An island hot-gospeller," the girl said. "He doesn't have a church; doesn't seem to belong to any particular denomination, anyway. He goes from village to village holding open-air meetings. Lots of singing and hand-clapping. God's own showman."

"My daughter's a bit hard on him," Milson said. "He's sincere and I think he does some good. He certainly——" He broke off, turning his head sharply. His face registered surprise, followed by disapproval and annoyance. At least, that's how I interpreted the variations of expression. So I turned—and saw Judith Milson.

The reason for her delayed arrival was obvious. She'd changed her dress. It was a significant change, too, I felt, because she'd selected one which challenged the island background. It emphasised that she didn't belong there, that she was of a different and more sophisticated world. And the sparkle in her splendid eyes was not without a certain defiance.

As she came forward I mentally withdrew my reservation

28

about foundation garments. She had no need of them. The filmy black material of the gown concealed very little.

"Apologies for keeping you waiting," she said.

"We haven't waited," Milson said. He didn't raise his voice, but it was harsh.

"I'm so glad." Very deliberately, she smiled. "I could use a long drink myself. Give me one, darling."

For an instant I actually thought he'd refuse. They were looking at each other and the clash of wills was evident. Then he turned to the cocktail cabinet. He gave a jerk of his shoulders which could have been exasperation, but it was wasted. Her smile was more natural now and she was directing it at Keefe.

I left the telling of our story to Keefe. This was after we'd dined and were relaxing in comfortable chairs. A time or two he appealed to me to confirm something or other, and once he said: "Randall can tell you what happened next." I took over, as he wished, but as soon as I could I threw the narrative back at him. I was more interested in noting reactions. I felt sure Milson was accepting us at face value. I didn't know about his daughter. There was a reserve in her manner which I'd yet to understand. Her mind might well be preoccupied. I sensed that she disapproved of her mother's present behaviour.

Judith Milson had indicated where we should sit and had so placed herself that Keefe inevitably looked at her. She'd been clever about the lighting. There was electricity in the bungalow and the bulbs were pleasantly shaded, cutting out any harsh illumination. It was soft on her uncovered shoulders. The upper curves of her breasts were exposed by the low-cut gown, and the shadow between them was soft also. She appeared to be listening intently, but I suspected her interest was less in what Keefe was saying than in the man himself. What I didn't like was the way he appeared to be talking to her rather than to anyone else, and something reciprocative in his manner.

29

At last he finished with, "That's the lot, I think."

"Not everything," she said. "What do you do next?"

Milson cut in rather crisply: "All very interesting. Quite an ordeal."

"It could have been had it gone on much longer," Keefe said. "Supplies were getting low—particularly water. However, it's over now." He turned back to Judith Milson. "We're not sure what we do next."

"You've had no time to consider the future." Milson frowned at his wife as though rebuking her for having asked the question. Then, somewhat illogically, he continued: "I take it the misadventure will at least postpone your project. You'll need to find another boat and provision her. Or will the whole thing be cancelled? There are, naturally, considerations of time and money."

Keefe was non-committal. "As you say, we've not had time to think about it. While we were in the open boat we were pretty well obsessed with the prospects of survival. We weren't optimistic enough to look beyond that."

Milson stroked his chin. "You can't pick up a new craft here. You can get passage to Australia in the company's ship; but she's not due for some time. About four months. There's a small steamship that visits the islands from time to time. Skippered by a man named Lacoste. So far as I know, he's the owner, too." There was an expression of disapproval on his face. "He's a trader and he comes to the store on Okama, which is the second largest island in the group. I can find out from Chang Yu—he's the trader on Okama—when he's expecting Lacoste." He leaned back in his chair. "Apart from those two ships there's nothing."

Keefe smiled. "Then that seems to decide our immediate future." He glanced at me. "Well, we wanted to look around some Pacific islands. We hadn't this group in mind, but chance has made the choice for us. Don't you agree?"

I nodded.

Keefe turned to Milson again. "Any hope of hiring a boat of sorts?"

Milson hesitated. Then he said: "I've a cabin cruiser which I use when I'm visiting the plantations. She's being repainted at the moment; but I'm due to make my routine calls in about a fortnight. You're very welcome if you'd care to accompany me. The disadvantage is that I have to work to a tight time-schedule and there won't be much opportunity for sight-seeing. On Okama, for example, which has some wonderful scenery in its wild interior, we've only two small plantations and my stay's only a matter of hours."

Keefe said: "Thanks for the offer, anyway. We would, of course, like to see as much as possible; but we'll have to be limited to what the circumstances offer."

Pat Milson interjected: "What about that man Hooley's lugger, Dad? Couldn't it be chartered?"

The suggestion wasn't well received. Milson gave his daughter an acid glance, but obviously couldn't ignore what she'd said. "There is a lugger," he confirmed reluctantly. "You might be able to charter it." After a pause he went on: "I can't offer to arrange anything for you. The fact is, I have nothing to do with Hooley. On the face of it it seems wrong to ostracise a fellow white man, but Hooley's a drink-sodden scoundrel. Fifty years ago there must have been plenty of his kind knocking around the islands of the Pacific. Fortunately, there aren't so very many of them now." He frowned. "I wish I could be rid of him, but there's nothing I can do. My company doesn't own the islands. I've had it out with Trubshaw more than once. He's an assistant district officer and does a duty tour every three or four months. He says he can't step in unless Hooley commits some crime. The difficulty is that Hooley's not a down-and-out. He owns this old lugger and also a small bungalow with a patch of land on the other side of the native village. He has property on Okama, too. Either he has some money salted away or he's got a hold on Chang Yu. He never does any work, so far as anyone can tell, but he's certainly not destitute." He paused again. "Hire the lugger, if you're set on it. But I strongly advise you not to trust Hooley. I've no legal proof but I'm convinced he's as crooked as they come. My private opinion is that if Trubshaw bestirred himself he could dig up enough to get the chap deported. Trubshaw's pleasant enough, but he carries the sleeping-dogs policy too far."

I wondered if we'd heard the whole truth of the matter. My guess was that Milson's strong dislike of Hooley had a firm, although hidden, basis.

Keefe was saying: "There's another possibility. You've given me the impression that for the sightseer Okama's the island." He looked questioningly at Milson, who nodded and said: "It's the largest of those that can be regarded as not commercially developed. All the islands are volcanic, which means a certain amount of wild and rugged scenery in the interior; but where there are sizeable plantations the scene's changed considerably. Land cleared for the planting of new groves, rough roads made, and villages cleaned up. If you really want a glimpse of the islands as they've been before development, Okama can give it you."

"Is there anywhere to stay?" Keefe asked. "I'm not expecting a hotel—but could the trader you speak of provide us with accommodation of sorts if we move over there?"

Judith Milson intervened swiftly. "We wouldn't hear of such a thing. You could rough it over on Okama for a few days. But you'll make this your headquarters. Life's uneventful, and we're certainly not going to lose any guests without a struggle." She directed a look at her husband. I wasn't sure whether it was challenging or demanding his support.

He said: "That will be the way to do it. And as soon as the launch is in commission again I can take you across to Okama."

Before Keefe could say anything Judith Milson exclaimed:

"I think that's a splendid idea, Oliver! We could all go. I've not been in the launch for ages."

"Yes, we could arrange that," her husband said. He didn't sound enthusiastic.

"It's a grand scheme," Keefe said. "But are you sure it won't be inconveniencing you, Milson?"

Again it was Milson's wife who interjected: "Of course it won't inconvenience him. He works much too hard and a little time off's long overdue."

Milson said: "We'll go into details later. The boat's not available yet."

I felt that he was regretting having put forward the suggestion. But what concerned me more was Keefe's falling in with it so readily. It was essential we should have freedom of movement, and this plan wasn't going to help us much. But there was no opportunity for discussing this with him until we'd retired for the night.

When he was lying on his bed, smoking a cigarette and with the filmy mosquito netting still raised on one side, I pulled a chair near and said in a low voice: "We don't want a passage to Okama and back—we want to be free to go *any* place and at a time to suit ourselves."

"True enough," he said calmly.

"But you agreed to Milson's suggestion."

He smiled at me. "We'll be free enough to pry around on Okama, which will be a start."

"I doubt if the answer's on Okama," I said.

"Agreed. No harm in making sure, though. But you're overlooking things, Randall. We keep in with the Milsons, which is important for the moment. We establish ourselves, under his patronage as it were, as potterers. If we've pottered openly around Okama we're not going to be regarded with such suspicion if we're unlucky enough to be discovered pottering around on another island. Right?"

"Fair enough," I conceded. "But there is the item of a boat. By falling in with Milson's suggestion I think we've made it difficult to go to Hooley without it looking a bit queer."

"It may not be so difficult. Hooley will approach us, of course. From what we overheard, we know he's eager. I can't think of any reason, other than a desire that we should charter his boat. Now then—as there's some antagonism between Milson and Hooley, I think we can bank on Hooley keeping his mouth shut for at least as long as he believes he's putting one across Milson. Right?"

"Sounds reasonable to me," I said. "But if we push off to Okama, what then?"

"Hooley can reach Okama more easily than we can, thanks to his lugger. He doesn't have to wait for anyone. So we can meet him there by arrangement. If he's not been able to contact us before we leave here, I think it's a safe bet he'll turn up on Okama."

I nodded. Some of the annoyance I'd felt towards Keefe evaporated. I'd misjudged him in thinking that his interest in Judith Milson was obliterating all else. There was more proof that little was escaping him when he continued: "I don't get the answer to a discrepancy. Milson takes it for granted that Hooley hopes we'll charter his lugger—yet he emphasises that Hooley doesn't want to work and doesn't need to work." He blew a smoke ring. "I'd like to know what Milson's really got against Hooley." He smiled. "But we're more likely to find out what Hooley's got against Milson. We'll hear that, for certain."

My thoughts went off at a tangent. "You noted that Milson mentioned Lacoste."

"Yes. Natural enough that he should. It's early to express opinions, but I doubt if he sees Lacoste as anything other than the owner-skipper of a small trading steamer."

"Somebody knows different," I said. "I kept wondering while Milson was telling us of various people. Asking myself which one."

Keefe reached out lazily and flicked ash from his cigarette.

"Milson himself unlikely. Nothing suspicious on him in the report; though that's not conclusive. But we have Hooley, the Reverend Swale, and Dr. Porter."

"And Chang Yu, the trader on Okama," I added.

"Doing business with Lacoste, no doubt. I think the contract's too open for there to be anything deeper in it."

"What about double bluff?" I reminded him. "Personally, I'd regard Chang Yu as—in racing terms—the best outsider."

"I'm not going to quarrel with that," Keefe said. "We'll certainly look him up when we get to Okama."

"You didn't get a report on him?"

"No. He wasn't mentioned. Actually, the information I received was rather sketchy. Can't blame the man who compiled it. He didn't have much in the way of opportunity. He visited the islands with that assistant district officer Milson mentioned. Trubshaw. Ostensibly, he was fact-finding, collecting odds and ends for inclusion in the Administration's Annual Report. The odd interest paragraph to make the statistics a little more palatable. He had to fit in with Trubshaw's programme and only spent six days here. So we can't think of his stuff as presenting more than a general picture. It certainly doesn't answer our questions for us. We'll have to find out the lot." He yawned. "There's no desperate rush. The first thing is to get ourselves accepted by everybody as a couple of amateur voyagers who've suffered shipwreck. We've made a good enough start." He yawned again and said sleepily: "Shall I leave the light to you?"

"Yes," I said.

He pulled down the netting, turned over, grunted something and appeared to be asleep within a few minutes.

I wasn't able to follow his example. I was still feeling the effects of the boat journey, and it was a relief to stretch out on a comfortable bed; but my mind was far from being drugged by tiredness. I looked through the film of netting to the bright moonlight and my thoughts settled on our mission. Somewhere on these islands, or so we believed,

Sergius Kabanov was in hiding, and we had to find him. Kabanov was not so Russian as he sounded. He'd been born in Shanghai. His father was a White Russian émigré and his mother a Chinese who was euphemistically described as a hostess in a place of entertainment. Kabanov the elder, by all accounts, had existed in a state of nostalgic gloom alternating with periods of boisterous and feckless enjoyment on the rare occasions when he happened to be in funds. His marriage had arisen out of one of these. He quickly tired of his Chinese wife and within a few years died of ennui or drink, or a mixture of both. She returned to her old form of life, though on a lower plane. Eventually she died. There were no details, but it wasn't difficult to imagine the pattern of her last few years.

It was natural that Sergius Kabanov, the Eurasian, should have a weighty chip on his shoulder, the corroding hatred of the poverty-bound for all those able to live luxuriously. Natural, too, that he should turn some of this hatred against the memory of his unhappily inept father. Nothing was known of his childhood. The first reliable information about him was that as a youth he'd joined a band of hooligan-type criminals operating near the dock area. Later, he seemed to have abandoned crime for political agitation. He had certain mental faculties, in that he was quick at languages and had somehow learnt to read and write.

Details of his career were sketchy. He fought against the Japanese in the ranks of the Eighth Route Army, which was a temporary reorganisation of the Red Army of China. Later still he worked for the new regime in China and had some semi-political position. Eventually he turned up in Moscow. And that was why I'd been the one selected to join Keefe on this present mission. Quite by chance I'd seen Sergius Kabanov in Moscow. He was still comparatively obscure and no one was particularly interested in him. Since then he'd become important but always as a person behind the scenes. His journeyings were furtive. He was the shadowy figure in

36

the back of a darkened car; the unnamed, heavily-wrapped passenger in the specially chartered aircraft. There were no available photographs of him. The forces of publicity were used in reverse, ensuring that people never heard of him.

Slowly and patiently our people had penetrated the secrecy. It was known that he was operating somewhere in these islands. Known, too, that Lacoste was a member of his organisation. On paper, Lacoste owned his ship, which had the offensive name of *La Garce*, and so he was free to voyage at large, covering the coasts of South-East Asia and ranging into the Pacific. Here and there, unobtrusively, he took on additional new crew. Young men, specially selected. When they returned to their home ports, after an absence of several months, they'd received intensive training fitting them for their rôles as members of the hard core of the various nationalistic movements. They had become experts in terrorism. And the man who'd supervised their training was Kabanov.

I recalled my first serious talk with Keefe, in Charles Lewis's bungalow.

"It's going to be our job to find his Academy for Cut-throats and close it down. A tough assignment, because he'll not only be well hidden but well protected. Sure to be an instructor or two as well as a batch of virile young students. You'll be able to recognise Kabanov?"

I nodded: "I think so."

"I hope you can," Keefe had said quietly. "I want to be sure of killing the right man."

2

TO WALK IN DANGER

Milson took us to his office early the next morning. We went to the small jetty first and saw that our dinghy was properly secured. Milson stared down at it and said: "Three days in that. My God!"

I looked out towards the wide gap in the reef and the immensity of the sea beyond, and felt that he'd some reason for being so impressed.

"It's the seaworthiness of the craft," said Keefe. "Not her size."

"Plus skill in handling her," Milson said. "I'll stick to my cabin cruiser. Nothing smaller or unpowered for me. But I'm no seaman, I confess to that."

He showed us the launch. She was drawn up on a slipway near the storage sheds and was beginning to gleam with new paintwork. Against this the black fuzzy hair and dark skins of the native boys working on her were strongly emphasised. All of them were stocky in build. Their only garments were brief shorts, but near to them were some vivid American-style shirts.

"Good workers," Keefe said.

"Not bad," Milson agreed. "At least we're spared labour troubles here." His tone suggested there were plenty of other problems.

The plantation offices, two long white-painted huts, were on higher ground behind the storage sheds. There was an open space where coconut cutters were slicing the flesh from the shells. Both men and women were doing this work and my attention was immediately attracted by a veritable giantess. She wore a gay print dress, pulled up high so that her massive thighs were exposed. The muscles on her great arm rippled as she used the long heavy knife. The bosom of her dress billowed out almost to bursting point. Her face was negroid, her hair hidden under a gaudy turban. She gave us a broad grin and her strong teeth were wonderfully white.

Milson surprised me with a lapse from his rather prim manner. "That's Big Bertha," he said. "The despair of Pastor Swale. Any man can have her, provided he's able to take her in a wrestling hold and throw her on her back. It's risky. We've had no end of dejected suitors with sprains and bruises. A broken-arm case once." He continued with a curious blend of amusement and distaste: "Hooley tricked her. Put her down in two seconds with a judo throw. Gave her the shock of her life, because Hooley's not particularly big or powerful. She was mystified, but in the end she worked it out that 'strong devil-devil belong 'im fella' and she's been in awe of Hooley ever since."

We entered Milson's office. It was austere and comfortless, the only real concession to bodily ease being a great three-bladed fan rotating overhead. He flung off his jacket and took his place at a table littered with papers.

"I suppose in the old days," he said complainingly, "a planter was a man who looked after a plantation. Now he's a poor devil who spends most of his time filling up returns. God knows what head office does with 'em all."

In the next room a typewriter was being tapped spasmodically, with little rushes of speed.

Keefe nodded in that direction and asked: "How do you manage for office staff?"

"I've one islander who shows some promise. He's performing now. All the other clerks are Chinese. Kim Lee shipped them over. I think they're his poor relations. They and their womenfolk form the major part of an isolated community living just beyond the storage sheds." He reached for some papers. Then glanced up to say: "The map on that wall may interest you."

It was a large-scale map, and Keefe and I studied it carefully. The islands formed a rough arc, the lines of a partly sunken volcanic range. Main Island was at the northwestern tip. The second largest was about halfway down and was Okama. From the contours we could see that all the islands were lofty in proportion to their size, the peaks some six or seven thousand feet. Most of them had a single peak, but on Okama there were two, while Main Island had three.

Keefe turned from the map. "I take it the red patches are plantations. I notice they're numbered."

"That's right," Milson confirmed, not looking up from the papers he was frowningly studying.

Most of the red patches were on Main Island. Two small ones were on Okama. Three islands were without any colouring.

"And the blue?" Keefe persisted.

Milson gave us his full attention for a moment. "What we call black soil areas. They're covered in kunai grass. For some reason no trees will grow in that soil." He lowered his head. Then he grunted in irritation. "Damnation! This won't do. The trouble I have with these blasted reports!"

"We're no help—only a hindrance," I said. "Thanks for letting us take a look at the map."

"You're welcome," he said. It sounded perfunctory.

As we moved towards the door he checked us by saying: "Oh, there's one thing." He hesitated, and it was evident he didn't want to speak loudly. When we reached the table he said: "About Hooley. I expect you saw I wasn't enthusiastic over the suggestion that you might arrange something with regard to his lugger."

"It doesn't seem to be here, anyway," Keefe said.

"It's about two miles down the coast. There's a small inlet reached by a break in the reef. Just out of sight from here.

She's sure to be there. Hooley has a bungalow on the far side of the inlet."

"And so——" Keefe looked at him questioningly.

Milson scowled. "You'll understand better when you've seen the man, which I'm afraid is inevitable. It's no concern of mine whether you do any deal with him, once I've warned you he's not to be trusted. But if anything does develop it will provide him with an excuse for coming to the bungalow to see you about one thing or another. I don't like the idea of that. I've Judith and Pat to consider—particularly Pat."

I nodded. "Understandable, after the story you told of Hooley and that Big Bertha woman."

"There's more to it," Milson said. "Unnecessary to go into details. Sufficient that Hooley dislikes me intensely. If he could harm me or cause me acute distress, he'd do it like a shot. That's why I have to be vigilant and why I can't tolerate him at the bungalow."

Keefe said: "He'll get no encouragement that way from us, I assure you."

"Thanks. And what I said about not trusting Hooley goes for his crew, also. In particular the bosun, a half-caste named Jimmy Prak. He's a cut-throat, no more or less."

"Thanks to you for the warnings," Keefe said.

We left him at this and strolled back to the bungalow, where we found Judith Milson on the verandah. She greeted us gaily.

"So Oliver didn't keep you long! I didn't think he would. I hope he wasn't downright rude. He never means to be, but as soon as he's within reach of work he forgets everything— and everyone—else."

"There were complications over some report," I said.

"There always are," she said. She still smiled; but there was a trace of bitterness, or resentment. I wasn't sure which.

"If I were in his shoes," Keefe said, "the plantation business would undoubtedly be neglected." The way he was looking at her added significance to his words.

Judith not only understood but responded. "So I imagine." She spoke slowly, her voice low-pitched.

I felt uneasy. I didn't like the way things were developing. There seemed an irresponsible streak in Keefe. Perhaps the long sequence of successes had made him careless; perhaps he'd always worked hard and played hard, mixing the two according to his fancy. I didn't know him well enough to be sure. My own feelings were clear cut. Sergius Kabanov was on the islands. It was our job to hunt him down. Until we had achieved this I was strongly against any side-tracking. Afterwards Keefe could do what the hell he liked. But not now.

They were still looking at each other, talking with their eyes. I thought coarsely that he wouldn't find it necessary to throw *her* down on her back as a preliminary.

Perhaps something of my disapproval communicated itself, for she suddenly turned in my direction and said: "You must see that Oliver and I are badly matched. It's not easy to conceal such things in this part of the world, where there are no distractions. Once the setting has palled—what's left?"

"There's not much wrong with the setting," Keefe murmured. "The long beach and the sea."

"But it has to be a setting for something," she said, and bitterness was really in her voice now. Momentarily she hesitated; then went on quickly: "You see, at the start Oliver was full of enthusiasm. Going to put in a lot of hard work, build up the plantations, and get rich quickly. It's the getting rich part that hasn't come off. I've no head for business so I can't give you details, but there were other projects which the company has abandoned for one reason or another. And the area under cultivation isn't as big as was intended. On this island, for example, ground was scheduled for coconuts; but the truth is you can't grow a tree. There's something wrong with the soil. All that will grow is a spiky grass. Somebody didn't realise it." She spread out her hands. "Other things have gone wrong, with nobody in particular to blame. But Oliver blames himself, in a secret sort of way. It's made him devote himself more and more to his work, and he's become less and less the man he was." She shook her head. "I don't think there's a thing anyone can do about it. I admit I've failed." Suddenly she stopped and demanded: "Why am I telling you this?"

"Because you've had it bottled up for too long," Keefe said. "A natural reaction. You need a break." His smile suggested the opportunity was here.

"What shall we do?" she asked. "A swim? You'll find that unless you're somewhere up in the mountains your body feels sticky from early morning until sunset."

"Jolly good plan," Keefe said. "But—unless you have advanced ideas here—you'll have to provide trunks for us. Or do we send for Kim Lee?"

"No need to trouble him."

She hurried away, her steps brisk and eager. I wondered whether to make some attempt at stressing caution; but Keefe deprived me of the chance. He said: "That map in Milson's office is interesting. I think we can rule out the islands where plantations preponderate."

"Which leaves us Okama—and three small islands."

"Did you notice anything about the one immediately beyond Okama?"

"Not much in the way of beach, and a relatively high proportion of jungle. Oh—and a number of mountain ridges that could be bare rock."

"Good man," Keefe said. "But there's something else. The reef continues right from Okama to the tip of the island. That should help a smooth crossing for a small boat."

"Are you thinking *we* might reach it that way? Or that there's probably a secret ferry service?"

Keefe grinned broadly. "You're quick, Randall. Actually, I'd both in mind."

"If there is a ferry service," I said, "Chang Yu won't be in ignorance of it."

43

He nodded. "Yes, I think you've got something there. He becomes a bit more than a likely outsider, doesn't he?"

"I've got supplies in mind. It's possible Lacoste lands everything that's needed, but there'd be the risk of discovery if he lies for some time off an island. Always a chance of being spotted by the plantation schooner, or Milson's launch. Much safer to unload everything more or less openly at the jetty on Okama, leaving somebody else to do the small-scale deliveries. And who more likely than Chang Yu?"

"Which sounds reasonable. If it's right, though, it follows that Chang Yu is going to be extremely suspicious of strangers. We have to be perfect in our parts, old chap. Quite a lot may hinge on it if we're not to disappear as completely as our boat's supposed to have done." He broke off, listening. There were quick steps, lively feminine voices, and then Judith Milson and her daughter appeared.

On our way to the beach we had a closer look at the native village. The houses were atap-thatched and on traditional lines. "Though much cleaner and more sanitary than the homes of their ancestors," Judith Milson said. She told us that at the back of the village and slightly higher up the mountain slopes there were other buildings which had been put up by the company. These were long and barrack-like, housing plantation workers who had been recruited from more populous islands.

In the centre of the village was one large building, not unlike an outsize park shelter of thatched roof pattern, except that it appeared to be mostly roof. This, we were informed, was the village meeting house. Pat Milson added: "Pastor Swale's far from certain that everything going on there is Christian; but he's had the sense, so far, not to interfere."

We didn't actually pass through the village. We saw it through a gap in the palms, a gap forming a broad avenue down to the beach. We crossed over this and went for some distance along a fairly well-defined walk which brought us eventually to a shallow crescent of gleaming sand. Palms growing almost to the water's edge at the points of the crescent enclosed it, while those at the back, growing more thickly, gave an impression of privacy.

"Perfect!" I exclaimed.

"Practically our private beach," Pat Milson said. "All the natives keep away from it. They seem to have a natural delicacy, at least in some directions." Then she laughed. "Perhaps I give them too much credit. It could be they don't consider us in the least attractive."

Keefe said: "I promise we'll be more appreciative."

She didn't answer him, and I saw the cautious expression was back in her eyes.

There were no rocks on the beach to give cover; but it wasn't needed. The two women had only to slip out of their dresses and kick off light sandals. Judith Milson had a minimum of concealment in the two close-fitting pieces of a bikini. She donned a bathing cap as she ran to the water, turning back to call to us: "Don't be long—or we'll come back and drag you in."

Keefe stood watching for a minute. When he turned to me his eyes were twinkling. "I congratulate myself, I really do, on having thought up this particular rôle. I'd no idea it would work out so well. The kind of chap who sails across the Indian Ocean for fun is practically certain to appreciate other sorts of fun." He looked towards the sea again. "You must agree the right material's here."

"I'm not so sure," I said doubtfully. "You could be getting a bit involved with Milson's wife—and that's certain to lead to complications."

He stared at me. Then he laughed. "But it's perfect, old chap! Milson's let his job swallow him up. Anyone can see he'll never hold his wife; she's the wrong type for him. Well —if we work things right and she comes with us to Okama we're going to have the finest screen possible. Chang Yu, Hooley, any others who matter, are all going to be so busy having a quiet chuckle at Milson's expense that they'll forget to probe after any deeper significance in our movements."

There was something in what he said, of course; but I still didn't like it. There wasn't anything I could do about it, though. It was primarily his show.

He said: "Come on—don't look so solemn. You should thank me for being unselfish in the interests of the cause. I'm leaving the more attractive one to you. She's younger and has an even better figure, though she tends to keep a trifle more of it covered."

"She's the reserved type, too," I said. "You'll have to go carefully, Keefe. She doesn't miss much."

"Then I'll rely on you to keep her attention distracted," he replied cheerfully.

We stripped off our clothes and pulled on the trunks Judith Milson had produced for us. I noticed that she'd remained in shallow water and, unlike her daughter, didn't keep her back scrupulously turned on us. Once or twice she waved impatiently.

There was no chill shock as we plunged into the water and I struck out towards Pat Milson's bobbing head. As I drew level with her she called: "Race you to the reef!"

As an above-average swimmer I started confident of victory, but I quickly realised she was pulling away from me. Although I went all out, the best I could do was to hold things as they were. I couldn't cut down her lead. She won by about three yards.

"You win!" I gasped. "Jolly good."

She laughed, and sounded carefree for the first time. "It was that spurt at the start. Otherwise a dead heat, I'd say."

When we'd recovered a little, we dived. It was my first experience of swimming from a coral reef and I was fascinated by the brilliant colouring of the clusters and the gala appearance of the multitudes of small fish which didn't seem very alarmed by our presence. I longed for underwater gear and wondered if Kim Lee could supply it.

After a time we swam back to the beach. There was no sign of Judith Milson or Keefe and their sandals were missing. We crossed to the shade cast by seaward-thrusting palms and stretched out. I was very conscious of the girl's loveliness. She had long shapely legs, the flawlessly smooth skin sunburned to a golden tan. She was propped on her elbows and I was admiring the curves of her shoulders and her round firm breasts when she suddenly threw me into confusion by saying: "Tell me about your friend, John Keefe."

We'd prepared our background stories carefully, but they were so far away from my present thoughts that I had to grope. I covered as well as I could, aware that she was looking at me with curiosity.

I said: "Odd that you should say that. I'm just realising I don't know such a lot. We met in England about three years ago. I'd joined a sailing club in Essex. I was rather in the novice class, but I hoped to get a few chances of sailing with experts. Keefe joined at about the same time. He had his eye on a boat and wanted to buy, but was hoping to find someone who'd share. It was just what I wanted, of course.

"Most of our sailing was at week-ends and it only lasted a matter of months. Work took me to France and he was about to accept a post abroad, so we sold the boat and that was that.

"He's the world's worst correspondent, so I heard nothing from him. I'd no idea where he'd gone. It was quite a surprise when I ran into him in Colombo a few months ago. I'd just finished work on a book of sorts—a rather heavy thing about the racial problem between the Sinhalese and the Tamils. Keefe was just about due for a long spell of leave—he's something in shipping—and he suggested this small boat venture. It sounded tempting. He didn't have much difficulty in persuading me to team up with him. And here we are."

"Is he married?" she asked.

This time I was able to give a truthful answer. "I don't think so. He's never mentioned a wife."

The rather troubled, reflective expression was in her eyes. Once more she surprised me. This time by saying: "Perhaps he's wise. Marriage can be very complicated. You must have realised that there's one of those situations here."

I didn't quite know what to say. I did my best. "Your mother and father don't seem well matched."

She smiled wryly: "That's an understatement. I think it had an unreal start. My impression is that Dad was over-optimistic. Give him his due; I'm sure he was ready to work hard. But he expected to make a sizeable pile pretty quickly. It was shortly before the war and Europe looked a mass of trouble and uncertainty. I think Mother was frightened of the horrors of war and eager to go on having a good time. They emigrated to South Africa, and when the war came along she certainly did have a whale of a time. I'd a good nanny, and she was free to make the most of the war-time social life. Dad was adjutant in a S.A.A.F. squadron and she was left in Durban. With the constant arrival of troop-ships—well, you can imagine!"

"All of which must have made it very difficult for her to settle down afterwards," I said.

She frowned. "I don't think she's ever succeeded. When the war was over, Dad had the suspicion—and he was right, wasn't he?—that conditions were going to change a lot in South Africa. We moved on to Australia. And then the home, which had never been firmly established, broke up. I was away at school. Dad came out to the islands. Mother divided her time between Australia and here. I used to see her at intervals; but I spent quite a lot of my holidays with an uncle and aunt in Sydney. Then, after college, I began to start making a life of my own."

"And is this a part of it, a change of direction, or just an interlude?" I asked.

She said very quietly: "What can I do here? Two people who know, inside themselves, that they've failed at making the life they set out to make. Dad, secretly embittered, slaving away just to prove to himself that comparative failure isn't due to slackness on his part. Mother, dissatisfied, restless, fearing she'll soon be losing some of her attractiveness and then there'll be nothing except memories." She sat upright and looked straight at me. "I don't know why the hell I'm blurting all this out to you!"

As I moved also, I could see Keefe and Judith Milson coming from the palms. They were moving slowly, so close that I thought at first he had an arm round her. I said: "I think it's because you're worried about what's likely to happen and you know I'm aware of some of it, too."

"I suppose so." She looked along the beach and then smiled. It was a smile which brought a little twist to one corner of her mouth. "Perhaps it's too late already," she said, in little more than a whisper.

I was wondering the same myself and when they came up to us I was almost certain, because Keefe didn't look at me and there was a glint of triumph in Judith Milson's eyes.

"Let's go back to the bungalow and have a long cold drink," she suggested. "We can come down for another swim later on. It's the only way I know of countering the sticky heat."

We moved back to where we'd shed our clothes. I was pulling up my slacks over my bathing trunks when Pat Milson exclaimed: "There's somebody coming! It's—it's that man Hooley." Then, slowly, she added: "Mother, I'm not at all sure he doesn't do some snooping around here. Last time I came for a swim I had a horrid feeling that somebody was watching."

Judith Milson said: "That's quite possible." I noticed she adjusted her dress quickly.

"It could be he's interested in us this time," Keefe commented. "I'm bearing in mind what your husband said about his lugger. Perhaps it would be better for us to see him here and now, rather than have him follow us to the bungalow."

"Oliver would be furious if he did that," Judith Milson agreed. "I've never talked to Hooley and I'd prefer not to give him any opening. Do you mind if Pat and I clear off?"

"Of course not. Best thing you can do," said Keefe. It suited us perfectly, of course.

"Don't let him keep you long, will you?"

"I won't," he promised.

Hooley was still some distance away. We ignored his approach and had finished dressing when he was near enough to hail us. By this time the two women were out of sight.

"Good morning!" Hooley called.

The thick voice was familiar. But he wasn't as I had pictured him. He was short and tubby. As he removed a limp panama and mopped his head I could see he was almost bald. A few long black strands of hair not only failed to hide the baldness but, by their failure, emphasised it. His face was round and very red. His eyes were beady, his nose podgy, and his mouth, even when widened into a smile, was small.

"I'm Hooley," he announced. "Heard all about you losin' your yacht. You'll be surprised how fast news travels. Had a bad time of it, did you?"

"It was hardly a pleasure trip in the dinghy," Keefe said.

"It wouldn't be, it wouldn't be. Well, you've survived, so that's lucky. But it means a loss, don't it? You was insured, I suppose?"

He directed the question at me, and I said, "Naturally."

"They'll swindle you," he vowed. "You can be sure of that. Big business is always the same. Cheat the small man every time." He finished mopping his head and face, replaced the panama, and pushed the handkerchief away into a pocket of his crumpled and shapeless white jacket. "Your names didn't come over the jungle telegraph." He paused, inquiringly.

Keefe indicated me and said: "Randall. My name's Keefe."

Hooley smiled. "Mr. Keefe and Mr. Randall. Glad to make your acquaintance, gentlemen. Couldn't help noticin' you was with the ladies from the bungalow. They sheered off as soon as they saw me. Well, that's how it is. No welcome there for poor bloody Hooley. And what harm's Hooley done? The answer to that is: none."

"It's no concern of ours," Keefe said brusquely.

"No offence meant," Hooley was quick to say. "An' I don't hold it against the ladies, anyway. It's Milson. You don't know him yet. He's a stuck-up, stiff-necked blighter if ever there was one."

"He's our host and treating us very kindly," Keefe said firmly. "If you've come all this way along the beach just to tell us what you think of him, you've wasted a lot of energy."

Just for a second Hooley looked angry. Then it was gone and he was smiling again. "Very proper feelings on your part, Mr. Keefe. I did speak a bit out of turn. But you needn't feel you owe Milson much. He'll charge you up to expenses, don't you fear. But you're wrong about me. I wouldn't expect you to share my views. You're new here. You'll find out about Milson as time goes on, an' find it out for yourselves, which is the best way." He shook his head. "No. What I come to ask you about was your own plans. There ain't much on Main Island. You wouldn't be far wrong in describin' it as a plantation surroundin' a mountain ridge. But there are some islands well worth takin' a look at. If you're minded to do that an' let me know, I can arrange things for you. I've got a lugger—an' you needn't have no fears of a second shipwreck. I know the islands like the back of me hands. Every inch of them." He paused expectantly. Then he repeated: "Every inch of them. What's more, I'm welcome everywhere—except at Milson's place—because I'm a man as minds my own business."

Keefe frowned. Then he glanced at me inquiringly. I

knew it was acting and that Hooley was watching us closely, so I shrugged my shoulders.

Keefe said to me. "I suppose we might consider looking round a bit. Or have you had more than enough of voyaging for the moment?"

"Whatever you feel," I said. "How's Milson going to take it, though?"

"Have to find out," Keefe said. He turned to Hooley. "Sorry we can't give you a definite answer. I expect we'll be here until the company's steamer arrives and then take passage in her to Australia. But we've made no plans yet."

"Think about it," said Hooley. "Better make myself clear. It's a friendly offer. I mean—there's no money angle. I don't take payin' passengers. Tried that lark once, but never again! Chap called Blackstock. His pal wasn't so bad; he was a foreigner and didn't seem to speak English, so he couldn't make a nuisance of himself. But Mr. Bloody Blackstock lorded it as though he'd bought me an' the lugger outright. Never again, I told meself. So what I'm suggestin' to you is just this—I'll be sailin' for another island called Okama one of these days soon. If you care to come along, you're welcome." He pulled out his handkerchief and mopped his face.

"That's very generous," Keefe said. "I confess I did misunderstand you. I thought you were after a bit of business."

"Anyway," I interposed, "we couldn't accept on that basis. Have to pay our way."

Hooley shrugged his shoulders. "I'm not takin' money. If you want to be obstinate about payin' for your keep, you'll have to work that out with Jimmy Prak. He's my bosun or what have you. He'll swindle you a bit—but serve you bloody well right." He added quickly: "Not meant offensive, like. He swindles me, too, an' serves *me* bloody well right for not havin' kicked him over the side long since."

Keefe said again: "Very generous. But I don't see why you should go out of your way to offer us a cruise."

"Don't you?" Hooley grinned. "For the same reason Milson's makin' himself agreeable. There ain't many of us here an' we're sick to death of each other's faces." He paused, as though to make sure we grasped this fully. Then he said, in a coaxing tone: "Now then, what about it?"

"I'm afraid we can't decide immediately," Keefe said. "As I've told you, we've made no plans."

Hooley nodded. "Take your time." He pointed back along the beach. "You go that way until you come to a pocket-sized harbour. You'll see the lugger there. I'll most likely be aboard, or in my bungalow. You can't miss that, either. Chance I'm not around, ask for Jimmy Prak. He's got so much mixed blood he can't claim to belong anywhere, but he can talk an unholy mixture of Yank an' English." He came a step nearer and quite unnecessarily lowered his voice a little. "An' if you don't feel like the walk, give a message to Kim Lee." He chuckled. "He's Milson's storekeeper; but don't let Milson hear you. Quite a lot of things Mr. Bloody Milson don't know, an' all about Kim Lee's some of 'em." He stepped back again. "Well, that's the lot an' I'll look forward to hearin' from you."

We watched him for a minute or so as he hurried along the beach. Then Keefe turned to me and said: "What do you make of it?"

I was puzzled and admitted it. "He couldn't have come here specially to see us. It might be that Judith Milson and her daughter generally bathe about this time and he's making a habit of watching them—or, of course, that he guessed we'd be with them." I thought for a minute and added: "It doesn't tie up with what Milson said. Unless Hooley's tempting us with free passages and expecting to make financial demands later."

"I don't know," Keefe said. "It might be no more than a trick to find out our intentions. He was offering us just what we want—apart from his company. If we'd jumped at it, shown eagerness, there could be grounds for suspecting we're not quite what we make ourselves out to be. I'm possibly being over-cautious; but it's a certainty that Kabanov's going to be interested in any newcomers."

"And Hooley could be working for Kabanov," I murmured. "If so, it means there's quite a good intelligence set-up. We'll have to watch our step."

Keefe nodded. "To walk in danger; but to know you're walking in danger. . . ." He gave a slow smile and said: "Let's get back to the bungalow."

The company's schooner returned unexpectedly that afternoon. It was raining at the time, a steady, relentless downpour that was heavy on the roof of the bungalow and cascaded from the verandah. It cut down visibility drastically, and the ship was making the passage of the reef before any of us sighted her. She was under shortened sails, was rolling badly, and looked miserably bedraggled.

Milson had finished his midday rest and gone down to his office just as the storm was starting. "He'll be furious!" his wife exclaimed. "He hates anything to go wrong with the schedule, and I'm sure the ship wasn't expected to return until next week. I wonder what it's in aid of." She gave a tight smile. "No doubt we'll hear soon enough and probably hear nothing else. When Oliver has a grumble he grumbles."

Her forecast wasn't far out. We didn't see Milson until around sundown. He came briskly into the big main room of the bungalow. His face looked tense, and with barely a greeting to any of us he exclaimed irritably: "Lodge is an old woman! Back with only half the copra he should have collected. And all because of her not responding to the wheel properly! That and some trouble with the auxiliary engine."

"Steering sounds important," Keefe said quietly.

Milson grunted impatiently. Then he said: "Could be it was something serious; but Lodge is afraid of his own shadow! He's always finding excuses for postponing sailing or putting back!"

"You don't have to forget, darling," Judith Milson said, "that if Captain Lodge loses the schooner he's likely to lose his job. And the chances of another command—even the command of a small schooner—are pretty slender."

"And what of my chances if the company's steamer arrives and I haven't got the copra ready?" he demanded.

"You've every excuse if the schooner's under repair."

Milson raised his hands. "Excuse! They don't want excuses at head office. They want returns showing that copra's coming along according to schedule." The edge of his irritation seemed blunted and there was weariness in his voice as he continued: "Big business hasn't any time to listen sympathetically. It demands results, and if the results don't come—somebody's going to get kicked. No use saying that Captain Lodge did this or that Captain Lodge didn't do that. It's my job to see he does *his* job. If anything goes wrong out here I'm the one who has to answer for it. I'm responsible. I assure you there are times when I envy the natives." He glanced towards where Keefe and I were standing. "Sorry," he murmured, "I shouldn't be inflicting this on you. It's just that things have been exceptionally trying recently. Getting me down a bit, I'm afraid." He straightened his shoulders, making it appear an effort. "I'll take a shower and get changed. I'll feel better then."

Judith Milson said: "I'll have a drink ready for you."

"Good." He attempted a smile. "I've invited Lodge, by the way. Felt I couldn't do otherwise."

"Of course," she said quickly.

He left us and there was a short silence. Then Pat Milson said: "Things are getting on top of Dad. Any idea just what's been going wrong?"

Her mother shook her head. "None whatever. I don't suppose it's any different from previous times, though; just an accumulation of irritations and minor worries. He

55

broods over them and in consequence they seem to increase."

Keefe said: "I suppose there are many things against him. The climate, for a start. I'm new to it, but I'm pretty sure it saps mental as well as physical energy."

"It certainly does," Judith Milson answered. She crossed to the cocktail cabinet. "Let's shake off indolence and do something about these drinks."

"I'll help you," Keefe volunteered.

I moved nearer to Pat Milson and asked her in an undertone: "What's Captain Lodge like?"

She smiled: "A mournful spaniel."

It wasn't a bad description. Captain Lodge arrived soon after Milson rejoined us. He was a man of medium height but looked shorter because of his marked breadth of shoulder. He was dark, his eyebrows were bushy, and he had a thick brown beard. His eyes expressed sadness. I felt he was a man who'd received plenty of kicks from life and was left with a pathetic and unfulfilled desire for kindness.

Milson, on introducing us, explained what had happened to us. Or, rather, what he believed had happened. Captain Lodge nodded gravely. He gave a drawn-out "Ahhh." And then he said gloomily: "Uncharted reefs."

It seemed he'd accepted us completely. My earlier apprehensions were unjustified. He displayed no curiosity, asked no questions. I wasn't sure whether it was out of consideration, the natural tact of one who has himself suffered, or whether it was lack of interest.

While we were dining and neither of the white-jacketed servants was in hearing, Judith Milson told her husband of Hooley's appearance on the beach when we'd gone for our first swim. He looked across the table at her with sharp suspicion. "What did he say to you? Did you talk much?"

"I did *not*. Pat and I cleared off when we saw him coming. It was probably a bit obvious; but that couldn't be helped."

"Of course it couldn't." Milson seemed disproportionately relieved. He looked towards Keefe and said: "What did I tell you? I warned you he'd try to get in with you at the first opportunity. That's why he came along the beach, you can bet."

Captain Lodge had proved no conversationalist. He'd concentrated on the food put before him. But now he glanced up and said: "Hooley's no good. What I can't understand is that he's a beachcomber type who, so far as anyone can find out, should be on his beam ends. But he isn't. Sails round in that old lugger; but does damn all."

Milson ignored this. "Did he get a word with you?" he asked Keefe.

"Yes. Introduced himself. Didn't seem to want anything in particular."

I took my cue from Keefe. He was chancing the possibility of Hooley giving a different version to either Milson or Lodge. If that did happen, we'd a good line of defence in saying we simply hadn't taken Hooley seriously. It seemed the lesser risk. I said: "He told us he lived along the coast and owned a lugger. Rambled on quite a bit. All seemed rather pointless."

Milson frowned. "I'd have expected him to put forward some sort of business proposition," he added sourly: "With a view to swindling you."

Captain Lodge said: "Doesn't seem to do anything to make money, yet neither does he ever seem to be short of funds. Gets all his supplies from Chang Yu on Okama. I'd say Hooley's got some hold over Chang Yu but for the fact that I've never heard of anyone succeeding in victimising a Chinaman—apart from another Chinaman."

Again Milson ignored him. He said to Keefe: "And he didn't try anything on?"

"No," said Keefe. Then he looked thoughtful. It was well done, but I knew he was acting. He said slowly: "There was something, though. When he talked about the lugger he said he'd once had a couple of people hire it. Someone named——" He stopped and looked at me.

"Blackstock, I think. Yes, I'm practically certain it was Blackstock."

"Blackstock," Milson repeated. He shook his head. "Doesn't mean anything to me. There's nobody of that name on the islands." At last he took notice of Lodge, flinging a question at him. "You ever heard of a Blackstock?"

"Not me," Captain Lodge said. "To the best of my knowledge Hooley's never chartered his lugger. He's been away for longish spells, though. Nearly a year once. Could have happened then—wherever he was."

"That might be the answer," Milson said. "Or it might have been sheer invention. As he didn't come out with anything openly he may have been trying to sow the seed in your minds. Obviously he'd be in a better bargaining position if you went to him." He was looking at Keefe again.

"Perhaps that was it," Keefe said. "He did go to the trouble of explaining where we could find him."

"Did he? Then I expect he'll be sitting back waiting for you, and the chances are you won't be pestered by him for a while." Milson appeared satisfied and Hooley wasn't mentioned again.

Soon after the meal Captain Lodge shuffled uncomfortably for a minute or so, then said: "I think I should be getting on board, if you'll excuse me, Mrs. Milson. Your husband's anxious for me to sail to-morrow, and the crew always start slacking when my back's turned."

Milson said quickly: "At least the unloading of what copra you'd got went quickly and without a hitch." He stood up. "I think I'll come with you. Then we can clear up a few final details." He glanced at his wife. "All right, darling?"

"Of course," she said. "Will you be very late?"

He hesitated. "A bit, I'm afraid. I want to look in at the office again. The accounts should be ready very soon and there's a discrepancy that's bothering me. Why they can't spare me a competent book-keeper defeats me. I've no clerical staff worthy of the name and yet I'm expected to cope. Don't wait up for me."

When they'd gone Judith Milson gave a sigh of exasperation. "If it isn't the accounts it's some sort of statistical return, or a report on the plantations—always something. I often suspect he makes work for himself during the day so that he can be kept busy into the night!"

I said: "I suppose there must be a great deal to do and considerable responsibility."

"There's all that," she agreed. "But he makes the most of it, you know. And worries unnecessarily." She turned to Keefe: "You're getting an insight into the romance of life on the islands! As you said, the setting's not bad—the palms and the gleaming beaches and the magnificent swimming pool inside the reef. The climate's endurable. But when it comes to amenities—my God!" She raised her hands and let them fall limply.

Keefe's smile was sympathetic. "I can imagine it palling. You need more residents, a hotel. A few bright lights. Though, even with a small community here, you'd grow very tired of the same faces, the same conversation."

"Conversation! It would be wonderful for a time. You've had a sample to-night. I assure you Captain Lodge was positively garrulous. He must have spoken nearly a dozen times!"

"The mournful spaniel," Pat Milson murmured.

"It's a description that fits him better than his uniform," I said.

She smiled and then looked serious. "I'm really rather sorry for him. I've often wondered what he broods over alone in his cabin. He lives on the schooner all the time, flatly refuses the offer of a small bungalow. I've a feeling that he's had a pretty harsh life and he's reached the stage of thinking of hope as a—a sort of barren illusion. He doesn't look forward to anything, because there's nothing ahead for him."

"Does he drink much?"

"He's not an alcoholic, if that's what you mean. He hits the bottle sometimes. My idea is that he uses it as a safety valve. Life becomes just about endurable again." The expression on her face changed, the seriousness deepening into something not far removed from sadness.

I realised we were alone. Keefe and Judith Milson must have withdrawn quietly to the verandah. So I said: "You're not getting much of a break yourself, are you?"

She looked up at me, her eyes very wide open. "You don't —you *can't* know half of it," she whispered.

I certainly didn't, because I could swear there was fear, both in her eyes and the way she said the words. I didn't know how to reply. It seemed she was making an appeal of sorts. But how was I to respond? What I did say, eventually, was: "There hasn't been much time. I've seen the surface, or perhaps what's just below the surface. What else there may be I've no idea."

She was silent for so long that I thought she was going to leave it at that. She'd lowered her head again. I moved a fraction nearer. The lights were bringing out the coppery glints in her otherwise dark hair. They also added a little to the gold of her sun-tanned, uncovered shoulders. The soft material of her dress clung and I could see the rise and fall of her breasts. She was breathing rather quickly. If I had more of Keefe's recklessness, of his seeming capacity for playing hard without burdening himself with the thought of where it would all lead. . . .

She interrupted my thoughts, just as by glancing up she checked me from moving still nearer to her.

"There are things I can't explain, because I don't understand them," she said. "It's something that isn't tangible— and how can that be put into words?"

"The relationship between your parents?" I suggested.

"Highly personal and very involved. You can't hope to understand it fully."

She surprised me a little by shaking her head. "No, not that. It worries me, but I know I'd be stupid to get too involved in it. If I'd been with them more it would be different—or if there was a strong family sentiment that absorbed me when I came into its orbit. No. By heredity I'm hooked up with them; by environment I'm quite separated. That probably sounds a mix-up. It is a mix-up, I suppose." She glanced round the room. "You didn't see what happened when they left us?"

She was, of course, referring to her mother and Keefe. "No. I suddenly realised we were alone."

"She looked at him and he looked at her. That was all that happened—on the surface. She's offering herself. And he's accepting."

It was cold and matter of fact, and it shook me a little. "I'm sorry," I said. "I could be fatuous and offer to use my influence, to speak seriously to Keefe. But I've no influence and I'd only make a fool of myself to no purpose."

She shook her head. "I wouldn't wish you to. It's nothing to me who presses his body hard against her. Coarse?"

"No. Realistic. Honest."

Her head was averted. I fancied the colour had risen in her cheeks. She went on quietly: "Sooner or later Dad will be away, visiting one of the plantations. Or you'll go over to Okama and Mother will come with you and she won't return with the launch. One way or another it will happen. So how very foolish to feel shocked or—or—well, to feel anything about it." She smiled, but there was bitterness. "I can vaguely remember Durban. There were handsome men in uniform who were introduced to me as uncles. I didn't guess at the truth until long afterwards. At school in Australia. Then there was something another girl, an older girl, said, and I had one of those flashes of revelation. The way you do learn the big, vital things when you're young. I felt sick at first, and somehow tarnished; but it wore off. I suppose it's made me a bit hard-boiled in my mind about sex matters."

"I'm sorry it happened that way," I murmured.

She shrugged her shoulders: "It might have happened in a worse one."

We'd drifted from what she'd started to say or to hint. I wanted to get back. I was puzzled. I said: "But the intangible things you mentioned. I've guessed and guessed wrong. Can't you tell me more?"

"I don't know. In a sense, there's nothing to tell. And if I try to explain you'll think it's nerves, that the real strain of one sort is causing imaginary anxieties—that I'm neurotic, in fact."

"No," I said.

She looked at me, very steadily. "You're certain of that? Without knowing a thing of what I'm likely to say?"

"I'm certain." And I meant it. Young as she was, this girl had faced up to unpleasant realities intelligently and with courage. The insecurity of adolescence and her ultimate acceptance of the complicated situation in her home had made her perhaps a shade too outspoken, a little hard-boiled, but these were her armour.

She continued to look at me, and I looked back at her. At last she decided. "Very well, then. I'm afraid. Yes. Afraid."

"I suspected that. But I can't guess what it is you fear."

She stood up. "I've asked myself that time after time. But I can't find the answer. It's a feeling of frightened uneasiness, and I can't explain better than that. I've read about people travelling in jungle, who've been conscious of watching eyes, even though they themselves could see nothing except the dense undergrowth. . . ."

I'd not only read of it, I'd known it—or something very similar. I couldn't tell her so, because it would have invited questions I wasn't prepared to answer. I said: "I've read of it, too. And you have this awareness of being watched?"

"Yes," she said quietly.

"You've mentioned it to anyone?"

She shook her head. "I've mentioned that I suspect Hooley watches us on the beach—but that's very different. If he dared, he'd probably creep up to the bungalow and try to peer through the slats and gaze at me undressing at night. I'd feel anger, disgust. But not fear."

"Anger, disgust," I repeated.

She smiled. "Because of what Hooley is—what I feel about him, anyway. But I don't mean it prudishly. I mean—if a man gets the idea he'd like to see me stark naked, I've sufficient vanity to reckon it a compliment."

"Now what the hell do I say to that?" I exclaimed.

She started to laugh softly. Then she broke off abruptly and turned away. When she faced me again the colour was definite in her cheeks. She looked at me quite firmly.

"I didn't mean to be provocative," she said very quietly.

I thought I understood. She was unhappy and in conflict. And there was something in the sultry tropic night which aroused desires. She had the disturbing knowledge, too, of how her mother and Keefe were responding to something similar. I said gently: "Of course you didn't."

"I meant——" She broke off, raised her hands and then dropped them helplessly. "I don't know."

Her defences weren't strong. If I were more like Keefe I could break through them, I felt sure. The devil of it was I was sufficiently like Keefe to feel the temptation. There was civil war in my mind. Part of me insisting I must remember the job. Keep disentangled. The other part jeering at me for being a fool. It ended in an uneasy, compromise peace. There would be other nights, other opportunities.

"Why haven't you told your father about your vague fears?"

I hadn't realised how much tension there'd been in the room, until it began to drain away from the moment of my question.

63

"Dad," she said. "Yes, it ought to seem natural to go to him. He should be able to put me at ease, or find out what's wrong. That looks the simple way; but it isn't. Oh, dear! It's so difficult to explain this to you without giving you the impression I'm just a hysterical girl imagining this and that."

I shook my head. "I'm quite prepared to accept that there is something. Perhaps I'll notice it myself if we're here for long."

"You've seen a little of what my father's like. I'm sure there's something worrying him. It may be the same thing, only he's conscious of a different manifestation of it. If my guesses are right, he's baffled by what's troubling him. So what could he do? I'd only make him feel it's even more serious without achieving a thing." She hesitated. "There's another reason. I'm not on confiding terms with him. Don't mistake me. There's no antagonism; it's just"—again she made the helpless gesture with her hands—"just that there's nothing."

And for the same reason, I was sure, she'd been unable to approach her mother.

I said: "I'll be alert myself; but if there's any confirmation of these vague fears I'd like you to come to me immediately. I'll do what I can."

"You can't imagine the comfort in those words," she whispered. She moved slightly. In my direction—and I don't know what would have happened but for the voices just outside. Judith Milson and Keefe were back.

They came in gaily.

"There's a great big moon and John feels like a swim." Judith Milson's smile in his direction was openly possessive.

He said: "What about it, Paul?" We rarely used Christian names. I think he did it this time to cast a protective cloak of friendliness. The less formality, the less his relationship with Milson's wife obtruded itself.

"Suits me," I said. "It's an excellent idea."

Judith Milson said: "We'll grab swim-suits. Safe enough to change on the beach. Hooley doesn't prowl nocturnally. By all accounts he regards this as drinking time."

We were able to walk more quickly to the shore than in the morning, when the heat had reduced us to a lazy saunter. The moon was full, covering the water with sequins.

"We'll trust you to keep your backs turned," Judith Milson said, laughing.

"She's quite a girl," Keefe said in an undertone.

"You mean woman." I didn't feel any too pleased with him and had a perverse desire to say the wrong thing. "She can give you a few years."

He chuckled. "Experience is the older woman's strong suit. I remember a woman in Saigon who was well into her fifties, and she practically held court. I doubt if any of her admirers was much over thirty. But she was French, and French women know how to make the best of themselves. She demonstrated the full meaning of soignée and made the average glamour puss look a bungling novice. She knew how to give as well as promise." He chuckled again. "By all accounts, that is. I can't speak with first-hand knowledge because I only saw her once. I was a bird of passage, and it was one of those spots of business that didn't permit delays."

"Unlike this," I muttered.

"Don't go sour on me! I'm putting in some good work."

"With considerable zest," I said.

"My dear chap! Judith's a very bored woman. The more bored a woman is, the more inquisitive she becomes; the more likely she is to watch with an eagle eye and talk plenty. Believe me, we'll gain from this in the long run. So don't needle me out of a puritan conscience."

"Oh, it's not my affair," I said irritably.

"I suppose it would have been less shocking if I'd made the passes at the daughter. Proves my devotion to the job, old chap. Pat may be the ingénue, but she's so superlatively equipped otherwise as to make that unimportant. The potentialities are there. Or do I have to tell you?"

He didn't realise it, but I felt like taking a swipe at him. I knew all he could tell me about Pat—and more; but I was holding myself in check. And Keefe wasn't completely selling me the idea that his motives were all tied up with our mission. I didn't say anything, though, and he went on: "The girl's safe, all the same, as far as I'm concerned. I'd guess that Judith has quite a capacity for jealousy, and what I've already said about bored women applies to jealous ones—only more so. And a woman who's both bored and jealous is one sent straight from the devil."

Judith called: "Sluggards! We're ready!"

This time there was no race out to the reef. I'd already decided to play safe as my emotions were in a combustible condition. So I tried to keep near to Judith Milson, caring not at all whether it aroused Keefe's annoyance. But it didn't work out very well. The two of them drew away and I found that Pat was swimming alongside me all the time. As we came out of the water together our arms brushed accidentally. Then her hand was in mine. I interpreted it as a gesture of groping her way out of harassed isolation. She needed someone she could trust. And there was something of this same element in her action of sweeping up her flimsy garments and keeping with me, so that she dried herself and then dressed practically at my side. There was nothing provocative in her manner, but there was no attempt at concealment either. For a few moments she was naked in moonlight. I looked at her, holding my breath. Unhurriedly, she began to slip on her clothes.

We were ready to leave the beach by the time Keefe came splashing through the shallows. He'd caught Judith Milson up and was carrying her. We heard her laugh.

"Do we wait?" I asked Pat.

"I think not," she replied, making the decision sound unimportant.

So it came about that we returned to the bungalow ahead of the others. There were lights on; but those along the verandah had been switched off. As we came through the tall and bushy shrubs there was a harsh call that sounded like some night bird.

"What was that, Pat?" I asked.

"I've no idea. I don't think I've heard it before. But I'm no expert on the wild life of the islands."

"So many sounds are new to me. There were frogs kicking up an abominable racket last night. I heard them once when I awakened."

"There *is* a swamp patch. It's quite a distance away, so it just shows how far their croaking carries. But you've heard frogs before."

"Not with such brassy vocal cords. This lot——" I stopped and gripped her arm. I drew her back into the shelter of a bush.

To her credit she didn't cry out or panic in any way. "What?" she whispered.

"Someone leaving the bungalow. Wait here."

I moved forward as quietly as I could. I wasn't mistaken. A small, white-clad figure dropped from the verandah to the ground. He started to run. Although the moonlight was so bright, the light was deceptive and played tricks. I couldn't get a good look at the intruder. I'd no idea whether he was white or coloured. But whoever he was he knew he was being chased. He sprinted and disappeared in a thickish patch of palms. I reached them a few yards behind him, and he'd already vanished.

I stood still, listening hard. At first there was nothing. Then I thought I heard a scuffle over on my right. I began to move in that direction. It was more a sixth-sense warning than seeing or hearing anything which made me jerk aside. There was a searing pain high up in my left arm. A throwing knife of some sort, not a bullet. I heard it strike the tree behind me.

I dropped low and groped. Found it and was ready to meet any follow-up of the attack. But none came. I was aware of a warm trickle down my arm. I felt a bit limp and leaned against the tree. Then I heard Pat calling, her voice urgent: "Paul! Paul! Where are you?"

I'd forgotten her in the intensity of the brief chase and its unexpected ending. I felt there was not any danger now; but I didn't like the idea of her being alone so I went back in search of her. As I came from the patch of trees I staggered slightly, probably due to shock from the wound or from losing blood quickly.

I saw her immediately, running towards me.

"Paul! You're hurt! What happened?" Then she saw the knife and whispered hoarsely: "God!"

Fear was unmistakable in her widening eyes. "Only a flesh wound," I assured her.

It wasn't necessary, but she insisted on supporting me as we made for the bungalow. I glanced at my sleeve. It was stained and the colour was increasing. As we climbed the verandah steps Pat called to the servants, but there was no answer. I went through to the kitchen with her. I insisted I could fix the wound, but she ignored my protests. She worked quickly and skilfully. It was, as I'd thought, only a flesh wound, but the gash was long and fairly deep. As she finished the bandaging I said: "We must have disturbed a thief."

"I've never heard of thieves here. Petty pilfering of stores, perhaps; but I'm sure there's never been any attempt to rob the bungalow."

I had my own ideas, but I was keeping them to myself. I said: "There always has to be a first time. Remember the call I thought was a night bird? I'll bet it was a warning signal from an accomplice who was keeping watch. So there were at least two of them."

"I can't think what's happened to the servants," she said. "There! That's the best I can do. Now we'll go into the

68

lounge and I'll give you a drink. Oh—of course! You should
have tea or coffee in case there's any shock. I'll soon make
it."

I laughed. Incautiously I said: "This is only a scratch.
No serious shock—just a flutter of it that's quite gone now.
No. I'll have a gin-something, please."

She gave me the steady, intent look which was now becoming familiar. "You've been in spots of trouble before."

"Run into the odd thing."

To my relief she didn't ask questions. We went to the
big lounge and I was taking a pull at my drink when Keefe
and Judith Milson came in. They were laughing, but Keefe's
gaiety vanished the instant he saw me.

"What the hell's happened?" he demanded.

I told him. The knife was on the table. He picked it up
and tested its balance. Judith Milson had turned very pale.
She whispered: "Put it down. It's horrible."

"A lethal little toy," Keefe murmured. "Lucky you dodged,
Paul. This, properly aimed and thrown . . ." He shrugged
his shoulders and let the knife clatter on the table.

Judith Milson was shuddering. "This is ghastly!" she
exclaimed. "There's never been anything like this happen
before. Oliver must be told at once. Pat! What's become of
the servants?"

"I don't know. They're not here."

"Oh, I remember. They asked if they could have time off.
Kim Lee's throwing some sort of a party. One of the many
anniversaries, I think. I said they could go." She looked
uneasy. Then she turned to Keefe. "I wonder—would you
go for Oliver? He's certain to be in his office."

"Of course," said Keefe. "But let's just check on what's
been stolen, if anything. Then I can give him more information."

"I hadn't thought of that," she confessed. "I'll take a
look in my room right away. I haven't much jewellery; but
there are a few precious items." She hurried away.

69

Keefe turned to Pat. "What about your room?"

"I've nothing that matters."

"Check, all the same," he said.

She went; but reluctantly, I thought. The moment we were alone Keefe said quietly: "It was our room, of course."

"I should think so. I've had no chance of making sure."

"I'll do it now," he said. I started to rise from my chair. "No. Stay here. Don't want to give the impression we're very anxious."

He was back quickly. His thoughtful expression was sufficient confirmation.

"What's gone?" I asked.

"The intruder found the canvas bag. Only our papers are missing. None of the money's gone. It was scattered on the floor." His eyes narrowed. "Just the papers. Somebody's very interested in us. But who?"

3

THE LAST COMMAND

I lay on my bed watching Keefe walk restlessly about the room. He'd just lit his fifth cigarette. "For God's sake stop prowling!" I said.

He grinned at me. "Inaction. Always gets me this way. A feeling of being caged. I'm every lion behind the bars in every zoo."

"There's been plenty of action of a sort," I said, "what with Milson in a state of snappy agitation and Sergeant Ilala turning everything upside down and inside out."

It was Milson who'd insisted on sending for the sergeant, who represented the law on Main Island. Ilala had the build of a heavyweight. He looked far more capable of quelling a riot than of investigating a robbery.

"I wouldn't mind having that native sergeant at my side in a tough spot," said Keefe. "Did you notice his muscles straining the seams of his tunic?"

"I did. But what about his mental powers? Do you think we managed to sell him the idea that the thief was disturbed and departed in such haste he dropped the money but clung on to the valueless papers, not realising just what he was doing?"

"I hope so. I don't think he spotted anything which would put a different theory into his head."

I laughed. "It wasn't for the want of trying. He reminded me of a black labrador on the scent of a bone."

"My guess is the papers will turn up. After some interested person has studied them, of course. They'll be dumped where the sergeant will be pretty sure to find them and it'll look as though the thief discovered they were useless and threw them away."

"Leaving an unsolved mystery, presumably. But what worries me is that Sergeant Ilala seemed certain the culprit— or culprits—didn't come from the village. He doesn't seem to suspect any other of the plantation labourers, either."

Keefe nodded. "Fair enough. I expect he knows the potential crooks and the sort of job they'd try to pull off. But what's got you worried?"

"I don't see Ilala as the man to give up easily. He's going to cast round in wider and wider circles until he gets on to something. If he succeeds, what's going to happen to him? If our suspicions are right, there's a formidable organisation here. Likely to be ruthless. And he won't have a clue. He'll push his nose slap into it."

Keefe shrugged his shoulders. "That's his funeral."

"Funeral's apt enough. I don't like it, Keefe. The poor devil won't stand a chance."

"An occupational risk," Keefe said slowly. "I don't see that we can do anything. We can't warn him without telling him about Kabanov, and that's out of the question."

He was right, of course; but it didn't alter my feelings.

Keefe stubbed his cigarette and went on: "Our best way of saving him is to get the job finished before he uncovers anything serious. Which brings me back to this frustration of mine. There's damn all we can do at the moment. It's essential to sit tight and act natural. I think we can take it as certain that Kabanov's security organisation is vetting us."

"You think Kabanov's definitely suspicious? Or do you regard it as routine?"

"Routine, I'd say. It's most unlikely that he's on this island. Even allowing for his having really first-class communications laid on, he can't have received enough information about us to get any strong ideas one way or another. So he's only making sure. But my guess is he's not had reports yet, and that leads to the obvious conclusion that he has an agent on Main Island. I'd bet it's his agent who laid on to-night's business."

"Kim Lee's party," I suggested. "Had that been fixed for some time, or was it a sudden arrangement made in the hope of getting the servants out of the bungalow?"

"Opportunism might enter into it. After all, nobody could have been certain we'd go for a moonlight swim. I see it this way. Somebody knew the servants might get permission for time off. So it was a favourable night for sending watchers to the bungalow, in the hope we'd go for a stroll or a swim. Of course, if the intruders were sufficiently skilful, they could have entered while we were all in the lounge, playing cards or something. Risky, but still on."

"And the money was deliberately scattered to give the impression of an interrupted robbery?"

"I think the scene would have been set more effectively. Articles taken from other rooms, for example. Only you and Pat returned too soon and so the disturbed robbery became more realistic than they'd anticipated."

"And the attack on me?"

"Don't forget our automatics were hidden and the intruder didn't find them. So you *could* have been armed, and you might have got in a lucky shot. That had to be prevented."

"True. And that brings us to Kabanov's agent, the man who, if our theories are right, is probably going through our papers at this very minute. Kim Lee? Hooley suggested there are facts about Kim Lee that Milson doesn't know."

"While we've had it from Milson and Captain Lodge that Hooley's financial status is a bit suspicious. That could be significant."

"So could the lugger," I said. "I'm thinking of the ferry service between Okama and the next island."

"*If* we're right about that next island," Keefe cautioned, "Kabanov may well be on Okama itself. It's barely culti-vated. The interior's wild. There are two peaks and formidable ridges, if I've read the map correctly. Resourceful men could hide away pretty effectively—especially with an efficient intelligence organisation working under cover on the coast and on this island."

I was thinking hard. "Reverting to Kabanov's agent, do you think there's anything in the unexpected return of Captain Lodge? I don't quite see how he could have heard of our arrival; on the other hand, Milson's complaining that the schooner's not in bad enough shape to justify her having put back."

"But that's just Milson. Living proof that it's not only the feminine sex which goes in for nagging. Look how he grizzled to-night about Judith's permission for the Chinese boys to go to Kim Lee's party. You'd have thought he suspected her of being an accessory before the fact."

"If he's really deeply in love with her and anxious to keep her with him," I said, "he certainly goes about it in a damned queer way. But perhaps he knows it's hopeless and stabs when and where he can. It's significant they have separate rooms, isn't it?"

"Yes." Keefe stood up, lighting another cigarette. "Damned if I feel sleepy. I'm going out on the verandah for a spell."

"Beware of knives," I warned him.

"Perhaps you're right. I think it's unlikely—but no harm in being prepared." He fumbled under the mattress and produced his automatic. I watched him as he fixed an underarm holster and tucked the weapon away. As he crossed the room he asked: "Shall I switch off the light?"

"You might as well."

He used the door which led directly from our room to the verandah. Through the open slats the moonlight was bright. I lay and watched his shadow passing and repassing. It was so regular that it gave me the idea I was being guarded by a sentry. But he didn't keep it up. I decided the moonlight had tempted him to go for a walk.

I'd intended to undress and settle down for the night; but

I seemed to have caught some of his restlessness. After a time I got off the bed and looked out another shirt. Kim Lee had provided us with several, as it was essential to have a number in this climate. My arm was rather stiff, but I managed the changing operation. Then I went outside.

There was no sign of Keefe. When I rounded the corner of the bungalow I could see the lighted window of Milson's office. Evidently he'd gone back to complete his interrupted work.

I turned round. Then I stiffened and drew close to the bungalow wall. There was movement in the bushes. Of course, it could be Keefe; but I doubted it. I watched, wishing I'd taken the advice I'd given him. My automatic was still tucked away under my mattress.

The bushes moved again and a powerful stocky figure stepped out into the moonlight. My tension relaxed. It was Sergeant Ilala.

I emerged from the shadows and he saw me immediately and came over. In spite of his weight he moved very quietly.

"Still investigating, Sergeant?"

"I have to go on looking until I find something, sir. That's my duty." His English was good, spoken in a deep, quite musical voice.

"Any luck?"

"There were two men here, sir. One kept watch outside. He did not stay all the time in the same place."

"And he was the one who gave that harsh call I mistook for a night bird—feathered variety."

His teeth flashed white. "I think that's the way it happened, sir."

"What about the men? They weren't from the village?"

"They were not from the village, sir."

"You sound very sure."

"The knife, sir. You will not find a knife like that anywhere in the village. I have never seen such a knife before."

He paused. "And there is no man from the village, or among the other plantation workers, who could throw such a knife with any skill."

"That doesn't leave you many people, Sergeant."

"No, sir. The Chinese. The crew of the copra schooner. And the crew of Mr. Hooley's boat."

"The lugger. H'm! If you start looking around there, isn't it likely you'll run into trouble? I mean there may be more than two of them involved in this."

"It is my duty, sir. I must not let the prospect of trouble stop me from doing my duty."

There wasn't much more I could say without openly warning him. I made one last attempt. "I hope you'll be cautious. I wouldn't like you to come to any harm just over our papers."

He gave a broad smile. Then he clenched a powerful fist and held it before me. "It's not me, sir, who will be harmed if there is rough behaviour."

I laughed. "Well, take care of yourself."

"With respect, it is you who should be doing that. You should be in bed and resting."

"Perhaps you're right, Sergeant. Good-night."

"Good-night, sir." Moving silently, he went back to the bushes and disappeared.

I returned to my room. I wondered what had become of Keefe and was afraid, remembering the lighted window of Milson's office, that I knew the answer.

The schooner was still alongside the jetty the next morning and Milson, his eyes undershadowed, was full of irritation.

"Typical of Lodge. He should have sailed at dawn or shortly after. He's in one of his difficult moods. He'll go on finding this wrong and that wrong until in the end she'll be in for a complete overhaul and refit. I don't like the idea of throwing him on the rubbish heap—that's what it would amount to—but if he doesn't mend his ways I'll be forced to put in an adverse report."

Pat protested: "Oh, Dad! You couldn't do a thing like that. He's a bit past it, I know. But you might do worse. It wouldn't be easy to replace him immediately and you'd only have head office instructing you to give the job to that horrible type Hooley. If he got wind of anything he'd put in an application just to get you hopping mad."

"Don't mention Hooley to me," he said irritably.

"Better the devil you know. . . ."

Judith Milson said: "Of course, there's a chance the company might send out a younger man." She ignored a suspicious glance from her daughter and continued: "There are probably some ex-Navy boys knocking around in office jobs who'd jump at the chance of captaining a schooner in the tropics."

This suggestion didn't please Milson, either. He scowled. "Yes. I'd do well with some smart know-all working out how much better he could run everything, and writing letters to head office behind my back At least I've some sort of a hold over Lodge. He'll come to heel if I threaten to kick him out." He shot up from his chair. "I'll go down and hear what kind of feeble excuses he's prepared."

Keefe and I walked a little way with him for the exercise. It was as well we were not doing it for his companionship, for he didn't speak until we had a clear view of the jetty. Then he stopped and pointed.

"Swale's boat. Would you mind going back and warning Judith? I'll nip into my office. I don't want to be caught by the Pastor right now. You've no conception of the amount of work I must plough through."

After he'd left us we stood for a minute or two watching Swale's boat. She was obviously old, broad in the beam and sluggish in movement. She had a single mast forward and some sort of a cabin which appeared to be constructed of canvas stretched over metal frames. Her engine plop-plopped monotonously.

"I don't think we'll try to talk him into hiring her out to us," I commented.

"That damned engine would give us away all the time," Keefe said. "And I doubt if she's any good under sail. She's best suited for inshore fishing."

"Must be seaworthy, though, as he visits the different islands."

"After a fashion. When I think what her motion would be like I admire him for his stomach. He must be immune from seasickness. Well, let's get back and give the glad tidings."

"I've the thought they won't be so glad," I said.

"You've said it," he growled.

We were right. Judith Milson exclaimed: "Blast the man! I hope he's not making a long stay."

I looked at Pat. She merely raised her eyebrows.

When I met Pastor Swale I had the immediate impression that he should rightly be in city dress and carrying a brief-case. He had a brisk, business-like manner. His pale complexion defied the tanning powers of the sun. His nose was pointed and there was a severity about his face, but it was offset by the eyes twinkling behind rimless glasses. He had a wide, though thin-lipped, smile.

"Ah, the adventurers," he said as Judith Milson introduced us. "Yes, I've heard about you." He had little, if any, American accent.

"What? Has the news reached Okama already?" Judith Milson asked incredulously.

"I shouldn't think so, dear lady. I heard it last night, from our sinning brother Hooley."

"From Hooley?" She frowned. "I didn't know you were on visiting terms."

"I'm afraid we're not usually; but I had occasion to call on him."

"Sit down and tell me all about it," she urged.

78

He pulled a chair near. He rubbed the tip of his nose for a moment and then said: "I'm afraid it's not a subject for conversation, dear lady. One of those things better forgotten."

"Now you're making me feel even more curious," she protested. "You can't leave it like this. . . ."

"It's a sordid business," Swale said uncomfortably. "It concerns that man Jimmy Prak. The lugger put in at Okama last week and I'm afraid he caused some trouble. Chang Yu, our unconverted and therefore doubly sinning brother, supplied alcohol, and Jimmy Prak became drunk and assaulted a young girl from the village." He shook his head again. "As I say, a sordid business so you'll forgive me for not going into details. I felt it was my duty to speak strongly to Hooley who, after all, has a certain responsibility though he fails to appreciate the fact."

"So you didn't get anywhere," Pat suggested.

"Not very far. At first Hooley just laughed at me. I stuck to my guns, though. Then he suggested summoning Jimmy Prak and giving him a forceful kick on a certain portion of his anatomy. He offered me what he called a 'free kick', also." Swale surprised me by giving a cackle of laughter. "Had its amusing side, I suppose."

"Did you get your kick?" Judith Milson asked.

"No. I insisted that I couldn't countenance violence. In the end Hooley promised to keep Jimmy Prak short of money whenever they put in at Okama. But what that's worth I wouldn't like to forecast." He turned to look at Keefe. "Anyway, when that business was over, Hooley told me about you and your friend. Is it true you spent three days in an open boat?"

"Absolutely," Keefe said.

"Remarkable. And you landed here safely. It proves that Providence is more alert to our distress than most people realise." His eyes twinkled behind the rimless glasses. "Of course, Providence has to be given a fair chance. God, in

His wisdom, demands we shall fight for our salvation, physical or spiritual. You must have handled your craft with skill. I'm afraid that in similar circumstances my performance would have been very indifferent indeed. The uttermost parts of the sea would test me too hard. I'm useless in a boat."

"But you voyage between the islands, surely?" I said.

He smiled ruefully. "I'm but a passenger aboard my little vessel. I have to rely on the Lord's mercy, the boat's seaworthiness, and Challie's seamanship."

"Challie—that's an unusual name," Keefe said.

"It should be Charlie. It's his own mispronunciation and somehow it's stuck. He's a half-caste, or so he claims. I think he's only a quarter white, but I wouldn't hurt his feelings by suggesting it. Challie's invaluable. He's my personal servant, the skipper of my little boat, and he provides the music for my prayer meetings. He plays an accordion." His eyes were positively sparkling. "The tempo's a little ragged and he puts in bits here and there which would startle the original composers. Also, his enthusiasm carries him away and there's always the risk of his striking up some tune far from sacred in nature and quite out of keeping with the occasion. But I'd be in a poor way without him. That's enough of Challie, though. I'm very eager to hear your story." He glanced at Judith Milson. "You'll confirm, dear lady, that we have very few visitors. Fresh faces and fresh voices provide rare entertainment."

"Very true," she said. "And I'll whet your appetite by telling you that Mr. Keefe's a first-class narrator."

"Marvellous!" Pastor Swale exclaimed. "Mr. Keefe, I'm all attention."

He listened without interruption. When Keefe had finished he said: "Amazing. I admire your courage in setting off on such a venture. There were so many hazards."

Keefe smiled. "We found one. An uncharted reef."

"And you might have lost your lives there and then. If

you'd failed to launch your dinghy immediately and had had to swim around. . . ." He shook his head. "There are sharks in these waters, you know."

"One was following us for a time," I said.

"Indeed! You were lucky he didn't attack you."

Keefe said: "I didn't think there was much danger."

"I wouldn't be too sure," Swale told him. "There are two schools of thought about sharks. Some hold they'll keep their distance if you splash about in the water. Others swear they'll attack a small boat, let alone an active swimmer. I'm no expert, but from the various stories I've heard it seems to me it depends very much on the type of shark. They're not all killers, but the kind that are behave with appalling savagery."

"Just as well I didn't know that when I was in the boat watching the dorsal fin," I said. "I'd have been scared stiff."

"And what of the future? What do you propose to do next?" Swale asked.

I left the answer to Keefe, who said: "We've not got down to any definite planning. I expect we'll try to obtain passages on the company's ship when she arrives. Milson's pretty sure it can be arranged."

Swale said definitely: "And that would be your best plan. There's a trading ship which turns up periodically. She's skippered by a Frenchman; but I wouldn't advise you to approach him. I know I should be the last person to pass judgment on others; it's my job to seek out the best in them and encourage it. But I'm very much afraid this man Lacoste is something of a scoundrel. He'd be very willing to help you if he thought you had some money—but the main idea would be to transfer most of it to his own pockets."

Judith Milson said quickly: "Anyway, that belongs to the future. We're anxious to retain our guests as long as we can. So don't talk about the possibility of a government boat putting in, or suggest any other way by which they could leave here."

81

Swale smiled. "Dear lady, I understand perfectly. I know that your instincts of hospitality are starved."

She returned the smile. "And you'll pander to them by staying to lunch?"

"I'll be delighted to." He stood up. "The usual time?"

"Yes. But are you hurrying off?"

"I very much want a few words with your husband."

"You'll find him in his office."

"Splendid. I'll go there at once if you'll all excuse me."

He departed briskly, and as soon as he was out of hearing Judith Milson gave a sighing groan and said: "Which means Oliver's going to be in a bad temper for the rest of the day. He doesn't like the pastor much and simply hates having his work interrupted." She uncrossed her legs and rose from her chair. "If I'm to lay on a lunch I must turn domesticated female for a while. See you a bit later. Come and lend me a hand, Pat, will you?"

Pat followed her with a certain amount of reluctance. When they'd gone I said to Keefe: "Well, what of Pastor Swale?"

"Asked plenty of questions, didn't he? But then, these God men always do. I believe they feel a little bit out of it so far as the wicked world's concerned, and so have a compulsion to display interest in everything."

"Could be," I said. "I'm glad my bandage doesn't make a betraying bulge. That would have started off a fresh set of questions."

"What's the betting he knows all about it by lunchtime?"

"Too true," I agreed.

He grinned at me. "Well, it's your turn. I've done my story-telling for the day."

"Very successfully, too."

"Yes, I think so. Just as well for him to accept us without any reservations, because I expect he gossips wherever he goes. But for ladies being present I expect we'd have had the full story—oh so delicately expressed, naturally—of Jimmy

Prak's delinquency." He chuckled. "I like that bit he did venture—Hooley's offer of a free kick."

"Hooley's probably an engaging rogue once he's off the subject of Milson."

Keefe frowned. "Yes. You know, I doubt if Milson ranks high in the popularity poll anywhere. . . ." He ceased speaking as someone came round the corner of the bungalow. It was Kim Lee. He looked as immaculate as when we'd first seen him, but the effect was marred by an over-vivid cerise tie. He spoke to us for a moment with smiling amiability, and then continued on his way.

"I'm far more interested in him than in Pastor Swale," Keefe said quietly. "I know he's the genial Chinaman, but he's just too bloody pleased with himself."

It was nearing lunchtime when we saw the column of smoke rising from the harbour, heard excited cries and watched a stampede of natives towards the store sheds and the jetty.

"We'd better get down there," Keefe said.

I hurried from the verandah and saw Pat in the main room and told her what was happening.

"It looks a biggish fire," I said.

"I'll tell Mother and we'll come with you."

I waited. Keefe had already started, but we caught up with him at a point where there was a clear view of the harbour.

"It's the schooner!" he informed us as we joined him.

The smoke column had increased and thickened, so it completely blotted out part of the jetty and half of the nearest shed. We could see black figures darting in all directions. The after part of the schooner was hidden by the smoke, but we could see that some of the crew were still aboard. There was a lot of movement forward. Pastor Swale's boat was under power, and my first thought was that she was going to pull out from the jetty and danger. But no; she reversed, slowly and cautiously. The activity on the schooner's forecastle increased.

"They're going to try and tow her out!" Keefe explained.

"So they've given her up!"

"Looks like it," he said grimly. And as if to emphasise how right he was, we heard a dull explosion and saw a red burst of flame. Then the black smoke conquered again.

"Oil drums," I said. "At least, I expect so." I glanced at Pat. Her face was tense, her eyes full of tears. She stepped close to me and impulsively gripped my hand. "It's a terrible thing to see," she said, her voice a little unsteady. "I'd never thought the death of a ship would be so like the death of a human being. I'm expecting to hear her cry out."

"It's a bad enough sight," I agreed. "I'm going to the jetty to help—if there's anything I can do."

"Take care. Don't forget your injured arm."

Keefe was already running. I followed and soon overtook him, his progress being hindered by the swarms of excited natives. We were able to push our way through them, partly because Sergeant Ilala was hard at work restoring order and keeping them back from the jetty. I noticed he was pushing the men with rough vigour though with no signs of losing his temper. Women and children were hastened on their way with a quick and playful smack on the bottom which most of the former obviously enjoyed.

There were some casualties alongside the nearest shed to the jetty. Pastor Swale and a native were busy among them. I was relieved to see that nobody appeared seriously hurt.

The jetty itself was still swirling in smoke. A portion of it had caught fire and natives were fighting the weakening flames with hoses and stirrup pumps, and with buckets. Through a break in the smoke I saw the schooner was responding to the tow and moving smoothly away. There was now a lane of water three or four feet wide between her and the jetty. Against the human cries, the clatter of buckets, and the crackle of flames, I could hear the laboured plopping of the antiquated engine of Swale's boat. The smoke thickened and my glimpse of the schooner was over.

Milson came up to me, coughing and spluttering. His face was black, his clothes little less so.

"Thank God we've got her away!" he shouted. "If the sheds and the copra had caught we'd have burnt out."

There was another dull explosion and a red glow from the heart of the smoke.

"We'll be lucky if she doesn't blow up!" Milson gasped. "She's carrying a lot of oil drums in the hold." He darted away to encourage a native to greater effort in using a stirrup pump.

Keefe had gone to the front of a human chain passing buckets of water. I joined him in the task of containing the fire by saturating the timbers of the jetty. Once this had been achieved we switched over to attack. The flames were driven back and finally subdued. It was gruelling work, with smoke stinging our eyes and getting into our lungs; but at last it was over and we were able to look seawards, leaving to the natives the task of pouring water over the blackened timbers from which wisps of smoke stubbornly rose.

The schooner was out by the reef and burning fiercely. The leaping flames were visible now, and as we watched her main-mast fell, sending up a golden rain of sparks.

Swale's boat was returning. I was able to pick out the figure of Captain Lodge in the stern, shoulders bowed, staring back at his ship. I could imagine the bitterness of his thoughts, and selfishly hoped that I wouldn't have to meet him for a while—at least until he was over the worst.

Another explosion from the dying ship distracted my attention.

"She must have oil drums aboard," Keefe said.

"Yes. So Milson said. Taking supplies to the plantations, I suppose."

"Well, they had the presence of mind to do the right thing. Lucky Swale's boat was here, and that his man Challie kept his head. They couldn't have coped with the fire. Not much in the way of equipment."

"Or skilled fire fighters," I murmured.

"Very true. Let's see if there's anything else we can do to help Milson. My God! He's going to be in a state over all this!"

We found Milson near the first shed. Now that the smoke had cleared we could see he'd had the foresight to damp the roof and the nearest side. There were muddy pools everywhere. Milson himself was staring gloomily at the injured men. Pat had joined Swale and the native in first-aid work. She came across and said: "Nothing very serious, Dad. No really bad burns. Two men are suffering from shock and I think it would be an idea to rush them across the island to the hospital."

"Right. I'll get Kim Lee to take them." Milson hurried away.

"You're all right?" Pat asked me anxiously.

"Of course. There wasn't much we could do."

"Your eyes are red and streaming."

"The smoke was pretty thick. And I've swallowed more than is good for me."

"I've done all I can here. Let's get back to the bungalow. What you need for your throat is tea."

"Wonderful idea," Keefe said.

There was a cheer from the natives. Looking back I saw that Swale's boat had reached the jetty. Some men, I took them to be the schooner's crew, came wearily ashore. Then I saw Captain Lodge. He'd moved apart from the others and was staring towards the reef. I hesitated for a moment and then, overcoming my shrinking from the task, went along the jetty to him.

He seemed unaware of my presence. His face was smoke-grimed, his clothes filthy. One sleeve was badly torn and there was a thin trickle of blood from a cut just below his elbow.

86

"There's nothing you can do," I said. "Why not come away and rest? You're about all in."

Without turning his head he said: "It was Milson, you know. What does he do but come aboard and start creating about the loss of time! He'd expected us to be away, but we hadn't finished work on the auxiliary engine. There are some hazardous passages through the reefs, with the breeze likely to be treacherous, and the engine's essential. Another thing, a lot *more* time would be lost if we had a sudden calm. I've known it as still as the doldrums for three or four days. I've stood on the open deck and the smoke from my pipe's gone straight up.

"But there's no satisfying Milson in one of his moods. So he just hovered around, getting in our way and upsetting everybody. In the end I left him to it. Pored over the chart, working out the best way of picking up the rest of my copra cargo as quickly as maybe. Milson must have gone ashore. I didn't notice.

"Then I heard someone screaming. I came out on deck and saw Ali. It was horrifying. He was a human torch, his dungarees ablaze. He jumped straight over the side, giving a last frightful yell. I had the boat lowered, but the crew were over-excited and bungled the job. I was watching for Ali. He came up once—but went down again quickly. He didn't seem to be trying to swim. Perhaps he was too badly burned. I don't know. We couldn't find him, anyway, even though two of my boys dived from the boat."

"I'd thought there weren't any fatalities," I said. "Was Ali your engineer?"

"Yes. You might call him that. An Arab. Not bad at his job. He deserted from Lacoste's ship about a year ago, and we were glad to get hold of him because I'd had to try and act as engineer myself. None of the islanders can be left without supervision. Pretty useless that way."

He'd been talking quietly, his voice monotonously level and, for the most part, unemotional. I felt he was saying all this because it had to find utterance, not because he particularly wanted to confide in me. He stared at the schooner sombrely. Eventually he said: "That took all my attention. The horror of seeing him burn robbed me of my wits. It was only when they'd started to dive for Ali that the implication of the flames came home. I looked aft and there was a great cloud of smoke. Ali's two helpers came staggering out of it. Only just in time; there was an explosion as an oil drum went. We started to fight the fire, but it was hopeless.

"Milson will never admit it, but he's responsible. I know he is. Look—he's in the position of owner and I couldn't order him off the ship. It was typical of him, the way he wouldn't leave anyone alone to get on with the job. Went prowling around and nagging away. He'd make Ali and his two boys flustered and confused and clumsy. Oily cotton waste dropped around—a few splashes of oil. . . . Ali had been running the engine and she was overheating. . . . It wouldn't take much." His sigh became a groan. "And now it's all over," he said despairingly.

"Then come away," I urged again. "We're going to Milson's bungalow. You need a clean-up and a rest—and something in the way of a refresher."

For a moment I thought he'd agree. He half-turned, but then drew back from me as if to emphasise his decision. "I must share her ending," he said hoarsely. "It's my ending as well. She's my last command."

"There'll be another schooner," I said, doing my best to sound encouraging. "They'll have to replace her."

"And they'll replace me at the same time," he answered.

I was reluctant to leave him, but there was nothing I could do by waiting. As I left I heard him saying: "And this is the way it has to finish. The last command."

How long the schooner floated before burning down to the water I don't know. She lasted an incredible time, with smoke rising in a massive column and at its base the red flames leaping triumphantly. In the mid-afternoon, rain which earlier might have saved her came down violently, to the accompaniment of thunder and lightning. It blotted the ship from our sight. From the verandah we could barely make out the stark lines of the storage sheds and the offices. Water poured from the roof and it was like sitting behind a broad waterfall. Eventually we were driven indoors, because great raindrops were bouncing up from the ground with all the force of ricocheting bullets.

There had been only the four of us. Judith Milson and Pat. Keefe and myself. Then Milson came in, having changed his clothes but still rubbing his hair with a towel.

"Soaked to the skin," he complained. "These damned storms are on you without warning."

"Alone, darling?" his wife asked.

"Yes," he said curtly.

"What's become of Pastor Swale and poor Captain Lodge?"

"Swale's in the village somewhere. Comforting the injured and their families, I suppose. As for Captain Lodge—*poor* Captain Lodge—he's on the office verandah staring blankly out towards the reef. The rain's lashing at him but he takes no notice of it. He can't see anything of the schooner —doesn't seem aware of the fact, and just goes on staring."

"Do you mean she's gone down, Dad?" Pat demanded.

"Probably not. But her masts have fallen and she's low in the water. You can't hope to see anything of her, though, with this damned rain cutting visibility down to a matter of yards. I told Lodge, but it was sheer waste of breath. I wasn't sorry he stayed behind when I came away. Couldn't get a word out of him."

Pat said: "He's had a very nasty shock, you know."

"Damn it, he's not the only one," her father retorted irritably. "What about me? There's going to be the devil to pay over this lot. It means a full report, and it won't be possible to gloss over how the schooner came to have so much oil aboard. It wasn't essential for Lodge to put back here. He was being an old woman about minor defects in the steering and the auxiliary engine. The repairs could have waited. If he'd done that, the full consignment of oil would have been delivered to the plantations, and a full cargo of copra brought back. *Then* he could have done all the repairing and servicing he wanted—with no rush and no risk."

Judith Milson said: "If that's going to be the tone of your report you'll damn him completely."

"What else can I do?" he demanded impatiently.

"I think you're being a bit too hard on him."

"Hard on him! What you don't realise is how hard all this is going to be on me. What do I do now? How do I get the copra from the islands he failed to visit? I'll only have half the expected shipment ready for the company's boat. Can't expect *her* to do a tour of the islands picking up the copra *I* should have collected. She couldn't do it, anyway. No loading facilities." He gave his hair a final rub with the towel which he then threw aside impatiently. "If I could charter another schooner we'd probably get out of the mess. But there isn't one."

"Hooley's lugger?" his wife suggested.

"My God! Hooley's the last man I'd go to. In any case, his lugger wouldn't be suitable. She'd have to make endless trips. No, there's no way out of it. It's just a bloody mess."

He thrust his hands in his pockets and stood with his legs wide apart, looking down and scowling.

"It seems all that's left is to write one of your long reports." Judith Milson spoke coldly, and I expected an angry retort from him, but after glaring at her he swung round and hurried from the room. When he'd gone she turned to Keefe with a smile which had an almost malicious twist to it. "I said Oliver would be bad tempered for the rest of the day. It was an understatement. This is going to last. And when I say last, I mean last. As hostess, I'm glad the lunch didn't come to anything. It would have been a ghastly flop."

In the turmoil and excitement we'd all contented ourselves with a snatched bite of something—except for Captain Lodge, who'd not come near the bungalow.

"Sorry I can't suggest anything to help the situation, Judith," Keefe said.

"Oh, it'll right itself eventually. Probably when he's written his blasted report. I wonder if they're as sick of them at head office as I am! It seems to me that Oliver solves all his problems by sitting down and putting them into a report."

I said: "I'm sorry for poor old Lodge. He talked to me a bit and I'm certain he regards this as the finish of things for him. So an adverse report from your husband isn't likely to come as much of a shock."

"He knows Oliver always finds a scapegoat for anything that goes wrong," she said bitterly.

"Mother!" Pat protested. "You give the impression Dad's vindictive. I'm sure he isn't."

"Do I, Pat? I didn't mean it that way. No, Oliver isn't vindictive; but he has to be right, to justify himself to the company. I think he always believes he is in the right, too."

As suddenly as it had started, the rain ceased. There was a strange quietness.

It was broken by Milson calling irritably to one of the Chinese servants. Then there were his brisk steps as he departed, evidently returning to his office. I said to Keefe: "I'm a bit worried about Lodge. He's had no attention since the fire. No food or drink, either. Would it be an idea to have a shot at dragging him away?"

Keefe nodded. "Sure it would." He smiled. "Milson will thank us for it, anyway."

"Try to persuade him to come here," Judith Milson said.

"Perhaps your persuasive powers would be more effective," Keefe suggested.

"I doubt it. I fancy he's never been at ease with me. He's always seemed eager to get back to the seclusion of his cabin."

Pat said: "He's not only lost his ship; he's completely homeless. So far as I know, he's never had a place ashore. At least, not for ages. I asked him once about his days in the merchant navy. Apparently he was first officer on a tanker during the war. Then he became skipper of a ship trading in the Dutch East Indies, but political events put paid to that. Ever since, he's been taking the best that fate's offered."

"Fate not having been over-generous," I commented.

"Too true. But what I was going to say was that I gathered he's always stuck as near his ship as possible, volunteering to stay on board while in port, and when he couldn't do that, putting up at a hotel near the docks. I shouldn't think he's got any family. I'm awfully sorry for him because I can't see any happiness ahead. What's he going to do?"

Keefe said: "He'll take some miserable job on the water-front somewhere. He's a man totally claimed by the sea. Put him ashore and the life will slowly seep out of him—poor devil."

"All the more reason to do what we can for him now," I said, and asked Keefe: "Do I do it alone, or are you coming, too?"

"I'll walk with you," he said.

As we went down the sloping path we met Swale, coming from the village. He was accompanied by a short, youthful-faced man who wore a blue shirt and khaki slacks.

"This is Challie," Swale said.

Challie's hair was black, parted at one side, plastered down, and having a strong smell of cheap hair cream. He was no darker than a swarthy European, but his skin looked very smooth and I doubted whether he had to shave. His eyes were brown and restless. When Keefe congratulated him on his job of towing the schooner, he smiled delightedly and exclaimed: "Challie good seaman. Also good player of squeeze-box. Know all hymn tunes. Lock of Ages, Abide with Me, Jerusalem. Good cook, too." His voice was as high-pitched as a boy's, and sing-song.

Swale smiled. "I've tried to impress on him that great barkers are no biters, but to no effect." He became serious. "But that's beside the point. He did some excellent work to-day. The disaster might have been much greater but for his foresight. He was preparing to take the tow before poor Captain Lodge had realised it was the only course left."

"I'm sorry for Lodge," I said.

"A calamity for him," Swale agreed. "I've tried to give him a word of comfort, but he wasn't in the mood to listen."

"We're going to see him now," Keefe said, "in the hope of getting him to come back to the bungalow with us."

"A splendid idea. You may succeed where I failed, because he's never had much regard for me. Avoids me whenever he can. Possibly I should have persisted, but I was naturally reluctant. Or was I dodging an unpleasant task on the pretext that he's not, strictly speaking, a member of my flock?" He shook his head slowly. "It's very difficult when you attempt to get down to motives. We deceive each other, we deceive ourselves. With the best will in the world we do these things. The only one who remains undeceived is the Almighty, the All-wise. Perhaps in His wisdom He makes us a little blind to our faults—or who could live with his conscience?" He jerked his head. "Well, no profit in discussing the things beyond our understanding. Go and do your best with Captain Lodge. I may, perhaps, see you later. It was my intention to be away; but Challie tells me our little craft suffered some strain during the towing. We're on our way to inspect her." His eyes twinkled. "A formality. It's Challie's decision."

Challie giggled. "No wish to baptise Pastor all over again."

Swale said: "As I can't swim a stroke I've no wish to run any risks."

They departed in the direction of the jetty. We continued on our way to Milson's office. Lodge was standing at one end of the verandah, still grimy, his face expressionless, staring towards the reef. There was no longer any sign of the schooner, which must have gone down during the storm. Her blackened hulk was now caught in the harsh grip of coral, the beautiful but dangerous enemy of all smaller craft in these waters.

Lodge gave no indication of having noticed us, but Milson was near the open door of his office and beckoned. We stepped inside. He spoke quietly but in exasperation.

"For God's sake try to get that fellow away from here. He's driving me crazy. Been standing there for hours. I've tried to forget him, but he's got a dry cough from the smoke he's taken into his lungs and it forces my attention back to him every time he has a spasm." He offered us cigarettes from a box. I noticed that when he was lighting his own his hand was shaking.

"We've come for that purpose," I said. "It'll be something if we can get him up to your bungalow for a shower and a drink."

"It certainly will," he agreed. "Well, do what you can. You'll not only be helping him, you'll be saving my reason."

He called us back as we were making for the door. "There's something else," he said slowly. He was still keeping his voice down but the exasperation had gone from it. "I've been doing some thinking—about Lodge."

"You can see a way of letting him down lightly in your report?" Keefe asked.

Milson frowned. "No. That's impossible."

"Well, it's not for me to comment. Randall and I are outsiders. It's your affair, and it's up to you to use your sense of judgment—and of justice."

Milson didn't like that. His frown intensified and I quite expected he'd snap back; but he controlled his annoyance. "You don't know the full circumstances," he said. "This isn't an isolated incident, although it's far more serious than the many that have led up to it. There's nothing to be

94

gained by discussing that aspect. What I want to have a word with you about is Lodge's immediate future."

"His immediate future!" I exclaimed. "I don't see how that concerns us any more than the rest of this tragic business."

"It could do," Milson said. "I think we both gain by my plan. As you know, the schooner's boat was saved. They got it away when they tried to pick up that poor wretch who jumped overboard with his clothes afire. She's a cutter of sorts and she's fitted with a good outboard motor. Well, my launch is still on the slipway; but as soon as she's available I shall need her for emergency visits to some of the islands Lodge failed to reach—and I shall be in a hurry." He broke off, looked at us thoughtfully for a few seconds and said: "You can guess I'm thinking of your wish to take a look at Okama."

Keefe nodded. "Using the cutter?"

"No reason why you shouldn't find her satisfactory. She's thoroughly seaworthy and for most of the trip you'll be within shelter of the reefs. I can't pretend she'll be as comfortable as the cabin cruiser; but it will only be for a matter of five or six hours."

"That will certainly suit us," Keefe said. "It has the advantage we'll not be making demands on your time—and, talking of time, we'll be able to suit ourselves how long we stay on Okama?" He raised his eyebrows questioningly.

"Of course," Milson agreed.

"But there's a bit more to your proposal? You're going to suggest that Captain Lodge comes with us?"

Milson nervously flicked ash from his cigarette. "That's what I had in mind," he admitted. "Frankly, I'm going to have the devil of a time with Lodge hanging around brooding over the lost schooner. But there's also the thought that it will be much better for him to have something to occupy him."

It wasn't an absolutely attractive prospect. I couldn't see

Lodge being good company; but that, of course, was subsidiary to other considerations. I wondered how his presence would affect our activities inland. We certainly didn't want him with us at those times, and that was putting it mildly. We couldn't risk having him with us. But the chances were he'd be willing to stay with the boat. And we'd certainly have more freedom of movement. On the whole, I was inclined to regard the proposition with favour; so when Keefe glanced at me inquiringly I nodded.

He said: "It seems quite an idea. But will Captain Lodge agree?"

Milson's mouth tightened. "He has no option. He takes his instructions from me—until head office approves my recommendation that he be discharged from the company's service."

4

DEA-DINDA

We had less difficulty with Captain Lodge than I'd feared. At first he ignored us; but not offensively. After we'd spoken twice without response, Keefe placed a hand on his shoulder.

Lodge started. Recognition came slowly into his eyes.

"You can do no more here," Keefe said quietly.

Lodge's lips moved. I just heard the murmured words: "No. It's finished. Everything's finished."

"Then come with us," Keefe invited.

Lodge shrugged his shoulders and obeyed. He seemed to have no interest in where we were taking him. It was like escorting a condemned man still stunned by the dread sentence passed upon him.

When we came to the bungalow Judith Milson was looking out for us. As she descended the steps Lodge straightened up.

"I must apologise for my filthy appearance."

"You'll soon look spruce again," she encouraged. "Everything's laid on." She touched his arm gently. "I'm so sorry, so terribly sorry."

"You're very kind," he murmured. I sensed it was no more than politeness. He was indifferent to kindness. Indifferent to any further kicks from fate. He'd stopped fighting. He had the battered, helpless look of his ship when she was held against the reef enduring the process of destruction.

Judith Milson escorted him into the bungalow. I grasped Keefe's arm and impelled him towards our room. I wanted to know how he felt about the latest development.

"Let's have your reaction first," he said.

I'd not changed my mind since swiftly considering the prospects in Milson's office. The advantages of having the unconditional use of a boat, of not being shackled to Milson's time-table, were obvious. Lodge was likely to be a cheerless companion; but even this could benefit us, in that he would probably be unwilling to journey with us inland. He'd prefer to remain with the boat. His complete isolation of himself in his despair practically guaranteed there'd be no argument or unpleasantness.

These things I mentioned and Keefe nodded. "Fair enough," he agreed. "Much as I see it. And if we should want to visit other islands I can't visualise Lodge objecting." He sat down on the edge of his bed. "Yes, it should suit us well." He lit a cigarette and added: "Milson's certainly got his knife into Lodge. So much for the family idea that he's not vindictive!"

I said: "Are you sure that's the angle? Doesn't it all tie up with Milson's inner dissatisfaction? Being tough on any failure in others is a means of emphasising his own merit."

"Could be," Keefe admitted.

"Another thing—is Milson trying to kill as many birds as he can with one stone?"

Keefe frowned. "What are you driving at?"

"I grant the new arrangement is more convenient; he's free to use the cabin cruiser as he wishes once it's ready, without being committed to a couple of runs to Okama. But he rids himself of Lodge's irritating presence, *and* knocks on the head his wife's suggestion of taking a joy ride to Okama."

Keefe raised his eyebrows. "Meaning he has suspicions?"

"I prefer to put it that he knows his wife."

Keefe chuckled. "I wonder."

I hesitated, then said very deliberately: "Listen, Keefe. I'm not trying to interfere in any private fun and games, but we've got serious business on Okama and I don't see Judith Milson fitting into it."

"Oh, I agree," he said with bland calmness. "But it would help to have her with us for a day or so. Lull suspicions of one kind by raising entertaining suspicions of an entirely different nature."

"And how would you propose to rid yourself of her at the right moment?"

"A problem, I admit; but likely to be one of those imagined difficulties which never arise." He grinned. "However, I'll do no conspiring with the lady. Does that ease your conscience?"

"Not my conscience. My mind."

"Good." He stood up. "Shall we dutifully return to the social scene? I expect it's far from scintillating."

He was right. Lodge had rid himself of the grime and even trimmed his singed beard; but he hadn't freshened up mentally. He was sitting with hunched shoulders and might have been alone for all the notice he was taking of other people.

Undoubtedly Judith Milson had found the going heavy. She turned to us eagerly. "We're having dinner earlier," she announced, "as lunch was such a complete flop. I've sent word to Oliver, but he'll probably forget within five minutes. That's his lookout, though. Let's have a drink."

"I could certainly use one," Keefe said.

He helped her and I noticed they gave Captain Lodge a drink heavily laced with gin. He murmured his thanks but the act of swallowing seemed to be automatic. They could have given him cold tea.

Pat was near me. She said in cautious undertones: "I've tried; but I can't get so much as a grunt out of him. It was about as unrewarding as talking to a deaf mute."

"Still stunned by disaster," I said. "I think it's as well to more or less ignore him."

"I suppose so. You know, seeing him as he is now makes me feel guilty. There was a certain excitement in it all, mixed up with the tragedy."

"No need to blame yourself for a natural reaction. And don't forget that you rose to the occasion—did a good job of work."

"It was quite something to have the chance of being useful." She spoke with unusual bitterness.

I said: "This island isn't the right place for you."

A little of the fear I'd seen before crept into her eyes. "I'm scared of it. There's something insidiously destructive. Don't ask me to explain what. Or how I know. It's just a sensing, rather like being aware of the heavy atmosphere before a thunderstorm."

Unwittingly, she was being highly perceptive. But this was something I couldn't say. It was impossible to explain to her that somewhere in these islands men were being trained, in mind and body, so that they might become ruthless killers. Or that, because of our mission, an outbreak of violence was inevitable and having started there was no knowing how far it would spread.

Captain Lodge interrupted my thoughts by saying in a deep, mournful voice: "To her—God rest her." It was the schooner, of course. We all drank with him, but he didn't appear to notice this. It was as though he'd forgotten our existence. Indeed, he showed momentary surprise when Keefe took the empty glass from him and replenished it.

Pat whispered: "I hope this isn't going to be the beginning of a drinking bout."

"I doubt whether alcohol will affect him in his present condition," I told her. "Anyway, he's not hurrying it."

Lodge was just placing his drink, untouched, on a small table. Then he resumed his huddled attitude.

His presence had a dampening effect, making conversation lifeless. It wasn't possible to ignore him; that was the trouble. His moody silence oppressed us all, and Milson's arrival was a relief. He was accompanied by Swale, who immediately began a long explanation of why he had not departed.

Challie, it seemed, was still unhappy about the boat's engine and had announced his intention of going out on trial.

"As usual on such occasions, he refuses to have me aboard," Swale grumbled. "I suspect some hidden corner of heathenism. He probably has a superstitious fear that I'm destined to meet my death on water. So he takes every precaution. He's only to use a piece of cotton waste on the engine and I'm firmly put ashore while he goes out on test. This will be two nights in succession. I wouldn't have spent so long with Hooley but for Challie hearing a knock somewhere, doing an overhaul—with the inevitable sequel."

"Or was it night fishing on the sly?" Keefe asked.

Swale's eyes twinkled. "That's a possibility."

"Ever tried being really firm with him?" Judith Milson asked.

Swale rubbed the tip of his nose thoughtfully. "A time or two. I have to confess defeat. His line is that I'll be in charge when we set forth for Heaven; but meanwhile he's in charge for all seaward journeys. I've yet to find an adequate answer. He's a good man, though. Perhaps he takes advantage, but don't they all? Hooley was grumbling about Jimmy Prak sometimes sailing off in the lugger without so much as a by your leave."

With a flicker of interest Milson said: "So I've heard. According to rumour it usually happens when Hooley's drunk himself into a stupor. How true, I can't say. Any more than I know why Jimmy Prak should do it."

Lodge looked up and said sombrely: "Put a seaman ashore for long and he rots."

It surprised us all, there having been no indication that he was listening. And no one knew quite what to say. There was an uncomfortable silence, during which Lodge regarded us with an expression of gloomy defiance on his face. He'd wanted to disconcert us and he'd succeeded. Milson flicked a hostile glance at him.

Swale cleared his throat and said, too eagerly for it to appear natural: "Talking of Challie and the heathen corner in his mind, it's strange how hard primitive beliefs die. I'd have said that Challie, with only a proportion of native blood and being closely and intelligently associated with me in my work, would have been immune to local superstitions." He shook his head. "But no. I can assure you he avoids the stretch of sea to the south of Okama at night. In that way he's no more enlightened than the village fishermen."

"And why is that stretch of water to be avoided?" asked Keefe. It sounded merely conversational; but I knew he was keenly interested. So was I.

Swale said: "Oh, the Dea-Dinda," and gave a deprecating smile, as though in apology for even knowing of it.

"What on earth's that?" Pat demanded.

"A fabulous creature. A local legend, I suppose. I've found out what I can, but they're all reticent. An enormous creature believed to be half-woman, half-fish. She, or it, prowls the water on certain nights seeking human prey. My idea is that the name's a corruption of two words in the Bajau tongue, meaning the fish-woman. The Bajau, as you probably know, are Sea Gipsies, and a few of them may have settled here for a while long ago and brought their superstitions with them. But that's mere conjecture. I can't speak with any authority."

"Does anyone claim to have seen this creature?" I asked with an incredulous smile.

"One or two of the fishermen; but I couldn't get much sense out of them. Their stories were more or less identical. Owing to some misadventure or other their frail craft was still in that area when night fell. Suddenly there was a disturbance in the water, a rushing sound, and a great dark shape speeding past."

Milson said: "There was an old man I used to employ as night-watchman at the store shed. He's dead now; but he came from Okama and he mentioned the Dea-Dinda.

Claimed he'd heard his grandfather speak of having seen the thing."

Pat exclaimed: "But this is fascinating! Why have you never told me?"

Milson shrugged. "I didn't take particular notice of the story. Lot of nonsense, I thought."

"I can confirm about the grandfathers," Swale said. "I've heard much the same from older villagers. Then there seems to have been a long interval during which nobody saw, or imagined he saw, the Dea-Dinda. But the eye-witness stories have started again and the belief's back in full strength."

"But there must be a rational explanation," said Judith Milson.

"I think there is, dear lady," Swale said. "I believe the Dea-Dinda is no more nor less than a really big shark. Probably a white shark, which means it could be in the region of thirty feet. I've heard these great sharks have what might be called a regular run, appearing at about the same time each night and taking the same course. Seen from a frail outrigger such a creature would be quite frightening. On top of that there's the legend and the superstitious native mind."

"A likely enough explanation," Milson said briskly, evidently tired of the subject.

But Keefe didn't let it drop immediately. "Just where do you say this monster has been seen?"

"Between Okama and La Caverne. Incidentally, La Caverne was so named by the captain of a French ship which put in there about two hundred years ago. There is, I'm told, a vast marine cave. I've never seen it myself; Challie always insists the approaches are too dangerous." Swale turned his head. "You ever been there, Milson?"

"Never set foot on La Caverne. I believe a survey party from my company landed there; but it was before my time. Naturally, they weren't interested in the cave. They wanted to know about the plantation prospects on the island, and reported entirely adversely."

"There's a long reef between the two islands, isn't there?" Keefe asked. "I seem to remember seeing it marked on the map."

"Yes," Swale said. "With one clear break in it. And my theory is that the shark goes that way."

Judith Milson replenished our glasses. When she went over to Captain Lodge she saw that his was still on the table, untouched. She passed it to him. He took it, hesitated, and then said: "To poor Ali. We've had three of them who deserted from Lacoste's ship. He was the best of the bunch." He raised his glass and drained it in one great gulp.

Swale, standing between Keefe and myself, murmured: "The best? I don't know. Under other circumstances I'd dispute that." He glanced at his glass. He didn't take alcohol and was drinking lime juice. He sighed. "However, God rest him, poor fellow." He drank.

"You know Lacoste?" I asked.

"It's unavoidable that I should encounter him sometimes." There was marked disapproval in his voice. So much so that I didn't think he'd say anything more. But, after a brief interval, he described Lacoste to me, presenting the man more clearly than Keefe had done.

It seemed that Lacoste was in his early thirties, rather tall for a Frenchman. Dark, with a neat black moustache close-clipped to the upper line of his mouth. He smoked cigarettes, always using a small ivory holder.

"He has the sleepy, heavy-lidded eyes of a man who takes drugs," Swale added. "Whether or not he does, I couldn't say." Looking round quickly to make certain neither Judith Milson nor her daughter could overhear, he continued: "I can be more definite about other vices. Chang Yu, the trader, keeps a few Chinese girls in what he chooses to call his hotel. The place should be closed down; but Chang Yu's too cunning. I abhor a slanderous tongue and I hope I'm the last man to speak badly of my fellow-men. But there are things——" He broke off, shaking his head.

I wanted him to say more, so I pressed him a bit. "Is there nothing you can do?"

"Without proof? My dear friend, I haven't a shred of proof. I know, as surely as I know that I'm standing here at this moment, that Lacoste owns one of Chang Yu's girls. He's bought her—just as they used to buy slaves. But when Trubshaw, the assistant district officer, visits us I'm unable to lodge a complaint or lay information. Chang Yu can establish that she's a daughter by his second wife—which is true. But I can't establish that he sold the girl to Lacoste— which is every bit as true. It's all most shocking."

"Very shocking," I agreed. But that was an automatic response. I was wondering about Lacoste's Chinese girl. Was she part of the intelligence organisation? I was visualising the map in Milson's office and wondering if a symbolic silken thread, yellow in colour, could be laid across from Okama to this island. From Lacoste's Chinese girl to Milson's Chinese storekeeper.

"I'd been asleep some time when Keefe roused me gently by reaching through the mosquito netting and putting a hand on my shoulder.

"What is it?" I demanded in a whisper, as I sat up. It was an essential qualification for the job to be able to awaken fully alert.

"Nothing to alarm you," Keefe said quietly. "I've been lying thinking, and I've a hunch there might be some gain from a night prowl."

I laughed. "Not if we bump into Sergeant Ilala. I bet he hits first and investigates afterwards."

"I don't doubt it. Keep us on our toes, that thought."

I dressed quickly. The prospect of any action was welcome as a contrast to the drawn-out ordeal of the evening. Lodge had remained taciturn and firmly anchored to his gloom. Milson, while attempting to be pleasant when he remembered he was host, had been in the predicted bad temper, barely civil to his wife and treating Lodge with thinly veiled hostility. Swale had talked incessantly, probably with the intention of doing his best to restore a strained situation, but wearying everybody in the process. I, for one, was thankful when the time came that we could decently retire.

Both Lodge and Swale were staying the night. The former because he had nowhere to go, the latter because Challie came to the bungalow and announced that the engine was unsatisfactory and it would not be possible to sail until morning. Swale had protested about causing inconvenience, but Judith Milson had insisted and two camp beds had been put up in the main room.

Remembering all this I said to Keefe: "We'll have to be careful how we go. Swale probably sleeps soundly; but Lodge may well be wide awake. Walking about even."

"Quite likely," he agreed. "We won't risk going round the bungalow. We'll make for the nearest shrubs."

As soon as we were ready he slipped out cautiously, returning very quickly to report that the entire length of the verandah was deserted.

We reached the shrubs without incident. Then we worked our way under cover until we were some distance from the bungalow. We paused about half way down the slope leading to the harbour.

"Any plan?" I asked.

"Nothing very definite."

Aware that we were under observation, he'd been averse to any venture on our part which might arouse or increase suspicion. But I agreed with him that the situation was forcing our hand. Milson would pack us off to Okama as soon as he could manage it, if only for the purpose of ridding himself of Lodge. So anything we might discover on Main Island had to be discovered quickly.

"I thought we'd take a peep at Swale's boat," Keefe said. "At least go near enough to make sure Challie *is* working on the engine. We've only Swale's word for it that Challie said the job would take him most of the night."

"And after that?"

"The company's store, I think. Bearing in mind the Chinese angle you mentioned I'd like to check up on Kim Lee—if possible. I'm afraid he's too slick to leave anything incriminating around though. Assuming he isn't on the level, that is."

"According to Hooley there's something going on."

"It's always according to someone or other," Keefe complained. "We only know of Lacoste's girl according to Swale."

"You're suspicious of Swale?"

"Only on the principle of suspecting everybody. He's not my idea of the typical missionary. But then, he's Yank. And they tend to put their religious activities on a sound business footing. I bet his profit and loss account is as important as his return of conversions. It wouldn't surprise me to hear they reckon to do the job at so much a head!"

"On the same lines as economic aid plus cornering the market?"

"Yes. It's an instinct with them. Well, let's take a look in the direction of his boat."

We walked carefully to the side of the path. When we were able to get a clear view of the jetty we immediately saw the glow of lamps from Swale's boat, and as we watched we could distinguish dark figures moving about in her. The sound of voices carried across the water. There was also a metallic hammering.

"Seems just as it should be," I commented.

"No harm in having checked." Keefe sounded disappointed.

"Can't risk going nearer. We might be seen. There's plenty of moonlight."

"We'll try the company's buildings," Keefe decided.

We came to the offices first. They were in complete darkness. It occurred to me as rather surprising that Milson had not, during the evening, made the excuse of necessary work to escape from company which was only increasing his ill-humour. Perhaps, I thought, he'd been so much out of temper that even his precious books and reports had lost all appeal.

From the offices we approached the storage sheds. Added to the smell of copra was the acrid tang of charred wood from the near-by jetty. We kept well behind the sheds because of the risk of Challie or one of his crew stepping ashore to stretch his legs.

The company's store, Kim Lee's special realm, was at the end of the godowns, set back a little. It was immediately beyond the slipway where Milson's cabin cruiser was being repainted. The shed had large double doors and, at the end nearest the office block, a single one. Keefe went straight to this and to my astonishment produced a key from his pocket. It turned easily.

"How the hell do you come to have that?" I demanded.

He chuckled softly as we went inside. "I've not been wasting so much of my time as you imagine, old chap. Picked up useful bits of information from Judith. Milson has a positive phobia about losing keys. There's quite a collection of spares in the bureau at the bungalow. All neatly labelled. So I abstracted one or two at a convenient moment. This among them."

"Yes, you've been suspicious of Kim Lee almost from the start. When you roused me you talked of a hunch. Re the smiling Chinaman?"

As Keefe closed the door behind us and we stood in darkness, he said: "That's a difficult one to answer. Don't have to tell you how often a sensing of the moment gives results in our particular line. I've that sort of feeling about to-night. Propitious for making discoveries, as the astrologists might say. You don't have to warn me that I may be making a bloody fool of myself."

He'd brought a small torch. He used this to check that the slats of the shutters were firmly down. Then he switched on the light.

We were in Kim Lee's office. "Does himself well," Keefe commented. "None of Milson's austerity."

I nodded. The emphasis was certainly on comfort. There was even a small refrigerator in one corner. I pointed to it. "I wonder if head office knows their little power-house on Main Island supplies juice for this."

"I'm surprised Milson hasn't kicked," Keefe said. "And talking of surprises, it's going to be one hell of one if we unearth anything here. Too blasted neat."

He was right. Fifteen minutes convinced us that all we'd be able to learn would be matters of company business. Keefe switched off the light.

"So much for that and the value of this particular hunch."

"Where do we go from here?"

I was just beside him and I could feel him stiffen. He whispered: "Voices! Hear them?"

I listened hard. "You're right."

"We must get out as fast and quietly as we can. Leave the door to me."

So I went first, moving with my body pressed close to the wall so as to cast no shadow. I came to the corner, peered round it and moved quickly. This time shadows didn't matter, because this landward side of the store was all shadow itself. Not deep enough for full concealment, but I knew how to make the most of it. Stillness was the secret. I'd been trained to do what the wild animals do by instinct.

I could hear the voices more clearly. They were not raised unduly, but their pitch carried them. Chinese undoubtedly. I whispered this to Keefe as he joined me.

"Then what the hell goes on?" he whispered back.

I'd no idea. I was considering our position and not liking

it. The store was between us and the sea. As we stood with our backs to the wall, we faced inland. On our left were the copra sheds, the jetty, and Swale's boat. Over to the right was the huddle of compact buildings which comprised Main Island's miniature Chinatown. It was from this direction the voices were coming.

They faded out.

We waited, fully alert. Three or four minutes must have passed before we saw anyone. Keefe had heard the voices first, but I levelled the score by spotting the men. There were four of them and they were spreading out across the slope leading up to Milson's bungalow and the native village.

"Damned if I get what all this is in aid of," Keefe muttered.

"They're not after us, anyway. But they cut off our line of retreat all the same. I think we should move. We're too ruddy vulnerable here."

"Think we can make the slipway?"

I remembered there were tarpaulins over the launch. They'd provide perfect cover. Whether it would be a good observation post there was no knowing. We'd no idea what was going to happen, or where.

"Should be able to reach it," I decided. "Have to crawl. Otherwise, if any of those chaps looks this way he is going to spot us immediately against a shining background of sea."

Keefe said: "Right. We'll do it singly. I'll start. Be ready for a shooting match."

I was already taking my automatic from my under-arm holster. I hoped it wouldn't come to shooting. That would arouse everybody and about finish the deception we were practising; there didn't seem to be any explanation that would convincingly cover this night prowl. Fortunately, nothing went wrong. Keefe disappeared into the darkness of the slipway. I gave him a minute to settle down and then followed, feeling uncomfortably exposed and moving awkwardly in the attempt to protect my wounded arm. However, I soon joined Keefe under the stifling cover of the tarpaulin.

"Do we camp out for the night?" I asked.

"I'm baffled," he confessed. "While you were coming across I could only see one of the chaps up the slope. He appeared to be playing the same game as ourselves. Went into hiding in the bushes."

I felt a flicker of alarm, but it died down almost at once. It couldn't be an attack on the bungalow. That was fantastic. Besides, two of the men had been heading more in the direction of the native village. Then another idea presented itself.

"Not easy to judge in the moonlight and at a distance, but it seemed to *me* they were moving pretty cautiously. Could it be a reception for Sergeant Ilala? Are they expecting him to come snooping?"

"Might be. But would they know his intentions? I'm betting he keeps his plans very much to himself."

"They could have baited a trap."

"That's true," he admitted.

"I hope it isn't. We'd have to help him, if possible—which wouldn't suit our game."

"Suits it so badly that we do nothing," Keefe answered.

"Damn it! We can't sit by and——"

"I once watched three wretched villagers dragged out of their hovel and bayoneted to death," Keefe said, without any emotion in his voice. "A man and his wife, and a girl of about twelve. I could have saved them—but only at a cost. It was three lives against some thirty to forty. As simple as that."

"Simple to live with afterwards?"

"Until I was able to catch up with the Jap lieutenant responsible," he said, just as calmly. "I saw to it his ending was slow enough for him to have a chance to understand that it was retribution. I'm not sure if he did though. Their minds don't work that way. A Jap's like a wasp—dies with his sting out."

I wasn't going to let him divert me. "Keefe—I'm not being

an inactive witness to Sergeant Ilala's death. If it balls up our plans that's just too bad. We'll have to revise them."

"They won't kill him—too much fuss afterwards." Behind the assurance there was irritation.

We might have come to serious disagreement, but the unexpected happened and threw our thoughts on to an entirely different track. There were gaps between the tarpaulins and I was peering past the offices and up the slope. There was no movement; no sign of life. Keefe had shuffled over and was in a position which gave him a seaward view. He suddenly exclaimed in a hoarse whisper: "My God! This must be Hooley's lugger!"

I scrabbled across, not without bumping my head against the hull of the launch. Keefe pulled one of the tarpaulins back a little more, increasing the field of vision. I stared out at the black shape of the craft coming up just within the reef. There was sufficient wind for her to be gliding along under the two lugsails and her auxiliary motor was not running. There was something furtively sinister in the quietness of her approach.

Keefe muttered: "Damned if I understand this—any of it."

"Your hunch; I think things add up. Hooley's lugger, and Kim Lee's poor relations up on the slope keeping watch. With any luck we're going to learn what Milson doesn't know about Kim Lee. Remember Hooley's little teaser?"

"You may be right; but I've a feeling this isn't going to get us anywhere much."

"All knowledge is progress," I said. "Which sounds like a quote from Confucius."

He grunted.

We were sufficiently near the water to hear the anchor chains of the lugger run out; even so, the metallic clatter was lessened considerably by the background thunder rumble from the reef. Within a few minutes a dinghy was being pulled towards the shore. She was a good size and there were four men at the oars. As she came in, two men stepped over the side and waded through the shallow water.

"Challie!" I exclaimed, then realised I was wrong. "No. Must be Jimmy Prak. He's a half-caste, too, isn't he? They rather stand out amongst the natives. Have you noticed? Different build——"

"Different walk, too. Yes, I bet that's Jimmy Prak. Question is—is he on an authorised trip, or is this one of the times when Hooley's drunk?"

We stopped talking, even in whispers, for the two men who'd come ashore were very near. They moved out of my vision. I crawled along under the tarpaulin and then, lying flat, raised it enough to be able to peep out.

There were three men now and the third was unmistakably the dapper Kim Lee. He crossed to the store-shed and I heard a heavy lock shoot back. The doors were opened and all three went inside. Jimmy Prak and the native with him came out a minute or so later, staggering under the weight of a small crate. They carried it down to the dinghy, loaded it, and returned to the store for another.

The dinghy, lower in the water, returned to the lugger. It was obviously a heavier pull than the shoreward journey. Watching this, I'd returned to my original position near Keefe. The dinghy was lost against the black shape of the lugger, so we could only guess what was happening.

Keefe whispered: "Have another look at the store-shed."

I crawled back. The shed was closed again. I moved so that I could see up the slope. There were four figures hastening down it. I rejoined Keefe and told him.

"No sign of Kim Lee?"

"No."

"Cleared off as soon as he could, I suppose."

We waited in our cramped and uncomfortably hot concealment for another ten minutes. Then we emerged, stood up, and stretched ourselves. The lugger was already on her way down the coast. We watched her for a little while before climbing the slope to the bungalow. We paused once, look-ing towards the jetty. There was still activity around the lamps aboard Swale's boat.

"Kim Lee and Jimmy Prak didn't seem concerned about Challie's presence," Keefe commented. "True, being this side the long godowns they were hidden and it's just possible the lugger couldn't be seen from the jetty."

"Kim Lee no doubt knows that Swale's sleeping at the bungalow. There may not be much danger from Challie and the others; probably have a live-and-let-live arrangement. Working their separate rackets."

"Assuming Challie has a racket," Keefe murmured. "But why not? We're still more or less in the East, where to be in on a racket is as normal as doing the football pools at home."

When we came to the cover of the tall shrubs we stopped for a smoke.

"Well, there was something in your hunch," I said.

"Nothing really helpful though. The local set-up's clarified. To-night's business was no legitimate transaction."

"That's certain. We can be sure Kim Lee's cooking the store books to cover store goods which are passed on to Jimmy Prak, destined—I suppose—for Chang Yu on Okama. But is Hooley in on it?"

"I'd say he knows about it, hence the hint he dropped. He probably takes his cut, which may account for some of the comparative prosperity that so puzzles Milson and Lodge." Keefe paused before continuing slowly: "It would be in-teresting to know just what goods are in that store. You recall how easily Kim Lee equipped us—equipped us well—which suggests it's not a typical island store with the usual trade goods."

"Might pump Milson. You know, if this is organised and profitable pilfering the company's being bled white."

"Quite possible," Keefe said. "With the entire clerical staff, apart from one possible exception, beholden to Kim Lee, there's no knowing the extent of the falsifications. Don't forget, though, that Milson's a worried man. It may be he's on to something and scratching like a terrier."

"That's a disturbing thought, because what's going to happen when Kim Lee realises the game's up? Milson isn't the merciful kind and these others are likely to be a tough bunch when cornered."

Keefe put a hand on my shoulder. "There has to be a line drawn somewhere, old chap. We've enough on our shoulders without picking up other people's troubles. Over to-night's business we follow the example of the three wise monkeys. Agreed?"

It was more than a question. He was warning me and I knew he wouldn't accept any evasions. After a momentary hesitation I said heavily: "Agreed."

He smiled. "I was sure you'd see reason."

The domestic storm broke the next morning. Keefe and I were in the final stages of dressing when Judith Milson burst into the room. Her face was pale, but her eyes seemed to be afire. The heels of her ornate slippers clicked imperiously. She brushed against a chair and the silken robe she was wearing caught on the wicker and pulled open. Beneath it she wore nothing but the filmiest nightgown I'd ever seen, and in the strong morning light its transparency was complete.

I suffered a momentary paralysis and just stared. It was Keefe who reached out and adjusted the gown.

"A little too disturbing," he said softly.

"Oh, that!" She dismissed it with a shrug of her shoulders and burst out angrily: "Oliver's just told me the new plan for Okama. Getting Lodge to take you!"

"He made it sound the only way," Keefe said smoothly. "It seems all his plans are upset."

"What the hell do I care about his plans! It was settled that *we* should take you."

Keefe nodded. "I know. It's a disappointment; but that wasn't an angle I could stress." He added: "He seems keen to be rid of Lodge for a while."

"So he's told me." The lines of her mouth hardened. "Yes. *He's* told me. Why didn't you? You knew about it."

"Wasn't it better that it should come from him? Apart from the lack of opportunity for a quiet word with you, it's more discreet——"

"To the devil with discretion!" She flung herself into a chair. As she crossed her legs the robe parted again, high up, practically to her waist. Although she seemed unaware of it, I doubted this. My guess was she knew to a nicety the value of her physical attraction and was deliberately using it. "Give me a cigarette," she demanded.

Keefe did so. He struck a match and leaned towards her. "Suppose he came in here now," he said. "Wouldn't quite do, would it?"

"He's gone. Gone to his office. That's what he should have married—a nice, modern office with all the trimmings. Except a voluptuous blonde secretary. Curves don't appeal to him." She moved her hand slowly up the long curve of her thigh.

Keefe smiled. "More fool he." He flicked the spent match away. Then he said quietly: "There was nothing I could do, you know."

"Lost enthusiasm for seeing Okama—or would that be asking too much?"

"Wouldn't it have appeared mighty suspicious?"

"Everything's suspicious to Oliver. He's certain the entire world's against him." She gave a brittle laugh. "He's a sterling, hard-working character and his reward is a pittance. From his pay-packet to his bed. That's his bloody martyrdom, and he enjoys it in his perverted fashion." She drew on the cigarette, blew the smoke towards Keefe. "Don't get the idea he isn't suspicious of you, John. He suspects any man who comes within a mile of me. He has to, because it adds to his private and precious purgatory."

"You should know," Keefe said quietly.

"My God I do."

I'd been feeling more and more uncomfortable. A slight pause gave me my opportunity. "I don't think there's anything I can contribute to this," I said. "See you later."

She looked across at me as if only now made conscious of my presence. Then, unhurriedly, she arranged her robe. She smiled. "Do forgive my fury. I break out this way sometimes. I'll soon regain my hostess poise."

I returned the smile but said nothing. As I went out the gown was opening again and Keefe was stooping lower.

I found Pat alone at the breakfast table, her head bowed, her shoulders drooping. She looked up quickly as I entered.

"I'm glad you're first—and by yourself. The day's off to a lousy start," she said impetuously.

I pulled up a chair and sat down. "You don't have to talk about it. I know there's been trouble."

"She's with John Keefe now?" It was more a statement than a question.

"And may be there for quite a time," I said.

"Quarrelling?"

"Too complex for analysis."

"Like that?"

"Like that." I rather hoped she wouldn't press for more. To my relief she didn't. Belatedly realising that hostess duties had fallen on her shoulders she make a quick, confused apology and rushed to the kitchen.

When she returned she was frowning. "Everything seems to be going wrong," she said thoughtfully. "The Chinese servants can be very efficient; but they're definitely getting slack. And I've an uneasy feeling they'll turn insolent any time at all. Or am I imagining things again?"

"They probably have their moods." Saying this enabled me to switch the subject. "Talking of moods, how's Captain Lodge this morning?"

"I've not seen him. He and Pastor Swale were away early,

long before I was up. The pastor left a polite note, all thanks and apologies, explaining that Challie had sent for him; while the captain just told Ah Soong he was going for a walk. I suppose he's somewhere on the beach, staring out to sea."

Keefe and Judith Milson hadn't appeared when I'd finished breakfast. We didn't discuss them or the domestic crisis until we were sitting on the verandah. Then, when I'd given Pat a cigarette, she asked: "Knowing something of Mother's persuasive powers, what are the chances of John Keefe giving up the Okama trip?"

"It wouldn't do at all," I said quickly. "How would your father construe that?"

"The obvious way. Especially coming on top of this morning's row. It was particularly beastly. Throwing chunks of the past at each other." Her voice was a little unsteady. "It left me feeling that if they'd actually bashed each other physically it would have been much cleaner. Words can be so filthy."

"I'm sorry. Damned unpleasant for you."

"I just didn't know what to do myself. I tried to intervene once or twice, but they ignored me. I'd about reached breaking point when Dad, grey-white with rage, called her a blasted unreasonable bitch and charged out of the room. She stared after him and there was murder in her eyes. She'd managed to keep up a sort of disdainful calm; but when he'd gone her fingers were trembling as she twisted and twisted a loose button on her pyjama jacket Then she swung round and rushed straight off to see John Keefe."

Not immediately, I thought. She must have gone to her room first and changed into the all-revealing nightdress. So much for her tempestuous entrance!

It was about two hours later that I walked down to Milson's office with Keefe. There'd been no opportunity for private conversation, but as soon as we were decently away from the bungalow I said: "How did you make out with Judith?"

He smiled, and there was a hint of mockery in his eyes which told me more than his actual words. "Smoothed things over as well as I could."

"And what's she going to do? Sit around patiently until her guests return from their trip?"

"I think I managed to persuade her that would be the best plan. A pity it has to be that way; her presence would have helped us a bit. However, it's not sufficiently important to risk putting Milson into a poisonous frame of mind. I promised her it would be a very short absence—that we'd find some excuse for returning in two or three days."

"But that's impossible—unless you've a second trip in mind."

"Of course it's impossible; but I had to say something. A soothing lie's often preferable to an unpalatable truth."

"You'll have some difficulty explaining in front of you when we do return."

He smiled. "I'll cope. It'll be a violent storm but it won't last. She's not going to cheat herself of what she wants, either out of pride or temper."

I didn't answer. Words wouldn't do anything to his complacency and self-assurance. A hard kick was needed.

We reached Milson's office. His desk was strewn with papers and he seemed to have cast aside resentful and bitter thoughts of his wife, to concentrate on work. He looked up sharply as we entered, but the annoyance was only momentary.

Keefe said: "Won't keep you a minute, Milson. It's obvious you're busy."

He scratched his forehead. "Busy! You've no conception how much work there is here. If I'd a competent assistant . . . I don't know . . . head office seem to begrudge staff. They certainly believe in getting full value out of me! But never mind—what can I do for you?"

"This Okama trip. If we're going to explore the interior we'll need some gear. Camping stuff, and so on. What about your store? Is it any use having a word with Kim Lee? We'll be buying, of course. But the big question is whether he can supply."

"See him by all means. I expect he'll be able to fix you up." He smiled faintly. "You'll be surprised at what's there."

"We've been surprised already," I said. "I mean, the excellent way we were fitted out with clothes."

"Oh, luck entered into that. We carry material and two of Kim Lee's relations are tailors. He keeps them busy making up garments likely to be required. It so happened you're about the same build as Doc Porter." He turned to Keefe. "The things you're wearing were made originally for Wentworth. He was responsible for the power-house and training a few likely natives to work as engineers. He's in New Guinea now on another of the company's projects; but I expect he'll be back here sometime or other." He didn't sound enthusiastic at the prospect.

"I'm surprised you have such a range of goods in the store," I probed. "Surely it's unusual?"

He nodded. "It is." He was sufficiently interested to explain. It appeared that the company's original ideas had been ambitious and they'd visualised a small settlement of Europeans. They had sent a heavy shipment in anticipation of their requirements. "Most of the stuff's still on our hands," he added bitterly. "So much for ambitious plans! No use asking me what we've got—I leave all that to Kim Lee. I can't supervise everything." And this reminded him of the papers covering his desk. He reached for a sheaf secured by a metal clip.

I glanced at Keefe. We'd learnt enough to make sense of what we'd witnessed on the previous night. But Keefe frowned warningly. I understood. He was concerned about our possibly becoming involved, and for that reason none too pleased with my last question.

Milson looked up from the papers. "Anything else I can do for you?"

It was a clear enough dismissal. Keefe said: "No, thanks. We don't need a chit from you? Kim Lee will take our word?"

"Tell him you've seen me. That'll be sufficient."

"And what about Captain Lodge? Have you broken the news to him about this Okama trip?"

For the first time Milson sounded sour. He said: "I've given him his instructions. You'll probably find him mooning around somewhere."

In point of fact, we encountered Lodge on our way over to the store. He was making for the jetty, but when he saw us he came across.

"So you want to look at Okama," he said, regarding us without enthusiasm.

"Yes," Keefe answered. "Milson had volunteered to take us as soon as his launch is in service again; but I understand that arrangement's no longer convenient."

"Nothing ever is convenient to Milson," Lodge murmured. "Nothing that drags him off the chair in his office. He's limpet-bottomed." He stroked his beard. "It was his suggestion, no doubt, that I should take you there."

"Of course," Keefe said.

"It would be." He evidently realised this might sound strange, for he continued: "Now the schooner's gone I'm shorebound, and he hates the sight of me. So he leapt at the chance of offering you my services."

"If you're very unwilling——" Keefe began.

Lodge interrupted him. "No, it's not so. I might as well be kicking my heels on Okama as here. I've no feelings. From now on it's wiser for me to be without any. That way I won't be so sensitive to kicks." He fumbled in a pocket of his jacket and produced a small piece of charred wood, still sodden from the sea that had cast it up on the beach. "You see this. A tiny scrap of the schooner. Useless. Finished. A very proper souvenir for me to carry around." He restored it to his pocket.

"We're very sorry about that disaster, Captain," I said. "You've all our sympathy."

"Shipless ourselves, you know," Keefe reminded him. "There's a fellow feeling."

Lodge shook his head. "You didn't lose the purpose of your lives when your boat went down. Your futures didn't sink with it. There's a great difference." He straightened his shoulders. "How long are you planning to stay on Okama?"

"A few days, I suppose," Keefe said vaguely. "We want to strike inland. I've a fancy to work through that belt of jungle and perhaps climb one of the peaks. Whether we'll actually do so I can't say definitely, not having seen the place yet."

"I'd be no use as a guide," Lodge said quickly. "What's more, the peaks are rugged and I'm no climber."

"You'd be content to remain with the boat until our return?" Keefe suggested.

"I'm prepared to do that. My instructions are to place myself at your disposal." Lodge spoke a little stiffly.

Keefe frowned. "That's one way of looking at it, I suppose."

"Milson's way," Lodge muttered.

"Not necessarily ours. We'd like it to be on a friendlier basis. Couldn't you regard yourself as a member of the party?"

There was more to it than the words; Keefe was using to the full that warmth of comradeship which I'd only gradually discovered was part of his stock-in-trade, an alluring quality that he could switch on at will. He didn't succeed entirely, but Lodge responded to a certain degree. Against his mood and inclination, I was sure.

"Don't think I've got a grudge against you two over this. It's something between Milson and myself. But I can't undertake to be good company. Things have gone very badly for me. I've a heaviness, not only in my mind but right inside me. You have to understand that I'm a man who's lost everything. Everything."

"Getting away from the immediate scene of your troubles is the best thing you can do at the moment," Keefe told him.

"I don't doubt that. There's no pleasure to me in running up against Milson all the time. That's why, when I was back here for a few days, I always stayed aboard my ship as much as I could."

Keefe turned to me. "Milson seems an unpopular chap, doesn't he?" Then to Lodge he said: "When we met Hooley he spoke out against Milson pretty strongly."

Lodge nodded his head slowly. "Hate each other. That doesn't mean one's white and the other black. Hooley's a scoundrel, a man without any principles."

"What's at the back of the feud?" Keefe asked.

Lodge stroked his beard. "Can't give you the full story. It started before I came here—Milson's first days as manager. There were three company's men on the island for a while. Milson, somebody from head office, and an engineer named Wentworth. Hooley was the only other white man, because Doc Porter was away on long leave. Somewhere in Australia where his father was dying. It was the natural thing for Hooley to join the others at night—made up a bridge four-some. Milson's wife wasn't here then. There was no social life. I've heard it said that Hooley, who was only just managing to scrape along in those days, was after a job with the company. Then Milson caught him cheating at cards—and that was the end of Hooley. Hooley claims he was framed, and backs it up with some rigmarole I've never had patience to listen to. There've been other incidents since then and Hooley would like nothing better than to see Milson come a cropper. I expect that's why he's sneaking around this morning; come to gloat over the loss of the schooner."

"Hooley's around, is he?" Keefe asked sharply.

"Saw him up the slope about ten minutes ago," Lodge said.

He didn't regard it as important, but Keefe's reaction was

different. I knew at once what was at the back of his mind when he said to me: "I say, old chap! We're forgetting the message for Mrs. Milson. Would you go along and deliver it? Meanwhile, I'll see if I can persuade Captain Lodge to come over to the store with me. He'll be able to suggest what we'll need for the boat journey."

"I can do that," Lodge agreed. He added, with his usual dejection: "Help to fill in my time—has no purpose to it now."

"See you later then, Keefe," I said.

As I went up the slope my thoughts were centred on Hooley.

It might be, as Lodge had suggested, that he'd come to gloat over a reverse suffered by his enemy. But had that been so, I'd have expected him to push his way into Milson's office, with a mocking offer to give assistance with his lugger. It was more likely, and this was doubtless Keefe's immediate thought, that Hooley wanted to see us. It was a golden opportunity for renewing his previous overture. Not knowing of our objective he'd assume we'd favour a cruise, taking in all the islands. With the schooner lost, his lugger would seem to be all that remained to us.

We'd promised Milson that Hooley shouldn't go to the bungalow on our account, therefore it was up to me to do everything possible to prevent such an intrusion. The knowledge that he must have a considerable start on me, that he might well be there already, quickened my steps. There wasn't a great distance to cover, but by the time I was in sight of the bungalow sweat was pouring down my face and my shirt was saturated. This wasn't the climate for exertion. I wondered what state we'd be in when it came to pushing through the Okama jungle.

Looking towards the bungalow I discovered that my haste had been unnecessary. Hooley wasn't there. Pat and her mother were seated on the verandah, reading magazines. They looked attractively cool in their simply cut, sleeveless dresses. The distance was kind to Judith Milson. Anyone not knowing them would have taken them for women of similar age.

The natural impulse was to join them, but I had second thoughts. Hooley had had time to reach the bungalow, assuming it was his objective. So where was he? Hiding and spying? Waiting for his opportunity to do whatever he had in mind? He'd be at a considerable disadvantage if I was able to catch him off guard.

I began to make my way cautiously through the shrubs. I lacked Keefe's extensive experience, but I'd received sufficient training and practice to be able to move quietly. At intervals I stopped, listening. There were the distant voices of the plantation workers, but close about me there was a silence broken only by the flapping of leaves as a lizard scurried off, the drone of a large fly, the higher-pitched panic vibrations from one caught in a spider's web.

But eventually there was a louder rustling. I stiffened instinctively. As it was not repeated, I took a careful step which brought me to a tall palm. I waited. Then I moved to the cover of another curving trunk and peered cautiously. There was a patch of alien colour against the dull greens. It was brick red, and as I leaned forward I was able to see more. The red became squared by thick blue lines. I was looking at the back of a man who was watching the bungalow. From the vividness of his shirt I didn't think it was likely to be Hooley.

I concentrated on concealment, which was as well because, after a few minutes, the man backed away from the sheltering shrubs. I had a brief glimpse of him. Black hair, cropped in a manner resembling a crew-cut. A skin too light for a native. His build recalled the man I'd seen coming ashore from the lugger. I'd little doubt this was Jimmy Prak.

He went off through the bushes quickly and seemed to be making for the native village. I followed, rewarded at intervals by a sight of the vivid shirt. It was a short pursuit, because as soon as he came to a path he stepped out on to it boldly and stood with his hands sunk in the pockets of his khaki shorts. The attitude suggested he was listening for someone.

I moved very carefully, afraid that now there was nothing to hold his concentration the slightest sound might attract him. I made slow progress to the limit of the bushes and sank down behind one of them. I eased my position so that I was well balanced, my muscles unstrained. Then I looked out.

It was the back view again; but this time I noticed one additional thing. He had binoculars. They were back in their case, which was slung across his shoulder by a thin strap. It must have been fully five minutes before he turned round and I had a better sight of his face. His colouring was much the same as Challie's and he had similar dark eyes. But instead of complete boyishness of skin, he had a very black, thin line of moustache, and there was a darkness round his chin, particularly in a deep cleft.

He turned away again and began to whistle untunefully. A few more minutes and he became tired of standing. He came to my side of the path and I had to lean forward to see what he was doing. Then, satisfied he was simply squatting and still looking towards the village, I drew back under cover. I relaxed, relying on my ears to give me warning of any movement.

Nearly a quarter of an hour later Hooley came down the path from the native village.

"Hello, Jimmy, you vagabond! What the hell are you doin' here?"

This might be interesting, I felt. It suggested that Hooley didn't know Jimmy Prak had been spying on Milson's bungalow. And Jimmy confirmed this by his first words.

"Just walked up from the goddam jetty, boss. Jeepers, they had one hell of a fire down there. Mighta burnt out the lot."

Jimmy Prak's voice was a little shrill for a man, and he used what he probably imagined to be an American accent.

Hooley laughed. "Pity it didn't—with that bastard Milson in the middle of it."

I ducked low as they passed close to me.

Jimmy Prak asked: "You see the black cop, boss?"

"Yes. An' I didn't leave any doubt in his mind that I'm sure it was one of the plantation boys." He chuckled. "Now next time we collect from Kim Lee we'll give old Ilala some false clues an' have him right away from where somethin's really goin' on."

"You're goddam smart, boss," Jimmy Prak said.

Then I couldn't hear any more.

Some of what I'd just discovered wouldn't interest Keefe. In fact it was likely to displease him, because of his anxiety to avoid anything connected with the business of robbing the company's stores. However, I'd definitely tell him that Hooley was involved. But that was only incidental. The big problem was why Jimmy Prak had been spying on the bungalow and why he'd not admitted it to Hooley.

PART TWO

I

NIGHT HOLDS MENACE

Okama Harbour, like that of Main Island, depended on the reef for protection; but there the resemblance ended. There was a long landing stage with stubs of jetty at either end. Behind the landing stage stood a solitary shed with an ugly corrugated iron roof.

There was a broad curving beach to the north, with native craft drawn up on the dazzling white sand. Above the beach native houses were interspersed with palms.

Under Captain Lodge's guidance we went away from the village. "Have to put up at Chang Yu's hotel," he said.

"Will he expect us to accept the highly accomplished services of the girls?" Keefe asked with a grin.

"You'll barely see them," Lodge answered unsmilingly. "We'll be put in what he calls the Annexe, which you might describe as three small bungalows linked together. He'll keep the girls out of sight until he's satisfied you're not administration officials doing a snoop."

"Won't he take your word for us?" Keefe asked, raising his eyebrows.

Lodge growled: "Chang Yu wouldn't believe his own

mother without proof—which is saying a lot against a Chinaman."

The crowd of curious, smiling natives fell back as we approached Chang Yu's stores, which was a low, long, palm-thatched building on the road running parallel with the sea. We turned inland and went along a path to the terrace of the hotel. It was an impressive building for the islands, quite three times the size of Milson's bungalow. Flower beds were ablaze with colour along the terrace. The verandah was deep, with chairs and small tables in the inviting shade.

"Quite a place," I said. "Does he have many visitors?"

"Very few," Lodge said. "But that doesn't seem to worry him. The only time he's really busy here is when Lacoste arrives. There are often a few passengers aboard the ship and they get a couple of nights ashore."

"Surprising he keeps the place going," I remarked.

"He can afford it," Lodge growled.

"Profits from trading? Is business so good here?"

Lodge said: "Don't ask *me* where his money comes from. He's mixed up in some villainy with Lacoste. And if you think I'm exaggerating when I say he's lousy with money, just take a look at his ring."

It was certainly worth plenty, Chang Yu's ring. It was of gold, with a solitary stone, a magnificent ruby. In appearance Chang Yu was the antithesis of the dapper Kim Lee. He was a tubby man dressed in black silk, the smoothness of which emphasised the toadskin texture of his face. His eyes, under wrinkled fleshy lids, were reptilian in their glossy darkness. He had a thin wisp of greyish beard. He shuffled towards us on ugly feet that were encased in shabby sandals.

He welcomed us in a reedy voice, with some floweriness of expression and insincere apology for the hotel's short-comings. As Lodge had anticipated, he gave us rooms in the Annexe. These were comfortable and clean, and from the verandah there was an attractive view of the beach to the south.

We dined in the hotel, waited on by two Chinese boys who, to my unpractised eye, appeared to be identical twins. It seemed we were the only guests. As Lodge had predicted, we saw nothing of the girls. The food was excellent and Chang Yu appeared in person to present us with a bottle of first-rate white wine.

"Don't be taken in," Lodge growled when Chang Yu had shuffled away, "He'll include twice the price somewhere in your bill." After this warning he dropped back into the dreary silence which had prevailed for most of the uneventful boat journey.

About an hour after the meal Keefe and Lodge walked back to the landing stage. I remained on the verandah of the Annexe, just outside our rooms, ostensibly because I was tired, actually because we wanted to give the minimum of opportunity to anyone who might have the idea of searching our luggage.

I welcomed the chance of being alone. I wanted to sort out my impressions and clarify my thoughts, never possible when Keefe was around. And while on Main Island I'd been so closely involved in the tangle of human relationships and the various happenings that it hadn't been easy to see things in perspective. Likewise, I had been struggling to maintain an objective attitude.

I thought first about Chang Yu. Now we'd met him I felt we'd seen the principals in what might be called the local racket, the theft of store goods belonging to Milson's company. Kim Lee and his poor relations selected what was to be stolen and covered up by falsifying the books. Hooley and Jimmy Prak collected the goods and delivered them to Chang Yu. How and where Chang Yu disposed of them we'd as yet no knowledge, though I strongly suspected that what Keefe and I referred to as the Terrorists' Academy was their ultimate destination.

If so, Chang Yu became the link between the store thefts, which in themselves were of no interest to us, and the far more serious things which were taking place on the islands.

How far he was involved in these other matters wasn't easy to assess. It was possible that apart from doing business with the terrorist organisation he was completely detached from its activities. But I doubted it. Lacoste used this hotel as his island headquarters and his Chinese girl lived here. It was reasonable to regard Chang Yu as guilty. We were unlikely to be able to prove it and we'd never force admissions from him. He was old in sin; too experienced to make mistakes. If we tried spying on him we were more likely to betray ourselves than learn anything of value.

Our discoveries so far weren't highly encouraging. We'd not made much progress and there were teasing questions still unanswered. Who'd taken the papers from our room and attacked me? And, if these were the acts of underlings, who'd instructed them? Why had Hooley offered to take us for a friendly cruise? And why had Jimmy Prak been loitering near Milson's bungalow?

I could use my imagination and make this a guessing game; but there'd be no prizes that way.

I sighed and lit another cigarette.

So far I'd avoided thinking about the personal problems, but there was no escaping them. They were with me all the time, nibbling at my peace of mind. The most immediate was that Keefe and I were not proving a good team. I didn't doubt we'd be all right in the moments of action, but in the deeper sense of working together I felt there was an incompatibility which might prove serious. It could be that I was misunderstanding and being unfair to him; but he impressed me as a man living up to a successful past. He was probably sincere in seeing himself as he did, but I couldn't help feeling his self-picture was romanticised. He was playing it as a film star might. His affair with Judith Milson was an example. He'd put forward a reason or two for being on intimate terms with her, but I saw them as justifications after the fact. My interpretation was that a woman, disappointed in her marriage, bored, and aware that the years of her full physical charm were running out, had made passes at him. Passes which flattered his exaggerated self-conception and to which he'd responded with unwise eagerness.

I wasn't happy about Judith Milson either. After that one tempestuous scene she'd apparently accepted our departure for Okama calmly. I'd expressed doubts to Keefe, but he seemed genuinely satisfied that he'd persuaded her to behave prudently. "I've promised to make it up to her afterwards," he told me. "Had her eating out of my hand. You know, old chap, there's an art in taming wild women."

But had he been as successful as he imagined? Judith Milson had put on an act that morning when she burst into our room—even to calculated undressing for the occasion. Was her compliance afterwards also an act? She was a resourceful woman, and I was prepared to credit her with having some scheme in the back of her mind, with probably difficult consequences for us. So on this point I was as uneasy as Keefe appeared untroubled.

From Judith Milson it was natural my thoughts should go to Pat. But although they were more pleasant they were as disturbing in a different way. My memory carried a vivid picture of her when she'd stood beside me on the beach, the towel dropped to her feet, her beautiful body naked as she reached for a flimsy garment. I'd only to think of her perfection for my pulse to quicken. There were other pictures, too, no less upsetting to my attempted detachment. How her eyes screwed up when she laughed, the frankly trusting way they regarded me when she indulged in confidences. Her blend of almost outrageous frankness and refreshing innocence.

I knew how many times I might have kissed her and after each one I'd cursed my self-control. Cursed myself knowing that had I done so it would not have been a mere meeting of lips.

Well, I'd been on the brink and I'd stepped back and that was that. But I was not unscathed, and the last wound had come when Pat stood on the jetty and looked at me as I left her. Nothing had been said, but it was all there in her eyes, and it made me feel I was behaving abominably. She'd started to give, impulsively, perhaps. And I'd accepted. Then, when the rest of the giving was there, I'd backed away. From her point of view, in her ignorance of the circumstances, I could only be a heel.

Yet how could I have done otherwise? The satisfaction of the moment wouldn't have been sufficient for either of us. I knew this, however much I tried to keep my thoughts bound to the present and from wandering into the future. So it had to be this way because, assessed objectively, the odds were heavily against Keefe and myself. We believed we'd succeed in our mission; but for my part I was far from sure that success would also mean a safe return.

Knowing I'd done the right thing, though, didn't make me feel any better about Pat. "It's a lousy situation and I feel lousy about it," I muttered. Then I turned my heard sharply, hearing Keefe approaching.

He was alone. He dragged a chair near mine, flopped into it and stretched his legs.

"Lodge?" I asked.

"The hotel bar. Telling Chang Yu all about us, I hope. I fancy Lodge will be skilfully pumped."

"And I wonder what he'll say."

"Just what we want him to say, I hope. I anticipated Chang Yu would try to do some fact-finding in the bar; which was why I took a walk with Lodge. Gave him our cover story."

I nodded. This was not merely that we thought it would be fun to explore one of the islands; but that, to help finance our cruise, we'd undertaken a series of articles for a sailing and travel magazine and would like them to be capable of expansion into a book. Disaster having cut short our voyage we had to dig up some additional material, which we hoped Okama might supply.

After a pause, Keefe added: "As I say, I gave Lodge our story; but I'm damned if I know whether he took it in. He's so bloody indifferent to everything." Then he laughed softly. "I wonder what will happen if Chang Yu, knowing Lodge isn't an admin. snooper, offers him one of the girls. Somehow I can't imagine Lodge in his present mood . . . Or will he, as an act of desperation?"

"I wouldn't know."

There was a short silence. Then Keefe said pensively: "I wonder what Lacoste's Chinese girl is like. And how much she knows. Not that it would be any use trying it on—for information purposes, I mean. A Chinese girl concentrates on what she's doing at the moment. Ever . . . ?"

"No," I said, anticipating the question.

"There's sensual delight in their incredibly smooth skin. But there's more to it than that. A Chinese girl doesn't expect to have acquired you afterwards. It's all something to enjoy naturally, like going out to a slap-up dinner. No conditions, if you follow. Or so I've found."

I murmured: "I doubt if Judith Milson's Chinese under the skin."

He shook with laughter. "I'll give you that point," he said, and there wasn't even a speck of venom in his voice.

The next morning Keefe and I, laden with bulky ruck-sacks, set out, ostensibly to take a look at the approaches to Okama's southern peak, which was the higher of the two. Chang Yu wished us well with such impressive benevolence that we almost believed he sincerely had our well-being at heart. He offered us practical help, assuring us he could supply a reliable guide as well as two natives to carry our gear. Keefe insisted that for the purpose of the account we'd be writing later of our adventures, it would be to our advantage to manage alone even at the risk of making fools of ourselves and getting lost.

Lodge growled: "They're crazy, of course. I wouldn't accompany them for a pension." And this remark seemed to remind him of his own precarious future, so that he became moodily silent.

Chang Yu undoubtedly agreed, but was too polite to say more than was necessary to express his best wishes and his hopes that we'd succeed in accomplishing whatever we wanted.

Then we collected our rucksacks and departed, Lodge not even getting up from his chair to see us off. All he said was: "You'll find me here when you get back."

"In three days, I imagine," Keefe told him.

Lodge only grunted. I glanced back at him from the doorway and his bearded chin was sunk on his chest. His body was slumped in an attitude which suggested he was falling asleep.

We avoided the village and the curiosity of the natives by going round to the back of the hotel and making our way through the palms until we reached a path that was little more than a rough track. According to Chang Yu this led to a ridge from which we'd obtain a clear view of the peak and also of the jungle belt, which would be our main obstacle.

It took us an hour to reach and climb the limestone ridge. We rested on its crest in the welcome shade of trees. Ahead of us the jungle rose like a wall of solid green. High up it ceased in a clear-cut line and in its place was the dark contrast of naked rock, formidably jagged.

"I'm thankful we're not climbing up there," I said to Keefe.

He grinned. "You'll be more thankful still when you've sampled a bit of jungle."

Knowing that our real destination was the extreme southern tip of Okama, I said: "Can't we travel along the fringe of it?"

"Better to go the hard way. I rather think Chang Yu's

accepted us on the basis of what Lodge must have told him; but he may take it into his head to check. In which event I expect he'll send one of his servants to follow our tracks." He pointed to the great mass of greenery. "It's unlikely the chap will probe into that lot, or even have the necessary skill to attempt it. But until we're actually in jungle anyone with keen eyesight will be able to trace our progress—even when we stop making the job easy."

I nodded. So far, our seeming carelessness had been deliberate. We'd broken branches of shrubs overgrowing the track, flung down spent matches, dropped an empty cigarette carton.

Keefe lit a cigarette and said: "Now to outline the general scheme."

Anticipating, I said: "You're regarding it as a possibility that our man's on La Caverne."

He nodded. "I don't think we can overlook the two things we've learned since we decided this island was the best spec. First, it seems nobody visits La Caverne in the normal way of things. And second, there's been a revival of the Dea-Dinda nonsense which keeps local craft away from that stretch of water at night."

"The shark—if shark's the explanation—being a lucky chance of which someone's taking full advantage."

"Could be."

"And talking of Lady Luck, it seems to me we're hoping for a favour. Or have you a theory?"

"It's slender," he admitted. "Conditional all the way. If our man is on La Caverne and if the intelligence organisation considers our arrival here worthy of report a message might be sent."

"Couldn't that have happened last night?"

"I hope not, because that would suggest urgency and mean we're very definitely under suspicion. The normal procedure would surely be to wait and find out what we're proposing to do now that we're here."

"Which information Chang Yu can now supply. So to-night, or to-morrow night perhaps . . . But suppose nothing happens?"

Keefe said: "I'd be inclined to interpret it as meaning either that our man is not on La Caverne, or we're considered harmless."

I looked at the belt of jungle and sighed. "Personally, I wouldn't call that a big reward for our efforts."

He chuckled. "A sentiment you'll repeat with more feeling in two or three hours from now."

He was right. I'd had an amount of jungle training but I'd never encountered anything as punishing as this stretch on Okama. We left the bright sunlight behind us and plunged into a greenish gloom. But we didn't escape the heat; in fact we entered a concentration of it with the humidity so high that sweat was dripping from the leaves. Before we'd gone many yards my shirt was like something pulled out of the wash tub.

We were struggling along a hollow between the limestone ridge and the lower slope of the mountain. It wasn't swamp in the true sense of the word, but all the time we were trudging in a cloying ooze. The function of the trees seemed to be to support great dangling beards of moss and complex snares of creepers. Most of these and many of the small bushes were spiked, so it was impossible to avoid scratches. The oozing blood and the tang of our sweat attracted swarms of insects which nearly drove us mad. My rucksack became an intolerable burden, constantly getting hooked up and jerking me to a standstill with a violence that all but threw me.

Keefe was leading and I began to hate him for the remorseless way he plodded onwards. It seemed to me he was capable of going at twice my speed with only half the effort I had to use. When at last he halted and announced we'd have a rest I was past being grateful, I just cursed him.

He could still smile. "I know just how you feel, old chap," he said. "Believe me, although I'm accustomed to jungle I

138

find this one a stinker. Must be as bad as the Solomons, which are supposed to be among the world's worst."

I leaned against the trunk of a massive tree and eased my shoulders under the drag of my rucksack. "If Chang Yu did send anyone to check on us I'll gamble the blighter didn't venture far into this, whatever he claims afterwards."

"Very true. Moreover, we were careful when we changed direction. Only an expert tracker would have spotted any signs, and I doubt if there's one on Okama."

"Not even among the natives?"

He shook his head. "They're coast dwellers. I asked Lodge, and he told me he doesn't know of villages in the interior of these islands. There's a legend of a cannibal tribe on this one, but if it has any basis in fact they died out a long time ago. Perhaps they established contact with the coastal people and contracted some disease against which they'd neither natural resistance nor primitive remedy."

We rested for half an hour and then pushed on again. I lost count of the pauses exhaustion forced on us, just as I lost all idea of direction and the distance we were covering. Once, when we halted, I argued hotly that we were suffering unnecessarily; we could well afford to break cover and make the rest of the journey more easily.

Keefe agreed. But he added: "We'll have to do this sort of thing while we're searching for our man. And conditions may be even worse. So it's valuable training."

It was an unanswerable argument. Once again he was demonstrating his efficiency, his grip on the situation, making my doubts about him seem a little less well-founded. To what extent I was misjudging him I didn't know; the acute physical discomfort operated against clear thinking. Apart from the unpleasantness of sweat-saturated clothes, the soreness and smarting from scratches and insect bites, there were patches on my body which irritated fiendishly and I felt quite sure I was starting prickly heat. But the only thing was to struggle on and endure.

At last the jungle started to change character. There were fewer trees and in consequence a decrease in the parasitic creepers. The bush thickened, but the ground was firmer. Sky was visible again and there were lakes of sunlight.

"Nearly there!" Keefe panted.

"Thank God," I whispered.

The jungle silence was broken by the distant thunder of waves against reef. After a time we had glimpses of the sea, not only ahead but on either side. Finally, we were among friendly palms and the gleaming white beach was before us. We flopped down, wrenched ourselves free of our rucksacks, and for a while lay like men struck insensible.

When we'd recovered, we ventured as far as the most seaward of the palms. Going by the map in Milson's office I'd expected the southern tip of Okama to be a low, rocky point. In actual fact there was coral sand beach about half a mile in length, rounding off to both east and west, seeming in both directions to disappear into thickets of palms.

Between the beach and the sea was a sort of no-man's-land, a region of coral flats draped with seaweed, holding shallow pools, and presenting a mosaic of rich colourings.

"No chance of crossing that lot and getting a swim," Keefe said. "Our feet would be cut to ribbons and we'd get blood poisoning into the bargain."

Beyond the coral flats the sea was yellowish, but at a distance it changed to a deep blue, apart from the foam and the green water strip which marked the reef running from Okama to La Caverne. We used the binoculars to study the features of that small island. Although, according to the map, its summit was lower than either of the peaks on Okama, it appeared higher; probably because of rising sheer, with little or no coastal strip. It was exactly like the upper few thousand feet of an enormous mountain most of which lay underwater, and indeed, this was its probable formation. I could see no sandy beach. There were dark rocks and then unbroken green. Above this there seemed to be bare ridges which had a halo of fleecy white cloud.

"Best seen from a distance, I fancy," said Keefe. "That green mass will be a duplicate of what we've just struggled through, with a gradient to make it worse."

"Doesn't that rule the place out? Nobody would be mad enough to live in the middle of jungle."

"You're forgetting the black soil clearings. Life would be tolerable on the edge of those, especially where there's a ridge and a stream of sorts."

I nodded. We didn't discuss it further, but turned and trudged in silence back to our rucksacks. We searched until we found a well-screened spot from which we could keep the stretch of water between the two islands under observation. Then we set up our camp and prepared a meal. After that we slept.

We came properly to life towards evening. We were near enough to the jungle to get the full volume of the strident insect chorus to which the frogs added their quota; but it wasn't long before our ears became conditioned and its nuisance value decreased.

We arranged to keep watch in two-hour stretches. Staring across the moonlit sea was a strain on the eyes and the waves created patches of shadow which provided a succession of false alarms.

I took the final watch, and towards the end of it was rewarded by the lovely colourings of the dawn. Keefe joined me and for a time neither of us spoke; but at last he stretched his arms and said: "Well, that's that. Nothing doing."

"Not even a glimpse of the Dea-Dinda," I said. "Although about three times I thought I was going to see it. You know, I've a little more patience with the natives after this. It wouldn't be difficult to imagine things on any night when there's a moon."

"True. And you're not the only one who was caught, by

the way. More than once, for a few seconds, I was convinced I'd spotted something."

"And as nothing happened—any interpretation?"

"Assuming Sergius K. is on La Caverne, I'd say there's a little encouragement. There's been no urgent report on our movements."

"Unless it was done the night before last."

He grinned at me. "You'll finish up by being as pessimistic as Lodge."

The day passed slowly. We looked out at intervals and during the morning saw two native outriggers, neither of which behaved suspiciously. Time dragged. We'd put ointment on our bites and scratches, and were both fortunate in that no poisoning seemed to be developing. My skin irritation had died down and I felt little the worse for the jungle ordeal, although I didn't relish the thought of the return trip.

In spite of the covering of a thick bush we were both soaked to the skin in the early afternoon during a violent storm, but once it was over we quickly dried out.

At sundown we were eager to renew our vigilance.

"After last night," Keefe said, "the danger's going to be that we'll assume anything suspicious is just another optical illusion."

"Don't worry," I told him. "The Dea-Dinda has fired my imagination. I'm all enthusiasm to get a glimpse of the creature."

"Don't be so spellbound that you fail to give me a call," Keefe said.

And I did give him a call, during my second watch period; but not on account of the Dea-Dinda. I'd been investigating a black patch which had turned out to be the usual wave-created shadow and was lowering the binoculars when I noticed another patch, over by the reef. For a few seconds I watched without real suspicion, until I realised that, unlike the deceiving shadows, this one was persisting. I brought the glasses up to my eyes. A little quiver of excitement went through me.

I called Keefe.

By the time he was with me I was certain there was no mistake.

"A boat." I pointed and passed the glasses over to him.

He looked for several minutes. Then he said: "My God it is. Recognise it?"

"It's definitely not Hooley's lugger. Neither is it Lodge taking a solo cruise. I'd say it's Swale's boat."

After he'd watched a bit longer he said: "I don't think there's any doubt—or of where it's making for."

We took turn and turn with the binoculars trained on the black speck of the boat against the moon-sparkled water, until the small craft was lost to us amongst the black mass of the island.

Then I said: "Swale?"

"The missionary who travels freely around, with everyone taking his comings and goings for granted. Nice cover for the chief of an intelligence organisation."

"His background's vague. He doesn't seem to represent any Church in particular. Again, it could be very clever, for there *are* these American organisations for doing good. Usually regarded as a bit of a joke, of course. And Swale doesn't strike me as a man with a spiritual vocation there's a hard core of business in him."

"All very true, but it doesn't prove anything. It's going to be damned difficult to check up on him."

"There's Challie," I said. "I don't somehow think the few natives who make up the rest of the crew even have suspicions. An intelligence organisation's outside their mental scope. But Challie's different."

"A bright boy," Keefe agreed. "So bright he's probably in on it."

"Which means we daren't try to question him. Well, what's the next move?"

"Immediately, I think we both have to keep on the job. I've noted the time and there'll be some value in knowing how long the boat stays over there—assuming it's returning to-night. Then to-morrow we'll get back to Chang Yu's place and see what we can discover about Pastor Swale. Lodge may be able to tell us something."

"If there is anything and he's roused himself sufficiently from his apathy to notice."

"True; but he's a better bet than Chang Yu, who probably as a matter of principle never gives anything away."

An hour passed. The strain of gazing out across the water tired my eyes and I had to fight drowsiness. In an effort to stay awake I groped for some shells and passed them from one hand to the other, until I found the action began to have a soporific effect. Smoking would have helped, but this was denied. Perhaps we were over-cautious, but we both felt the glow of a cigarette might be risky.

At last Keefe spotted the returning boat. We watched it coming back along the line of the reef until it finally disappeared behind the palms at the end of our beach.

Keefe dropped the binoculars with a grunt of relief.

"That's the lot," he announced. "Let's snatch some sleep."

"There's still time for the Dea-Dinda before dawn," I reminded him.

"Damn the Dea-Dinda," he said wearily.

We slept until dawn when, after eating and covering up all traces of our camp, we packed our rucksacks and set off on the return journey. With speed a consideration we didn't plunge into jungle until we were very near the limestone ridge from which we'd surveyed the southern peak. There'd been few glimpses of the coast as, by keeping well in the bushes, we'd done our best to avoid the mischance of being seen.

Keefe was first to reach the top of the ridge, and after a glance seawards he beckoned me impatiently.

"What is it?" I demanded as I came up with him.

"Can you beat it? Just look down there."

We were high enough to have a view of the landing stage, although part of it was blotted out by palms and the solitary storage shed. I saw at once what had surprised Keefe. The lugger was at anchor. There was no sign of our own boat, or of Swale's; but they were probably right against the landing stage and so completely hidden from us.

"Hooley!" I exclaimed. "I wonder how long he's been here?"

"That doesn't worry me so much as his being here at all," Keefe said. "He's going to be too damned curious about us. And a bloody nuisance into the bargain."

When we reached the hotel the first person we encountered was Captain Lodge. He was on the verandah of the Annexe, and but for his chair being in a different position might never have moved since my last sight of him. Even the way he looked up was that of a man awakened from a deep sleep.

"Well, have you climbed your mountain?" he asked.

"We didn't set out with anything so ambitious in mind," I said. "This was a preliminary survey."

"And not as rewarding as we'd hoped," Keefe cut in. He threw off his rucksack and collapsed into a chair. "It's tough country."

Lodge contemplated us for a minute and said: "Yes. You look travel scarred. Do you seriously maintain you've got pleasure out of it?"

"There's a sense of achievement," Keefe replied.

"Achievement," Lodge echoed gloomily. He lowered his head again.

I pulled a chair near and sat down, stretching my legs and enjoying to the full the physical ease. Keefe broke the silence by asking Lodge if anything had happened while we'd been away.

"Nothing the first night," Lodge said. In a resentful tone he went on: "But yesterday was different. Pastor Swale arrived. His man Challie brought him ashore and fixed up a room with Chang Yu, which was unusual because Swale regards this as a place of sin and avoids it, preferring to sleep in discomfort aboard his boat. This time he'd no option though. A touch of fever. Challie put him to bed. He's better to-day, but still there."

I avoided glancing at Keefe, but I knew he must be thinking as I was, that our theory about Swale had been exploded.

"Is Challie any good as a doctor?" Keefe asked. I guessed what he had in mind and waited eagerly for the answer.

Lodge was irritatingly slow. He gave a few grunts which could have meant anything. Eventually he said: "I wouldn't know about his qualifications. He's a physic-and-prayer merchant. Give him his due—devoted. Kept on looking in at his patient. . . . Not that I saw him every time; but I heard him often enough. Praying away in his sing-song voice. Lot of rubbish."

"All through the night, you mean?"

"For a considerable part of it. Had a hell of a bad night, myself," he grumbled. "Couldn't turn in until very late; there was such an unholy row going on over at the native village. Hooley's blasted lugger had put in and the two crews were mixing with their pals ashore. A fine excuse for a party and a bit more scope than usual owing to the pastor not being around."

"And what was Hooley doing? Joining in with them?" I asked.

"Closeted with Chang Yu for a time—two precious scoundrels together! I walked along to take a look at the village revels. Didn't hurry; I was trying to get used to the feel of having all the time in the world on my hands. But when I came back they were still in Chang Yu's office behind the bar. I could see 'em with their heads together. Plotting mischief, I don't doubt."

"Good Lord! Does Hooley often come here?" I asked, feigning the traveller's interest in new surroundings and people.

Lodge scratched his cheek slowly. "I couldn't say how often; he gets all his supplies from Chang Yu's store."

"And what would he be plotting with Chang Yu?" Keefe asked.

"No idea," Lodge said. "But you can take my word that those two wouldn't get together for an honest purpose." He fumbled in his pocket for his stubby pipe and it was evident from his manner he'd done all the talking he intended for the moment.

Keefe and I left him. We went to our rooms and enjoyed the refreshing luxury of a shower. After this, I flung myself on my bed. Keefe came in.

"A sleep," I said firmly. "After that a long cool drink, and then I hope Chang Yu can produce something really good to eat."

"Not a bad programme," Keefe agreed. He crossed to the bed and, lowering his voice said: "I've just checked that Swale *is* in his room. The fever's genuine enough. He's certainly over the worst but he looks as though he's been through it. I only stayed a minute or so. Knocks our theory out, doesn't it?"

"Unless it's a fake," I suggested, but with little conviction.

"I don't think so. I've seen too much fever to be easily fooled."

"It can't be Challie, either—unless Lodge is mistaken. I'd thought of it as a possibility, remembering his habit of taking the boat out whenever he's done repair work on the engine."

Keefe nodded. He said slowly: "I'm not sure we could swear it was Swale's boat."

"It certainly wasn't the lugger. Or our boat. So by elimination——"

"Could be another boat somewhere."

"Owned by Chang Yu? Lodge should know the answer to that."

"We'll try to find out." He smiled. "But not right away. Have your sleep. I'm going to do the same."

Physically I was weary enough, but my mind had been stimulated by what Lodge told us, and so I was awake for some time. Not that the mental effort was rewarding. I merely propounded a number of questions which I was unable to answer. At last, though, I fell asleep, awakening just in time to join Keefe and Lodge as they made their way into the hotel bar. Chang Yu was not there and our wants were supplied by a young, smiling-faced Chinese boy. Having attended to us he went round the room lighting lamps. There was no electricity on Okama.

We took our drinks to a small table, and as we sat down Lodge asked: "What are your next plans?"

"Vague," Keefe confessed. "We'd like to have a crack at climbing the peak; but there's no hurry and we've had our fill of jungle for the moment. A sea trip might be an idea."

"I'm entirely at your disposal," Lodge said, a little stiffly.

"You know these waters," I said. "Would it be worth while to take a cruise round Okama?"

"If you wish to." His tone made clear that he didn't propose to recommend anything.

"We'll think it over," Keefe said, which was what I'd anticipated. La Caverne was our objective now; but to suggest it right away would be most incautious.

There was a silence, broken by Lodge saying gloomily: "I expect that by now Milson's written the report that's going to finish me with the company."

"Why are you so sure he'll be hard on you?" Keefe asked.

Lodge answered carefully: "It's one of those things that work up over a long period. Milson's a worrier. He's not only in charge; he has to be in charge every minute, if you get my meaning. There've been times when I've been forced to assert my authority as captain of the schooner. My having acted within my rights hasn't made him any less resentful. He nurses grudges and I've known for some time that he's only been waiting for an opportunity. Well, he's got it now, and he'll make the most of it." He stroked his beard. Then he shuffled in his chair and suddenly burst out: "I can't think when I'm ashore! Never can! You know, once you've decided on your plans and can spare me I'd like to take a short cruise—alone. Perhaps, that way, something may come into my mind."

Keefe said: "You've had an excellent opportunity while we've been away."

"I suppose so. But until yesterday I'd no intention of fighting against my present circumstances. Stunned by the shock of events, I suppose, the realisation of personal disaster. I was trying to resign myself to the inevitable." Lodge looked at us belligerently. "Any reason why I shouldn't fight?"

"You're the only one who can answer that," I said.

"H'm," he grunted. He looked at the empty glasses and stood up. "Let's have another drink. Have to chase up the boy—you could die in this place and nobody . . ." He was crossing to the bar and I didn't hear the rest.

Keefe leaned towards me. "What's changed his mood? It may be true he started yesterday to wonder whether he could do anything to save himself; but I'd swear he's only just come to a decision. Odd?"

"Damned odd. Let's not add it to our problems though. We've too many unanswered questions as it is."

Keefe grinned. "I think the way's paved for getting the answer to one of them without appearing over-curious." And he said, as soon as Lodge returned: "I've been thinking about your solo cruise."

"It probably sounds strange to you; but, you see, I've done most of my serious thinking at sea, uninterrupted on the bridge. Aboard the schooner I used to go for'ard during one of the night watches. It's possible to have a sense of isolation." He directed a challenging glance at Keefe.

"A man for whom I had a great respect always used to take his problems up a mountain," said Keefe. "You go off whenever you like. If we want a breath of sea air we could surely hire a boat from Chang Yu."

Lodge shook his head. "No, I'll fit in with your arrangements. There's no desperate hurry. Anyway, the only boat you could hire would be from the native village and as like as not you'd be in for a ducking."

"We won't risk that," Keefe said. "You surprise me, though. I'd have thought Chang Yu would own a launch —even though I didn't see one when we landed."

"Chang Yu has no stomach for the sea," Lodge declared. "It's said Lacoste always makes fun of him by inviting him to dinner aboard his ship—and that Chang Yu's never accepted yet." His fingers were combing his beard. "Hooley, I don't doubt, would be eager to oblige; but I'd advise against accepting anything from him."

"Why should he be eager?" Keefe asked. "You mean he'd hope to swindle us?"

"I wasn't thinking of swindling, though he'd do that if he thought he could get away with it. But Hooley's an outcast, and in spite of his thick skin that's a raw patch." Lodge paused to relight his pipe. "If he could contrive to place you under an obligation he'd have claims. Contrive's the word, because he'd use his craftiness to that end. Manufacture a situation. And then you wouldn't be able to cut him dead and you'd be in a difficult position if he called on you at Milson's bungalow."

"I understand," Keefe said thoughtfully.

Lodge actually smiled. "I'm not so sure you do, fully. Hooley knows just how bad Milson would feel about it."

Lodge maintained his more communicative mood over dinner; but we didn't learn anything of value. He talked mostly of incidents in his past, all dating back to before he

came to the islands. It was infinitely more pleasant to have
him behaving this way; but it left me puzzled by the complete change in his manner. It was as though he'd received
an unexpected reprieve, which certainly didn't tie up with
the facts as we knew them. Milson had been quite definite
about an adverse report, and Lodge not only appeared to be
taking one for granted but had still made no claim to have
thought up a way of countering it. That he proposed to do
some hard thinking didn't explain the striking departure
from his previous pessimism. I felt something else must
have happened, but what could it be?

After the meal Lodge returned to the bar, inviting us to
accompany him. I said I'd probably join him later, that I
was going for a walk first.

"On top of all the jungle travelling!" Keefe exclaimed.

"I suppose it does sound heroic; but I've a suspicion my
leg muscles may stiffen. Anyway, a little gentle exercise will
be in marked contrast."

Keefe smiled. "Don't suggest that I come, too. I'm for a
quiet drink, old chap." Very quietly, he added: "And to
size up Chang Yu if there's a chance."

"Do you need me?"

He shook his head. "Better this way, I think. Looks more
casual. Which is, I fancy, the prudent pattern of behaviour."

As soon as I was outside the hotel I heard sounds suggesting further festivities in the village. There was the
monotonous beating of drums, accompanied by hand-clapping, and the twanging of some sort of stringed instruments.
By the time I was half-way to the landing stage I could see
the glow of a large fire. Against it the palm trunks and
the edge of a native hut were intense black. There were
lively leaping shadows and, smaller, the figures creating the
shadows.

If I'd obeyed my natural curiosity I'd have made for the
village; but the thought came into my mind that Hooley
would probably be there. He wasn't, I knew, averse to finding

amusement amongst the natives, and I didn't relish an encounter which would give him an excellent opportunity to force his company on me. So I made for the landing stage. Near the storage shed this was littered with empty boxes and crates, so I'd no difficulty in finding a seat.

I must have sat a long time, undisturbed, smoking, deep in thought. Almost *too* deep in thought, because I had to move quickly when I suddenly heard someone approaching. In scrambling behind a crate I barked my shin and only just managed to choke back a full-blooded curse. The pain was swiftly forgotten, though, when I discovered there were two men and that they were Hooley and Jimmy Prak.

Evidently they'd come from the village, and I congratulated myself on my good sense in keeping away, especially as Hooley had undoubtedly been drinking heavily. He was in an argumentative mood.

"I don' wanna go to the ship. Wanna have a goo' time."

"You've had all the good time for to-night," Jimmy Prak asserted in his outrageous semi-American accent. "Yes, sir, you've had it. And how and how."

There was a scuffling, with one of them—Hooley, I imagined—gasping for breath. After that, a pause. Then Hooley demanded: "Wha's the bloody idea, anyway?"

"Boss, you're soaked. Too damn right you're soaked. And you open your mouth too damn big."

"Why shouldn' I? Talk's free."

"Too many ears on Okama now. Some other time you talk plenty and no risk. But this time you keep shut up. Get into bunk and sleep."

The scuffling was renewed, but not so violently this time. Hooley panted: "Can' fight you now. You wait till to-morrow. Belt your back into raw liver."

"Sure, sure. To-morrow," Jimmy Prak agreed cheerfully.

I'd not been to the edge of the landing stage and so hadn't noticed the dinghy; but I heard them scrambling down into it. There was a thump and Hooley yelled with pain and cried out: "You clumsy half-caste bastard!"

"Raw-liver bum to you!" Jimmy Prak shouted derisively.

I heard the oars in the rowlocks and the steady splash as Jimmy Prak pulled on them. I waited a while before looking out. Then I watched them all the way to the lugger, which was anchored close in. It had a cabin amidships, and after a minute or so a light shone through the ports. I guessed Jimmy Prak was putting Hooley to bed. I wished I could hear what was being said, and the thought flashed into my mind that it shouldn't be too difficult to find out.

I considered the risks and decided they were not formidable. There'd been no sounds from the lugger and I interpreted this as meaning that all the crew had come ashore to join the revels in the village. They'd be there for most of the night and the odds were on their dropping off to sleep under the bushes if they weren't lucky enough to find quarters in one or other of the huts. Anyway, for the time being there was no dinghy, so I couldn't be taken by surprise. On the lugger itself I'd only have to be wary of Jimmy Prak, and he was likely to have his hands full keeping Hooley from trying to get ashore again.

Even while I was working this out, I was stripping to my trunks. I stowed everything, including my automatic, inside one of the empty crates by the wall of the storage shed. It was a safe enough hiding place for a short time, I felt.

I crossed the landing stage over by one of the stumpy jetties so that I could clamber down to the water and avoid the splash of a dive. Then I struck out. Distances being deceptive at night, it was a longer swim than I'd anticipated, but not so long that I was exhausted. I rested my hands on the stern of the dinghy and then climbed aboard the lugger with the help of the mooring rope.

The deck was untidy and gave the impression they'd been taking on stores which they'd not yet troubled to stow. There were several loose coils of rope. If it came to a quick getaway I'd have to be careful; they'd be as dangerous as trip wires.

The cabin was reached by a companion ladder, and light shone up from the sliding door which was three-parts drawn back. I kept in shadow and crept over to a corner of the coach roof. The cabin ports were a little above deck level and unscreened. They were like so many lanterns. It didn't give me much space for free movement, especially if Jimmy Prak emerged suddenly.

For the moment, though, there was no danger. An argument was going on in the cabin, with Hooley complaining: "Nothin' but a bloody, interferin' spoil-sport. You should 've signed on with Pastor Swale."

Jimmy Prak laughed. "Sorry. No voice for singing, and the only songs I know too dirty for pastor. Yes, sir!"

"You're a bloody scoundrel," Hooley announced. "That's what you are, Jimmy Prak, a bloody scoundrel. You don' fool me. I know you're up to some black devilry. An' if you don' act more civil I ain' goin' on coverin' up for you. Wha's more, I'll tell——"

"You tell nothing," Jimmy Prak interrupted. "Hell's bells!" You talk and I'll spill the beans. And some! Put you on the spot if I open my mouth about the Chinese girls you bring in for Chang Yu. Get your bum kicked from here to hell!"

"I was only jokin'," Hooley protested.

"Lousy joke," Jimmy Prak retorted. "Now button up. Get some sleep."

Hooley muttered something, but I couldn't distinguish the words. There was movement in the cabin and I feared Jimmy Prak might be appearing at any second. I crossed the deck, slipped down the rope and into the water. I struck out for the landing stage, not without apprehension until I was a considerable distance from the lugger; but nothing untoward happened and it seemed I was safe. I finished the swim in a more leisurely way and perhaps not as cautiously as I should have done. My thoughts were concentrated on what I'd overheard.

I was climbing up, my head just about level with the landing stage, when the rapid pattering of steps warned me the night still held menace. I jerked my head quickly, but not fast enough to completely dodge the savage kick directed at it. The glancing blow inflicted a stabbing, agonising pain which blinded me for the moment and made me feel sick. I acted more by trained instinct than judgment in heaving myself up and grabbing at an ankle. My attacker was taken off guard and fell with a heavy thud. He was up again as though thrown back by a spring and I'd no time to brace myself properly. I did the best I could, jabbing a shoulder into him, and it checked the force of his charge so that, although I took some staggering steps I wasn't thrown right off balance.

Then we were at grips, fighting in silence broken only by our tortured breathing. He'd no skill as a boxer and that gave me an advantage as soon as I was able to thrust him away from me. I heard him grunt as I drove my fist somewhere near his heart. Then I tried an upper cut, but he was speedy on his feet and I only grazed his cheek.

He darted aside and at first I thought he was giving up and about to take to his heels. But I was wrong. He went into a crouch and sprang at me. I caught a glimpse of the knife, a wicked flash of steel in the moonlight. I swayed to the side and made a successful grab at his wrist. Then we were close together again, with the knife between us, he exerting all his strength for a swift lethal thrust, and I keeping the point down. Then I twisted his arm. He tried to stamp on my bare foot, but the shifting of his balance warned me and I swung him round so that he was in danger of falling. He'd have saved himself, but the cluttery of the landing stage was his undoing. He tripped and went down, taking me with him. He gave a choking cry. I rolled clear and shot to my feet; but he remained where he'd fallen. I

155

didn't bend over him at once, lest it might be a ruse; but his position was too unnatural, too still. Then, stepping nearer, I saw where the knife had gone deep into him.

I made no attempt to pull it out. He was dead right enough, and I didn't want blood gushing all over the planks of the landing stage. Carefully, I dragged him back into shadow. It was a gruesome task, but I pushed and prodded and folded him into one of the largest of the empty and slightly damaged crates. I closed the lid down on him. Then I found my clothes and dressed quickly.

After this, I searched for rope, found two lengths, and bound them round the crate. It was very heavy as I hauled it nearer and nearer to the edge of the landing stage. The festivities in the village were going hard and fast and there was plenty of background noise. Even so, the great splash of the crate as it struck the water was alarming. But nobody else seemed to hear.

There was a bubbling of escaping air as it went down.

I was exhausted and somewhat battered. I badly needed a brief rest, but I didn't dare take it. I went back to the hotel as fast as I could. Fortunately, Keefe had left the bar. I found him in his room, riffling through the pages of an old magazine. He looked up as I entered and his welcoming smile faded.

"What the devil have you been up to?" he demanded.

"I've just killed Challie," I told him.

2

LA CAVERNE

After demanding: "How the hell did that happen?" Keefe listened without interruption. He didn't hurry to speak when I'd finished either, but sat frowning at the lengthening ash of his cigarette. At last he said: "It's a bit sticky. Did anyone see you return?"

I shook my head. "I'm reasonably sure of that. On my way across I stopped to see if you were still with Lodge, but I stayed at the door and didn't look right in until the bar boy's back was turned."

"Good. So, provided Challie was alone, there's nothing to link you with his disappearance." He glanced at his watch. "I only had two drinks with Lodge and I've been back here for a good half-hour. You could have been with me all that time."

"I'm almost certain Challie *was* alone. I neither heard nor saw anyone else. Of course, there was Jimmy Prak on the lugger, but the odds are on his being fully occupied making sure Hooley wasn't going to give more trouble."

Keefe nodded. "That conversation you overheard is damned interesting. I expect you've the same thought—that Jimmy Prak's the intelligence agent we've been wondering about. Likely enough; he's undoubtedly a bright boy."

"There are two things that don't fit," I said. "It was Swale's boat that crossed to La Caverne. And I'm certain Challie's knife was a twin to the one thrown at me the night I disturbed the intruder."

"Both capable of explanation."

"I suppose so," I said. "Jimmy Prak might have borrowed or hired Swale's boat—or even taken it without permission. The knives could have come from Chang Yu's store, where both Jimmy Prak and Challie must have made purchases from time to time."

Keefe picked up the magazine which he'd let fall when I'd begun to tell my story. He put it on the bedside table, took a glass and poured some water from the chatty.

"You?" he asked. "Or do you prefer something stronger?"

"Water, I think."

He handed it to me and found another glass for himself. "What about the head? Aspirin?"

"Might be an idea, I think. It throbs. An unpleasant reminder that there's an important question unanswered."

"Why he attacked you?"

"Yes. What do you think?"

He didn't answer immediately. He found the tablets and then moved restlessly about the room. Finally, he came back and sat on the edge of his bed. "Did he mistake you for Hooley? Let's suppose he was at the village revels with Jimmy Prak and so knew that Hooley had started making a nuisance of himself and had been dragged off to the lugger. As time passed he wondered why Jimmy Prak was away so long and came to the landing stage to see what was happening. He saw you swimming ashore and jumped to the conclusion that Hooley had escaped. He might also think, as there was no pursuit, that Hooley had knocked Jimmy Prak senseless. Not relishing a fight he got a kick in first, hoping to stun Hooley and then fish him out of the water."

"But he'd known his mistake as soon as the fight started," I objected.

Keefe grinned. "I don't imagine there was much opportunity for explanations. Also, he probably lost his head. He'd let himself in for a charge of assault, so it seemed the safest thing was to put you out cold before you recognised him. It wasn't a long fight?"

"No. It was over pretty quickly."

"Then it warmed up so fast that he more or less went amok. Happens with these half-castes."

I frowned. "It's an explanation—but it doesn't convince me."

"Nor me," he confessed. "Just as likely he was up to some little game in no way connected with Jimmy Prak or Hooley—like a spot of pilfering from our boat. Which postulates a consciousness of guilt that panicked him."

"Or he might have reason for attacking me," I said. "Assuming he threw that knife at me outside Milson's bungalow, he wasn't to know I didn't see him clearly. Another encounter in moonlight and something might click in my memory." I paused. "My feeling, Keefe, is that we'll find he and Jimmy Prak have been in this intelligence business together. Both are half-castes, which is likely to be a bond between them. They hold similar positions with Hooley and Swale, and both make use of their respective boats for purposes of their own. I'd say that last night they'd arranged between them for Jimmy Prak to cross to La Caverne in Swale's boat. As for to-night, Challie was, as you suggested, with Jimmy Prak at first. You're probably right in thinking he came to the landing stage to satisfy himself all had gone well in getting Hooley to bed. When he saw me swimming ashore he didn't know what I might have discovered and felt the best thing was to silence me. Not too risky, really. With my clothes somewhere around it would look as though I'd been tempted into a swim. For the rest— cramp, a shark inside the reef. . . ."

"Or even snatched by your Dea-Dinda," he said with a smile. "Yes, you've got something. An explanation that at least covers more ground than any of the others." He stretched his body and rubbed his ribs. "If it's right, I wonder how much Hooley knows. I'm inclined to believe Swale's in ignorance."

"From the bit I overheard to-night I'd think Hooley knows enough to be dangerous when he's in drink and talkative, without knowing so much that it's necessary to silence him permanently. But the big problem is—what do we do?"

"I've been thinking hard," he said.

Listening to him, I had to concede that for all his play-boy diversions and his acting up to a theatrical conception of himself, he was quick to sum up an unexpected situation and work out what should be done. We had a breathing space, he maintained. There was little doubt Challie had the reputation of being something of a scamp, and his absence would, for a time, be put down to after-effects of the festivities in the native village. It wouldn't be until later on to-morrow that his disappearance was likely to be considered seriously. By then, it would be advisable to be away from Okama so that nobody could question us. But he didn't think we should clear out immediately. An unexpected departure would invite suspicion.

"We'll push off early to-morrow," he said. "I think the idea will be a cruise round Okama. We'll aim at a night landing on La Caverne, crossing soon after sundown and before the moon's high."

"How do you explain the new plan to Lodge?" I asked.

He stood up. "I'll slip over to his room immediately. I'll tell him we've decided to move off again before Hooley can start pestering us. It's a reason that should appeal to him. We'll make an early start. That way, if you're showing any bruises by morning, very few people will have the opportunity of noticing them."

"While you're talking to Lodge I'll attend to the damage. Not that there's a great deal, apart from the kick at the side of my head. Challie didn't strike out much. He depended on strangling me, and when that failed went for his knife."

In my bedroom I dealt with grazed patches on my legs and massaged some strained muscles. Then, after applying a lotion to suspected bruise spots, I flung myself down under the mosquito netting and relaxed. I was drifting gently off to sleep when Keefe returned.

I raised the netting lazily. He pulled a chair close to the bed.

"All fixed," he said.

"How did he take it?"

"Not badly. Didn't question that it was a good idea to slip away from Hooley's clutches. I've not mentioned La Caverne, by the way. Broach that later."

"Splendid!" I could see from his pleased smile that there was something else. I didn't have to wait long for it.

He leaned nearer. "I've learnt something. It arose casually, from talking about Hooley for whom, as you know, Lodge has no friendly feelings. After some slanderous comments he suddenly came out with it that Jimmy Prak's no better than his boss. I encouraged him and he told me—among other things—that both Jimmy Prak and Challie were deserters from Lacoste's ship."

I sat up. "My God! I remember now. Lodge talking of that man who died when the schooner caught fire. He said something about three deserters from Lacoste's ship, and that his man Ali was the best of them."

Keefe nodded. "I'd forgotten; but the bell tinkles faintly. Listen to the rest. He hinted that Jimmy Prak and Challie may be brothers. Apparently it's not common knowledge, but Hooley let something drop one time in the bar here. Lodge had come ashore from the schooner and found Hooley hitting the bottle."

I whistled, remembering the night when we'd been hidden near Kim Lee's store shed and Jimmy Prak had landed from the lugger. It was not that there was a close physical resemblance; but some similarity of movement or posture.

"Then we can be certain," I said quietly, "that the two

of them have been working together—that their desertion
from Lacoste's ship was a put-up job."

"Yes—and something else. Once Challie's body's discovered there's going to be hell to pay."

Our departure the next morning was effected smoothly.
By combing my hair differently I managed to cover some of
the bruise at the side of my head. Apart from this there were
no very obvious indications that I'd been in a fight, and the
solitary Chinese boy in attendance at breakfast didn't once
look at me with curiosity. So far as we could tell there was
no concern over Challie's absence.

We made our preparations and hastened to the landing
stage. There was no movement aboard the lugger and Swale's
boat was unoccupied.

"I expect his boys are still sleeping it off," Swale said.

Lodge had lapsed into his more customary uncommunica-
tive mood. He said very little until mid-morning when we'd
rounded the southern end of Okama and were sailing up the
east coast. The shore line was rocky, with occasional narrow
strips of sand. The low cliffs formed a thick black line on
which the jungle seemed to rest. Lodge pointed to a break
in them and said: "If you're minded to step ashore that's
the only place this side the island."

"Then let's try it," Keefe agreed.

It was a miniature, well-sheltered bay, but the entrance
was too narrow and the water too shallow for it to have any
potentiality as a harbour. There was a rock-studded beach
of horse-shoe shape, and as we walked across it we disturbed
an army of small crabs which scurried off in disorganised
retreat. There were palms and a thick growth of some
variety of true fern. Dense bush merged into jungle where a
stream had cut a gully down to the beach.

We sat in the shade for a while.

"Easy to imagine ourselves the only people on Okama,"

Lodge said. "If you want a hermit's holiday this is the place. I'd guarantee you no intrusions."

"What about La Caverne?" Keefe asked. "Couldn't we have an entire island to ourselves there?"

Lodge stroked his beard. "I suppose so. It's true nobody goes there. From the sea it looks most inhospitable. All mountain slopes and jungle."

Keefe turned to me. "That sounds promising for our purpose. An uninhabited island is just the thing to appeal to armchair travellers who read the magazine." He looked at Lodge again. "It *is* uninhabited, I take it?"

"Yes," Lodge answered reluctantly.

"You don't sound enthusiastic," Keefe said.

Lodge shook his head. "I'm not. I've never tried scrambling up a jungle-covered mountain, and I'm too old to begin that sort of game."

Keefe laughed. "I see what you're getting at. You wouldn't wish to accompany us exploring—and there'd be no comfort camping on the beach."

Lodge glanced up from filling his stubby pipe. "You're quite right," he admitted. "Mind you, if you insist. . . ." He shrugged his shoulders. "You know as well as I do that I've had my orders."

I felt it was time I contributed, so I said: "I've an idea. I'd very much like a good look at La Caverne. But there's surely no need for you to be with us, Captain. We won't pile the boat up on a reef, I promise you. We're very wary of reefs now."

Lodge lit his pipe before saying: "If that suits you it's clearly not in my interests to grumble. I'm well content to get my sleeping in a hotel bed."

"Splendid!" Keefe exclaimed. Then his expression became serious. Watching him, I gave him full marks for acting the part.

Lodge evidently had no suspicions. "What's troubling you?" he asked.

"Hooley," Keefe said. "If he knows we've gone over there he'll be after us, for sure. He's already tried very hard to persuade us to take a cruise with him."

"Hooley can be a damned nuisance," Lodge agreed. "Yes, he'd regard it as a golden opportunity, I don't doubt. But there's no reason why he should know. A little strategy . . ."

"Just what I have in mind," Keefe said. "Need working out carefully. So long as it's daylight and he's sober I think he'll be keeping an eye on our movements. Which suggests a night crossing."

"When you can be certain he'll be drinking," Lodge observed. In marked contrast with his earlier mood he was becoming enthusiastic. I assumed the prospect of pulling a fast one across Hooley appealed to him.

"We'll need a story to cover why we've pushed off and why you've been left behind," I said to him. "Have to say something to Chang Yu, and whatever he's told is likely to be passed on to Hooley."

Lodge grunted agreement. "The best yarn will be that you've gone back to Main Island."

Keefe cut in: "And reasonable enough after our inland journey. We've decided we need more gear. Doesn't explain, though, why you haven't gone with us."

"That's easy," Lodge commented. "Nobody's going to think it strange that I should have volunteered to wait at the hotel, keeping an eye on our stuff. It's common knowledge that I stay as far from Milson as I can. So this will be considered artful."

"Splendid." Keefe turned to me. "Then I propose we cross to La Caverne to-night, after putting Captain Lodge ashore at the landing stage."

Lodge pulled hard on his pipe, pressed the tobacco down with his thumb and announced: "Suits me." When the pipe was going satisfactorily he leaned forward, hands on knees, and continued: "Make your passage near the reef. Avoid the high cliffs and the rocks of La Caverne and don't be

tempted into going close in to find the big cave. Run down
the coast until you're past a strip of beach. It's the only sand
on the east side, but avoid it. It's quicksand. At the southern
limit of it there's a low spur of rock, a natural jetty. That's
the place for you, but don't pull in over sand. Go the other
side, where you'll find you've a fathom depth all the way."

Keefe nodded. "Thanks. With those directions we should
keep out of trouble. You landed there many times?"

Lodge shook his head. "Only once. A long time ago—just
for the sake of having set foot on every island. What I've
given you is mostly from the chart and what the natives say.
Any idea how long you'll be over there?" He added hastily:
"Don't misunderstand me. You suit yourselves. You know
my instructions."

Keefe gave me an inquiring glance. I knew what was expected and said: "Let's do the job properly. It's obviously
our best chance of exploring and we've ample supplies in
the boat."

Keefe nodded and said to Lodge: "Several days, then."

A suspicion of a twinkle came into Lodge's eyes. "If you
intend to climb the peak you'll need at least a week. I'd
advise that you camp near the boat for the first two or
three nights and limit your exploring to the lower slopes.
Don't be misled by thinking of the island as the top of a
sunken mountain. There's plenty of jungle and a number
of ugly looking ridges. Quite easy to lose yourselves and
have a bad time."

"We'll do it the careful way," Keefe assured him. Then
he asked: "But what about you and your wish to push off for
a solitary cruise in order to do some undisturbed thinking?"

For a moment Lodge stared, and I had the idea he was
nonplussed, that he'd completely forgotten this intention.
But he said easily: "Oh, don't worry about me. As a matter
of fact, as Swale's going to be in no condition to leave the
hotel for some days he'll let me take his boat."

"You're sure of that?" I asked.

"Certain. I've not much time for missionaries and Swale's a bit too much of the Yankee smart aleck for my liking, but he's a good fellow at heart. There'll be no difficulty. I've helped him out once or twice when his boat's been laid up. Given him a free passage—unknown to Milson. Yes, I can borrow his boat easily enough—and without having to take Challie along."

The words were natural, but they gave me a momentary jolt. Recovering, I wondered how Lodge would react if I announced: "You couldn't take Challie anyway. I killed him last night."

Keefe was saying: "That seems to cover everything. You'll tell Swale the same story, of course."

Lodge nodded. "But by the time he's in a condition to show any interest you'll probably be back."

Keefe stood up. "With so much ahead of us to-night I suggest we take it easy for the rest of the day."

In the thick bushes by the stream we found shadowy cover from the glare of the sun. At intervals we refreshed ourselves by swimming. Lodge plunged into the water with us and seemed to shed his worries and quite a few years with them.

Towards sundown we pushed the boat clear of the grip of the beach, clambered aboard and nosed out to sea. When we approached the familiar outline of the landing stage and the flanking stubs of jetty it was fairly dark, the moon still lying low. The lugger was at anchor with only a riding light showing.

"Hooley's ashore, I imagine," Keefe said.

"In the bar, trying to discover what's become of us," I suggested.

Lodge grunted. "More likely to be plotting mischief with Chang Yu. What these islands need is a clean-up."

"I'm not doubting Chang Yu's villainy," Keefe said. "But surely he doesn't get much scope here? I'd have expected to find him in a busier place, one with a cosmopolitan population."

"I don't claim to know what goes on," Lodge replied. "I can make a few guesses. As I see it, the big tie-up is with Lacoste—another who'd do anything for money. I'd say Lacoste often carries pretty hot cargoes. Gun-running—drugs —right up his street. And it's valuable, of course, to have some place where he can store stuff. There's always the risk of being stopped and searched, and he's too cunning to have all his eggs in one basket. It's my opinion that a raid on Chang Yu would bring to light some surprising things—and I don't mean the Chinese girls."

"Sounds reasonable," said Keefe. "But where does Hooley fit in?"

"Not involved in the big stuff." Lodge was scornful. "They wouldn't risk Hooley's tongue when it's drink-freed. But you can bet there's some crooked business. A sideline of some sort. Chang Yu can't resist a hundred per cent profit, even if it only amounts to pence." He added morosely: "He's probably rich enough to buy up everything on the islands and take over the company into the bargain. And they say crime doesn't pay! I'll tell you what doesn't— honesty."

And with that thought he left us, for we were pulling alongside the landing stage. He jumped up to it with surprising agility. I handed him the leather grip which had been his only luggage.

"See you in a few days," Keefe said.

"Ay. You'll be glad enough to be off that place. Don't forget my warning about the beach."

He raised a hand in a casual salute and strode away. The lane of water between us and the landing stage widened. It was in full shadow and very black. It looked as though it held secrets and I was reminded that I knew one of them. Somewhere down below there was a crate which held Challie's body. It wasn't a pleasant thought.

I moved aft, nearer to Keefe. We came round in a half circle and passed the lugger. Still thinking of the sunken

167

crate I said: "Lodge is going to walk right into excitement probably."

"Oh, Challie! Yes, he's surely been missed by now. I expect it will be assumed he went to the party, got too fresh with a village girl and was bumped off by a jealous rival. The sins of Jimmy Prak laid on his shoulders."

I wondered if Jimmy Prak would accept such a story, and if, later on, someone would send for Sergeant Ilala. I'd no personal apprehension. If I survived I could give my account of what had happened and it would doubtless be accepted.

When we were about level with the southern beach from which we'd kept watch in the direction of La Caverne, Keefe killed the engine. We rigged the small sail. There wasn't much wind, but sufficient to keep the canvas tight. There was an illusion of greater speed, the water disturbed by the bows was phosphorescent and creamy green. We were near the reef and the crashing roar of the waves breaking upon it seemed to make the air about us vibrate.

"Keep a sharp look-out for your Dea-Dinda!" Keefe shouted. I couldn't hear his laughter but I knew it was there.

We reached the gap in the reef and it was as though the sea suddenly decided to attack us. The boat rocked perilously and once, when we were sliding down a watery slope into a valley, I thought we were about to capsize. The realisation of survival was followed immediately by fresh apprehension as a wave swept us upward with such violence it seemed certain we'd be flung into the air. But this, too, we survived, and when we gained calmer water the worst that had happened amounted to a few bruises and a soaking to the skin.

"Lively while it lasted," Keefe panted.

We'd already wrestled with the sail, reefing it, and now we took it down. As we neared La Caverne we'd be less noticeable without it; but estimating the distance I felt Keefe was overdoing the caution. Not for the first time either. He'd cut out the engine long before any sound of it could possibly carry to the island, particularly against the competition of the reef. As I started to row my thoughts were still on this strange contradiction in Keefe, that in some ways he should be reckless, careless of the consequences, while in others he went to extremes in safety even at considerable physical cost. I'd not forgotten our hard struggle through the Okama jungle.

Gradually we drew near the black bastion of rock which Lodge had mentioned. I wasn't surprised when Keefe indicated that we should pull in towards the rock stretch where the marine cave was situated. A natural jetty beyond the quicksand beach was too obvious a place for landing. If they kept watch on La Caverne they would know this spot and we'd make an easy target for a hidden marksman. I'd no doubts about the quality of the shooting of Kabanov's trainees.

Lodge's warnings were justified. We were soon having to exercise the utmost care. Jagged rocks rose from the water all about us, and the spray from sea splashing against them filled the air so that it was like running into a thick mist. We progressed by using the boathook and an oar; gripping, hauling, pushing, squirming our way amongst the rocks. We sighted the big cave, its sharp edges and black interior eerily menacing. There were strange echo sounds from the water rushing into it.

We avoided the place, Keefe saying: "Not here. There should be others. We'll try to find something smaller."

It was an uncanny experience, the rocks rising threateningly all round us, the moon creating patches of intense shadow, the baffled sea making splashings and gurglings as it invaded crevices and retreated from them. At times the boat grated noisily against rock. Often, as I thrust the boathook into the water, thick seaweed clutched it with eager fingers. Once, in a moonlit patch I had a swift glimpse of sinuous tentacles as an octopus was startled into movement.

There were several smaller caves, and among them one that seemed ideal for our purpose. It was so low that we had to crouch as we edged the boat into it. Blackness swallowed us. Keefe switched on a torch, and by the light of this we managed to wedge the small anchor into a cleft. We'd already prepared our rucksacks and succeeded in hitching the straps over our shoulders in the confined space. Then, still forced to move with bent backs, we clambered from the boat to a narrow ledge along which we scrabbled and slipped until we emerged from the cave. Spray broke over us as we searched for a way up the cliffs. There were plenty of holds for hands and feet, but even so it was difficult going. The rock ranged from aggressive knife edges to treacherous smoothness. I was constantly grazing my skin or slipping, and as Keefe's progress was just as slow he evidently fared no better. At last we gained a wide ledge and, in exhausted silence, collapsed on it to rest.

We were in an exposed position. Any sentry above, observing our landing, could have picked us off easily; but for a while we were too spent to care about the risk. The ledge sloped upwards, and as soon as we'd recovered sufficiently to move again we discovered we could reach a V-shaped cleft which provided a less strenuous climb. At the top of the cleft we found ourselves in the thick bushes fringing the jungle and at last safe from observation.

Keefe said with satisfaction: "A successful landing, anyway. The boat's hidden, we've achieved deep cover, and there've been no bullets."

"But where do we go from here?" I demanded.

"Just follow me," was all he'd say.

My immediate thought was that he'd plunge straight into jungle, and every nerve of my tired body protested. To my relief, however, he kept to the bushes, making for the northern tip of the island, the top of the rocky bastion which overlooked the stretch of water between La Caverne and Okama. I didn't waste energy in discussing his purpose. Going through bush was easier than tackling thick jungle— but that was the most one could say in its favour. There were the ubiquitous spiked leaves and thorny ground creepers, the bushes were dense, and there was nothing even remotely like a track. Or if there was, we certainly didn't find it.

There must have been half an hour of quite arduous progress before we reached our objective; but at last the wonderful moment came when I was able to free myself from the constricting grip of the rucksack. We were not in anything of a clearing; it was no more than the space between two of the giant bushes crowning the summit of the cliff. I edged forward and looked seawards. It was a splendid vantage point, but I was thankful I'd a reasonable head for heights. The cliff was sheer and there was an appalling drop to the sea. Knowing the unwisdom of gazing down for too long, I concentrated on the more distant reef and the dark bulk of Okama.

Keefe passed me the binoculars, and with their aid I could make out the pin-points of light about the so-called harbour.

Keefe was so near to me that he was able to speak very quietly.

"We'll have to keep watch until dawn. Then—I hope—we'll rest."

"What's your plan?"

He explained. Although La Caverne didn't look very large on the map, the jungle area was considerable and, unless we were lucky, it was likely to take us a long time to discover a small huddle of huts or some cave dwellings in the great ridges of rock. Kabanov's quarters would surely be well camouflaged as protection against the chance passage of an aircraft.

Keefe was assuming that our suspicions of Challie and Jimmy Prak were correct. That being so, there was every possibility of Jimmy Prak coming to La Caverne to report Challie's disappearance. It was extremely unlikely he'd make the crossing by day, so we'd keep watch at night. We'd have to see just where he landed and hope we could get across to where he climbed the cliffs in time to follow him to Kabanov's hideout.

"There's a possibility," I said, "that Kabanov's men keep a night watch, and that when they see a boat arriving they'll go down to meet it. I know it didn't happen to-night—but it may be we were lucky and that only certain nights are arranged for communications."

"Doesn't make any difference," Keefe said. "If Jimmy Prak's met by anyone who descends the cliff, we've still someone to follow."

"And if Jimmy Prak doesn't turn up? We can't restrict ourselves to night watches indefinitely."

"Let's cross that bridge when we reach it. Reconsider the situation three nights from now."

"Fair enough," I said. "I'm in favour of anything that saves us a long jungle search. You know, they should have used troops for this job. Or a detachment of police accustomed to jungle patrols."

"It was considered. Before you came into the picture. It was decided, rightly I feel, that there'd be no hope of success. This training of terrorists isn't a local thing. It has ramifications all over south-east Asia, and elsewhere. It's the new strategy of bringing about world domination by so-called nationalist risings. Kabanov is a key man. Send troops or police and there's not a hope of keeping the operation secret. Kabanov would be warned and away before any of 'em set foot on La Caverne. The only way was by landing people like ourselves who can be vetted—as we've reason to believe we've been vetted—and still appear innocuous."

"Sounds logical. But, Keefe, one thing occurs to me. If Kabanov has a means of escape laid on, it follows he must have a boat of sorts. We can rule out aircraft. I'd say there's no possible landing strip on this island."

"There'll be a boat somewhere," Keefe agreed. "Sheer guesswork—but I think that huge marine cave's a distinct possibility. He can't rely on *La Garce*, with Lacoste only turning up at intervals. Swale's boat or Hooley's lugger wouldn't be much use to him either."

"Which suggests we should investigate the marine cave. It's the most likely place. It's vast, and I'd say there's deep water. Any hint of sailors at his establishment?"

"There's no information whatever," Keefe answered. "What's in your mind."

"I'm thinking of the importance of Kabanov being able to make a clean and undetected getaway at a moment's notice. And also of the strange reappearance of the Dea-Dinda."

Keefe laughed softly. "That damned thing's captured your imagination!"

"Perhaps. But—have you thought?—these islands are small and the natives didn't see much of the Japs during the war, so far as I can make out. A destroyer put in, according to what Lodge told me; but the Japs didn't do more than show the flag."

"And so?"

"It's unlikely any of them have ever seen a submarine. Now a small submarine—I don't mean a midget—could probably be hidden away very nicely in the cave. With the resources at the back of Kabanov it's not impossible for there to have been certain modifications to such a craft. I'm thinking particularly of carrying extra fuel and dispensing with torpedoes. They could cut down on deck guns and ammo. These savings would also reduce the crew to engine-room and navigation departments."

"It's a theory," Keefe said. "But where does the Dea-Dinda come into it?"

"Imagine a submarine seen at night by ignorant fishermen. Only partly submerged, perhaps, and with phosphorescence about her. Diving and coming up again. A bit of deliberate manoeuvring just to create the right impression, with Jimmy Prak having sown the seeds, as it were."

"You may well be right," Keefe admitted. "I'm impressed,

old chap. So impressed that we'll give the marine cave high priority."

It couldn't be done for a time though, because it would only be safe to make the descent of the cliffs under cover of darkness and we couldn't risk separating while there was the chance of Jimmy Prak arriving.

So that project was left for the moment and we arranged to split the watch for the remainder of the night, though we had no expectation of anything happening. In this we were perfectly correct. When dawn came up we drew back deeper into the bushes, prepared a meal, and snatched some sleep before the full humid unpleasantness of the day was upon us. Later, comfortable resting became impossible. The bushes prevented what current of air there was from circulating, and we were not sufficiently in jungle to have the protection of a dense leaf canopy. I suggested we might penetrate farther, but Keefe felt we should be able to look out across the sea from time to time, even though we weren't keeping a systematic daytime watch.

"I suppose you're right," I said, grudgingly.

When the full noonday heat was over we decided on a reconnaissance. Keefe went first, working his way back along the cliff to the cleft we'd climbed. At least, that was his intention, but he pushed on and was away so long I began to worry. On his return he explained: "I couldn't see an easy way down and I didn't like the look of the descent by means of our cleft. That started me thinking there must be a practicable route, especially if our suspicions about the marine cave are right. Eventually I discovered a gully, quite steep and bushy at the sides. There's an unmistakable path which drops to a point very near the natural jetty Lodge mentioned."

"A useful recce," I said. "Did you spot any signs of recent use?"

"I wouldn't swear to signs. If it's being used, it's being used with caution."

"Contemplating moving there?" I asked.

He shook his head. "Can't afford to miss anything and there may be another way down. So much for my do. Now you exert yourself."

I was to cross the tip of the island and take a look at the coastline on the other side. As Keefe had done, I worked my way through the bushes instead of venturing into the jungle. According to the map, this end of La Caverne was a rampart of high cliff forming a blunt tip a little over half a mile across.

I'd covered roughly a third of this distance when I heard sounds which made me drop flat and start wriggling into the cover of the nearest bush. Somebody was singing. It was the peculiar quarter-tone music of the East, a meaningless wail to my unattuned ears. After a minute or so it stopped and I heard voices; but I couldn't estimate the number of speakers.

I hesitated, wondering whether to go back to Keefe; but decided I had to know more for my report to be of much value.

The voices were ahead of me, and as they were neither fading nor increasing it seemed the speakers were not moving much. I tried a half-circle approach so that I should come upon them from the jungle, with thicker cover behind me.

My progress was slow. Penetrating into jungle I had to contend with the punishing tangle of spiky creepers, soft leaf-mould ground, and the occasional obstacle of a fallen tree with its rotting wood harbouring aggressive insects. I disturbed a venomous centipede and drew back sharply, sweating even more than the heat and exertion warranted. Small malignant ants attacked me and their bites were like the pricking of red-hot needles. Fortunately it was an encounter only with a few patrols. I managed to escape the excited and swarming main force.

It was necessary to keep within hearing of the hidden speakers, and as there were silences this entailed frequent halts. Gradually I began to locate their position. They were in

the narrow belt of bush between the trees and the cliff summit. It was when I judged I was more or less behind them
that I found a narrow track. I kept to its side, well under
cover, and from this comparatively safe position made my
next discovery. Right on the jungle edge there was a rough
shelter, palm-thatched and open at the sides. It was deserted.

I calculated the risks with my heart quickening a little
because deep down I was anticipating my decision. It was
essential to know how many men were stationed here and
whether they were equipped for a long or a short stay. On
the other hand, half a warning was better than no warning
at all. If I investigated and was jumped on it wouldn't be long
before there was a hue and cry after Keefe. A shot, though,
would alert him and he was too experienced a campaigner
to come blundering into trouble. I balanced the hazards
against the value of what I might learn and that was that.
I took my automatic from the holster and there was comfort
in the feel of it.

I crossed the path and dived into cover on the other side.
Then I worked my way towards the shelter. The voices were
coming from a little distance beyond, possibly about half-
way between it and the cliff edge. Crouching, I moved forward a few steps and was able to see into the shelter. There
were bushes on the seaward side, screening the talking men
from me and me from them. The danger lay in one of them
jumping up and returning.

I kept down and three awkward steps took me to one of
the uprights. I dropped lower still, a hand on the upright
for support. Kabanov didn't appear to include tidiness in
his curriculum. The place was a litter. There was an oil
stove and a drum of kerosene; also two hurricane lanterns.
A large dixie, uncleaned from a meal, had grains of rice
adhering to it. Of two metal boxes, one with a wire gauze
front contained food supplies; the other I had to reach across
and open. It held clips of ammunition for automatic rifles.
There were three sleeping-rolls and three very dirty and

crumpled bundles of mosquito netting. A large chatty of water stood by three water bottles.

Apprehension was with me all the time I was inspecting these objects. Twice a sudden raising of voices made me start back with accelerated heart-beats.

I withdrew as cautiously as I'd approached, but I retired no farther than the narrow path. I crossed this and then started to crawl through the bushes. I badly wanted a glimpse of the men, if only to check on the evidence suggesting there were only three of them. Unwittingly, they helped me. There was no natural clearing, but they'd made one by tearing up a few bushes which they'd piled high—fortunately on the side from which I was approaching. These provided an additional screen from behind which I was able to take a good look at my quarry.

As I'd anticipated, there were three of them. They were youths; not one, I judged, over twenty. All had dark, glossy hair and were slight in build. Their faces had the boyishness typical of Malay features in early manhood. They wore uniforms of a sort, between khaki and jungle green.

I withdrew carefully, and as soon as it was safe progressed as fast as I could back to Keefe. He listened with a frown of concentration. When I'd finished he said: "So all our suspicions are confirmed; they must be Kabanov's boys. They're certainly not a patrol searching for us, as it's a more or less permanent watch post." He smiled. "Pity you didn't see a duty roster. I'd like to know how long they put in at a stretch and when they're due to be relieved."

"We were damned lucky they didn't spot us last night," I said.

He nodded. "We've the human element to thank, I suppose. Probably a long period without alarms has encouraged natural indolence. Even rabid nationalism can't alter every characteristic."

"True. When I was spying on them they were deep in some kind of gambling game."

Keefe laughed softly. "There you are!" Then he was serious. "But the devil of it is they'll be unreliable both ways. They'll have their efficient periods—which means we're forced to be on our toes all the time."

The presence of Kabanov's men not only placed the burden of continuous vigilance upon us, but prevented our making any further expeditions. We decided against withdrawing to a safer spot, because we still hoped for a night messenger from Okama. It was true we now had an alternative method of finding Kabanov's headquarters as, sooner or later, the guards would be changed; but the risks would be high. We'd have to station ourselves practically on top of the outpost and it was a certainty the men there would be relieved during the hours of daylight. So we remained where we were, dividing a full twenty-four-hour watch. It was a strain, but unavoidable.

The day dragged wearily. Nothing happened during the night, and by the following morning we were a little dispirited. "Damn it!" I said. "Jimmy Prak must be worried about Challie by now. Why the hell hasn't he come across to report? Are we barking up the wrong tree, Keefe? Is it possible they use radio?"

"I've wondered," he admitted. "If there's a transmitter on Okama it will be hidden in Chang Yu's place, I suppose. But I don't think they'd use it except in emergency. There's always the chance of radio messages being picked up and somebody getting curious. Moreover, we do know they use a boat for communication. We've seen it for ourselves. I expect they have fixed times for making the run across, and only break the schedule for anything urgent. I'm not sure Challie's disappearance would grade so high—unless the body's been discovered."

"That's likely enough, anyway," I said. "The crate's right alongside the landing stage and it's not going to be long in disintegrating. It was already damaged."

Keefe said philosophically: "One thing—we're used to

sitting tight and waiting for something to happen. Makes up eighty per cent of our job."

He was right, just as he was right about the unpredictable vigilance of Kabanov's boys. We discovered it when disaster came unexpectedly that afternoon. It was during one of my spells of keeping watch. By day we didn't trouble greatly about the sea approaches; what we had to guard against was one or more of the guards taking exercise along the cliff summit. I'd gone a few yards from Keefe, in the direction of their shelter, and had settled behind a bush, relying on hearing rather than sight.

After about an hour of this I moved around, stretching my legs and fighting off the heat-induced drowsiness which was an insidious enemy. I ventured along the cliff edge and looked seawards. The sense of distance and the change of colour was a relief to eyes wearied by the closeness of green leaves.

But the relief didn't last long. I noticed something and stared incredulously. Then I whipped the binoculars to my eyes. A moment later I was back with Keefe, shaking his shoulder impatiently.

He jerked up. "What is it?"

"We're sunk! It's that bloody fool Lodge! In Swale's boat and making straight for here. What's worse, he's not alone. There are two females with him. Do I have to say more?"

Keefe whispered: "My God!" He snatched the binoculars and scrabbled away.

When he returned he looked grim.

"Well," I said bitterly, "we've been fooled nicely. So much for Lodge wanting to take a solitary cruise to get his thoughts sorted out. It was a put-up job. He went back for Judith Milson. Small wonder she took our departure so submissively! She'd worked out a scheme and knew bloody well she was going to get her own way."

It wasn't necessary to say in so many words that I blamed him. He'd created the situation by enjoying himself, and now the bill was being presented.

"So unlike Lodge," he said slowly. "I'd have sworn he was too immersed in his own troubles to have plotted with anybody."

"Remember how his mood changed?" I demanded. "We were puzzled. Surely it becomes clear now? She must have sent a message to him. Through Swale. A letter that Challie probably handed to Lodge as Swale was sick."

"That's likely," Keefe agreed. I'd never seen him look so dejected as at this moment.

"She probably offered an inducement. . . . Yes, of course! Not hard to guess. If he'd do as she wanted and say nothing about it to us, she'd undertake to kill that adverse report. That's why his troubles slipped from his shoulders. Knowing it doesn't help us any though. What are we going to do?"

He shook his head but didn't answer. He went back to the cliff edge. I listened carefully and was sure I could hear excited voices in the distance. I joined Keefe and said grimly: "They've spotted it, too."

The boat was now on our side of the gap in the reef.

Keefe still said nothing. I went on, after a pause: "He'll make for the natural jetty, and we can't stop him. If we thought up some way of signalling we'd only draw attention to ourselves."

He lowered the binoculars and crawled back to where our gear was dumped. It seemed to me there was a greyish tinge under his sun-tan. His eyes were narrowed and his mouth was tight. I squatted near and waited, feeling too angry about the consequences of his folly to help him out of his silence.

At last he said: "Much depends on what Lodge does. He'll expect to find our boat there and ourselves camped somewhere near, as he recommended." There was uncertainty in his expression. "It'll look to him as though we've gone cruising again; so there's a chance he'll put back to Okama and no great harm done."

"But if they come ashore?"

"Damned if I know. I can't picture Lodge searching the jungle on the remote possibility of finding us. If he's going to hang around in the hope we'll turn up, he'll stay down by the rocks."

"And Kabanov's boys?"

"They'll report the arrival, for certain. And watch what goes on. Kabanov's surely had descriptions of the residents, and he's not going to be greatly worried by the arrival of Judith Milson, her daughter, and Captain Lodge on some crazy picnic. It won't please him; but he won't take drastic action. Their disappearance would stir up too much trouble."

"I hope you're right," I said. "But if not, are you proposing to sit back and do nothing?"

He scowled and didn't answer.

I had the wild notion of trying to climb down and warn Lodge to push off again, though how I was to justify such an injunction I didn't know. Anyway, I realised it wasn't feasible. If Kabanov's boys were around I couldn't manage it unobserved—and that would be disastrous for all of us. I said: "We can't stop them; but at least we can sneak along the cliff and see what happens."

He shook his head. "Our friends from back here will be doing the same. Fatal to run into them."

"Of course it's dangerous," I said impatiently.

"I didn't ask Judith to follow me." He sounded resentful.

"But now she's arriving you've some responsibility. . . ."

"Damn it—I'm not accepting that! If there's trouble, she's invited it."

"If there's trouble, as you euphemistically term it, we're in a sticky position ourselves. Let Kabanov grab them for questioning and he's going to learn about us. They'll see no reason for holding out on him. Not that they could hope to do that, anyway. Do I have to remind you how quickly he could break Judith Milson down?"

Keefe winced. "Perhaps you're right," he muttered. "Let's

go." Then, with characteristic thoroughness, he hid the few items of our equipment deep in the bushes. When he straightened up his carefree smile was back. "I don't believe it's as serious as you think. Kabanov wants to stay hidden. Compared with that, satisfying curiosity's a trifle. He'll let them depart peacefully and rely on Jimmy Prak to discover later on exactly why they came here."

I didn't answer. What he said was reasonable enough, but I was filled with anxiety for Pat. I had to be certain no harm came to her. The knowledge that I was putting personal considerations ahead of the job only increased my resentment towards Keefe for having fooled around with Judith Milson and paved the way for this tricky situation.

We'd heard nothing to indicate what Kabanov's sentries were doing. The silence was nerve-tormenting. No doubt they were expert in moving quietly through bush or jungle country, so there was a definite risk of encountering them at any moment. As we set off, the only side we could afford to ignore was the cliff edge. Keefe went first and I followed at a little distance. It would be a fatal error for us to be close together. Nothing had been said, but in the event of trouble the one not in danger would use his discretion about intervening or withdrawing.

Without incident we reached the deep cleft we'd climbed on the night of our arrival. For a moment Keefe was in sight and he indicated that I should close in on him a bit. I obeyed, understanding what had prompted this. It would be fresh ground to me, but he'd surveyed it already.

When the ground sloped downwards I knew we must be approaching the deep gully which led to the beach quite near the natural jetty.

Keefe halted, and when I came up to him said very quietly: "This is where we'll need to be careful. Have to reach the cliff edge in order to watch—but we don't want to blunder into Kabanov's boys, or have them dropping on us in our observation post."

"Best plan is for one to watch the beach and the other to act as rearguard," I suggested.

He nodded agreement and then flashed a smile. "You go to the cliff edge. After all, your girl's in the boat."

We started crawling. Keefe gave me a friendly push. "I'll be right behind you," he said reassuringly. I continued between the bushes and finally pushed and wriggled forward until I could peer over the cliff edge. The boat was still some distance away, keeping well clear of the rock-studded water in the area of the vast marine cave. The canvas awning was partially rolled back, revealing some of the metal framework. Judith Milson and Pat were in the bows, and I could tell they were eagerly searching for any signs of us. Lodge was aft, at the tiller, with the box-like casing of the auxiliary engine in front of him. As I watched, he leaned forward and cut back the speed. He changed course, heading in for the rock jetty.

It seemed absurdly easy to stand up and wave to him to keep off, and infuriating that I couldn't risk it. I clung to the hope that, finding no sign of our boat, he wouldn't attempt to land.

It was a barren hope. I had the ordeal of watching him blundering into danger, and all I could do was to curse him with vigour and futility under my breath.

I dragged myself back and reported briefly to Keefe: "The bloody old fool's landing."

His face tightened. "Sod him!" Then he said wearily: "Right. See what else happens. Better you than me—I'd probably shoot him."

By the time I'd reached the edge and looked out again, the boat was alongside and they were landing. Lodge was giving Judith Milson a hand as she stepped ashore. Pat jumped gracefully to the smooth ledge. They hurried forward and started to climb the low rocks. Lodge followed, after bringing the anchor ashore and wedging it firmly.

I thought that if they came right below me I might risk

dropping a stone and then take a chance by leaning out and waving them away. But there was no opportunity. Lodge was already pointing to the mouth of the gully which was away to my left.

I watched in fuming impotence as the three of them steadily increased their distance from me. I began to consider what to do next. I might descend the gully, hoping I could keep clear of Kabanov's men. I wondered if Keefe would agree, or be stubborn about it. But before I had the chance of consulting him the unexpected happened. Two drably clad figures stepped out from the bushes at the foot of the gully. Automatic rifles were pointed threateningly. I saw Lodge's arm move. Then there was a single shot. Lodge swayed for a moment and slowly crumpled. Judith Milson threw up her hands and screamed.

3

A POINT IN TIME

Lodge wasn't killed. He came up the path, walking slowly, pressing a pad to his side. Pat was with him, giving him the support of an arm. Her mother was just behind them. One of Kabanov's men was leading, another a few paces in the rear, his automatic rifle levelled for instant use. Of the third man from the observation post there was no sign. Perhaps he'd gone direct to headquarters, reporting the sighting of the boat.

Keefe and I had descended the steep side of the gully to a position where, from the cover of bushes, we overlooked a stretch of the path. Action was forced on us, and the form it should take was a frying-pan or fire decision.

We could attempt a rescue, picking off the two terrorists before they'd a chance of firing a single shot. After that we'd have to make for the boat and lose no time in getting away from La Caverne. But even if we succeeded the cost would be high, virtually the failure of our mission, because Kabanov would be put fully on his guard and the chances of another undetected landing become very slender.

Keefe summed it up: "We'd walk straight into the bag."

The alternative was unpleasantly hazardous. I had to be taken prisoner as well, for that was the only way in which I could warn the others to make no mention of Keefe's presence on the island. Everything depended on lulling any suspicions Kabanov might have, and on Keefe's success in trailing us to the hidden headquarters.

As far as our ultimate escape was concerned, we made

what plans we could; but with so much uncertain these were very sketchy. There wasn't a lot that could be said and we lapsed into a depressed and anxious silence.

When the captives and their two guards came in sight Keefe said quietly: "Zero, old chap."

I'd already removed my under-arm holster. I handed it, and the automatic, to Keefe. His final caution was: "Try to approach them without obscuring my view. Then if they get trigger-happy, fling yourself down and I'll do the best I can." He reached out and pressed my arm. "Good luck."

"I've never needed it more," I said.

For a short distance I crawled among the bushes. Then, with a decidedly uncomfortable sensation in my stomach and my legs weakly reluctant, I stood up and strolled amongst the screening bushes towards the path. I tried to whistle. It wasn't outstandingly successful. My mouth was dry. I began to count my steps, wondering which would prove my unlucky number. Seventeen, eighteen, nineteen. The section of path directly ahead of me was clear. I had a crazy impulse to run. Twenty-five, twenty-six. The hairs at the back of my neck were standing up. The sweat bursting out on my forehead was cold. I'd forgotten how many steps I'd taken. Thirty-something. Stupidly, it seemed most important that I should know. Thirty-four, perhaps. My God! There was a definite rustling. Very near and over to my right. Would I know anything when the bullet came? Searing flame through all my nerves and then the blackness of extinction? If only I could remember just how many steps. . . .

There was an imperative shout in a high-pitched voice. God! This was it.

I turned slowly.

When I'd last seen him close he'd been playing a gambling game, rolling dice and laughing. A boy, a pleasant-looking boy. Now he was a disciple of death, his dark eyes menacing.

Keeping my hands well away from my body I raised them. He snapped an order. I shook my head. I tried to look startled, incredulous. I didn't have to try to look afraid.

He jerked his rifle in an unmistakable gesture towards the path. I obeyed. He backed away a little, on guard against trickery, ready to shoot me down at the first sign of it. But he didn't tighten his finger over the trigger and I could have shaken him by the hand for his restraint.

We came in sight of the others and there was an exclamation from Pat. She started to run towards me.

"Keep back!" I warned.

And the terrorist guarding the three of them swung his rifle menacingly. The nerve-straining moment passed. I kept moving at the same steady pace. Lodge said in a low, hoarse voice: "Randall—what the hell's all this about?"

Judith Milson began an urgent question but I cut it off by snapping: "Don't mention him." I hoped our captors didn't understand English. Although they appeared to be of Malayan stock they were most likely Indonesian. From their exchange of swift, perplexed glances I was pretty sure the present situation had them beaten.

I pointed to the pad Lodge was holding to his side and asked if I might fix him up more comfortably. They gave me the impression of trying to understand, but the words didn't seem to mean anything, which was the reassurance I needed. I explained by signs and they shrugged their shoulders; but I wasn't free to help Lodge immediately. One of them beckoned, and as I stepped towards him the other put down his rifle, came to my side and ran his slender brown hands over me expertly. Satisfied, he darted back and picked up his gun.

Pat was wearing a filmy slip underneath her cotton dress, and she ripped a strip from this.

"Only a flesh wound," said Lodge. "But a bit deep."

I fixed a bandage as well as I could and while doing it,

under cover of apparently giving instructions to Pat, who was helping me, I managed to put across the vital warning.

"The less you know the better. We're in for some rigorous questioning. Don't try to be clever. Tell what you know—but insist that I came over here alone and my pal's remained with Swale, who's down with fever. Understand?"

"Damned if I understand," Lodge complained. "But I'll do as you say."

"It's the only hope of being rescued," I said.

The bandaging completed, I stepped aside. Our captors gestured for us to move on. One went ahead, the other kept a short distance behind us.

Judith Milson appealed in a low voice: "Can't you tell us *anything*?"

"It's better for you to just act scared and bewildered when you're being questioned."

Her mouth twisted. "That's not going to need acting. I've never been so frightened in my life."

I didn't feel very sympathetic. I couldn't forget it was her scheming which had created this perilous situation. Most of my concern was for Pat. As we climbed the steep path she was near to me and whispered: "How bad is it?"

"Sticky," I said.

"But not so dreadful now you're with us."

"Nothing I can do right now."

"You walked into this deliberately. You let them take you."

"The less you think about that the better," I said.

"I can't help thinking of it. You might have been killed."

"Had to take a chance."

She glanced at me shrewdly. "An occupational risk?"

"You mustn't know, or guess, anything more about me. There's an ordeal of interrogation ahead."

When we came to the top of the gully we were in thick jungle. Our captors halted us and one of them slashed at some long creepers, joining them to make a rope. We were shackled together, with a double coil round our waists knotted several times. There was about a yard of slack between us. They'd put Judith Milson first, then Lodge, Pat behind him, and myself at the end. It was a clever arrangement. Had I wished to attempt escape I'd have been powerless with a gun at my back.

The narrow track just permitted us to scrape through in single file. Although some clearing had been done, the going was hard and we needed frequent rests. Our captors weren't unreasonable in granting us merciful pauses, but we could have done with more, and several times I heard Judith Milson protest. She gave this up eventually because, as I discovered later, the man who was guiding us merely reached back, grabbed her by the wrist and jerked her forward.

I found consolation in the thought that owing to our slow progress Keefe should be having no difficulty in following. Foolishly, I'd have welcomed some assurance that he was near.

We must have endured about an hour of this jungle travelling, climbing all the time but with the gradient really steep in only a few places. At the end of this hour we were given a longer rest. I soon knew the reason for it, because when we set off again we encountered a wickedly steep ascent, so bad that we had to make full use of branches in hauling ourselves up. Then, suddenly, there was no longer dense greenery in front of us but a bare wall of black rock. It was one of the ridges Keefe and I had seen marked on the map. We traversed it for about three hundred yards, to where there was a split in the rock, forming a miniature pass with steep sides.

We went through into a small valley. The rock, with trees and shrubs at its base formed one side of it, the wall of the jungle the other. In between was a grassy clearing. It was evidently one of the black soil patches; but I didn't think of this immediately. My attention was claimed by the huts. There were about a dozen of them, stoutly built and palm-thatched. They had a camouflaging of creepers and were well spaced out.

Our arrival, heralded by a shrill whistle from the terrorist who'd acted as guide throughout, caused immediate activity. Men seemed to spring up from everywhere and converge upon us. There must have been some thirty of them. The majority were Asiatics, all young and wearing the same uniform as that of our captors. The few others were Europeans, dressed in white. Their features were Slav, mostly bearded, and there was that about them which made me suspect they were seamen. This tied up with my theory of a small submarine in the marine cave. They tended to hang back a little and, though they stared at us with curiosity, there was also a certain detachment, as though our capture—and ultimate fate—was not in any way their business.

As I looked around, taking in all that I could, two men came from one of the smaller huts and with a quiver of excitement I recognised the leader. He'd put on weight since I'd last seen him but he was Sergius Kabanov right enough. There was the same stiffness of the shoulders, rather lurch-ing walk, the same puttyish lumpiness of cheeks, the bristly black eyebrows which had the appearance of being clipped. The man following him was unknown to me, but an arrogant military stiffness betrayed him as German.

The terrorist who'd given the whistling alarm hurried to meet Kabanov. He raised a clenched fist in salute, then half-turned and pointed to us. I could hear his high-pitched, excited explanations and fervently wished I could under-stand the language. They were sufficiently near for me to see Kabanov's black brows come together in a frown. It was obvious he was mightily displeased.

He growled an order, then turned away and lurched back to his hut, followed by the stiff-backed German.

Under escort of half a dozen heavily armed youths we were hustled in the direction of two small huts near the rock ridge. The creeper length stringing us together was removed, but we were not to enjoy complete freedom of limbs. Our hands were efficiently secured behind our backs with thin rope.

We were pushed with unnecessary roughness into one of the huts. The interior was gloomy as there was no window, the place evidently having been built as a store shed and used sometimes for this purpose judging by the empty wooden boxes which, it seemed, were to provide the only note of comfort.

The youths departed, leaving a solitary, sulky-faced sentry who looked in at us and patted his automatic rifle threateningly before starting to prowl just outside the open doorway.

We sat on the boxes and stretched our legs.

Lodge said: "This is a fine how-d'you-do. What happens next?"

"Who was the black-haired bear of a man who glared at us?" Judith Milson asked.

I decided they were questions better left unanswered.

That I should be the first one brought before Kabanov didn't surprise me. Two youthful terrorists escorted me to his hut, prodding me with their rifles on the way. Kabanov was sitting at a table, pen held in stubby, fur-backed fingers, a blank sheet of paper before him. The German stood just behind; a man with closely cropped fair hair and a jaundiced skin. His eyes, a light grey, regarded me with cold appraisal. Kabanov didn't as much as glance up until I demanded: "What the devil's the meaning of all this?"

Kabanov raised his head slowly. He'd certainly thickened a lot since I'd seen him in Moscow. He was more Slav than Asiatic in appearance, although the oblique setting of his heavy-lidded eyes hinted at his origins.

He said, in passably good English: "I ask all the questions." He gave an order. The guards released my wrists and pushed me roughly into a chair.

The interrogation began. Kabanov had a deep voice and a mannerism of jerking his head at the end of each question. He sounded a natural bully.

I answered clearly and, while avoiding hesitation, did my best to convey the impression that I was normally a slow speaker. Once I could get this accepted I'd gain valuable seconds for avoiding traps. I'd mastered my brief so thoroughly that I learned more from him than he did from me. The tenor of his questions was proof he'd seen the papers stolen from us when we were staying with the Milsons.

At first he kept plugging at how I'd reached the island, coming back to the question with every possible variation. Equally doggedly I stuck to my story that I'd hired a native fisherman who hadn't been eager and had driven a hard bargain. He was to come back for me three days from now, making the crossing early in the morning.

From time to time Kabanov made notes, but I suspected this was for psychological effect. Suddenly, while in the act of writing a sentence, he ordered me to stand up. I stared at him blankly, without moving. He'd spoken in German.

He resumed his writing. When the questioning continued, he switched to information about Keefe. The usual repetitions followed, interspersed with new questions. I knew I'd avoided mistakes so far but I didn't let myself drift into a self-confident mood.

Eventually Kabanov grunted at me and turned to the German. In that language he said: "It's a damned foolish blunder. You agree?"

"Most certainly." This was my first intimation that the German understood the questioning. I'd not been able to watch him during it, all my concentration being on Kabanov.

This exchange of views was good hearing; but I was careful not to betray that I understood. I did my best to look puzzled and said: "Am I now permitted to ask what this means?"

Kabanov ignored me. Still speaking German he went on: "You agree those guards have failed to discharge their duties efficiently in two respects? They didn't see this man land. And they wrongly arrested the people to-day."

The German nodded. "They must be put on trial."

Kabanov growled: "We'll take a short cut to the punishment."

The German shrugged his indifference. "As you will." He fingered a small scar at the corner of his mouth. "But what of these others? We can't afford to set them free. As prisoners they'll be a nuisance—and have to be disposed of eventually. There'll be a search for them, too."

Kabanov said: "Their boat must be discovered capsized on the reef—near Okama. There should be a body cast up on an exposed patch of coral. Hold one of them under water until drowning takes place. Then a little battering against the coral after death. Better to use one of the women for this; she won't struggle so much."

"A convincing picture," the German agreed. "An element of waste though. We keep no women here and both look attractive."

"We cannot afford to deviate from the main purpose," Kabanov said gruffly.

"That is appreciated fully," the German answered curtly.

Something like this was no more than I'd expected; but recognising it was forced by expediency didn't diminish the cold-blooded and brutal ruthlessness. It required all my strength of mind to maintain the attitude of a man bewildered and alarmed, to hide my surging anger.

Still ignoring me, Kabanov gave an order to the guards. They jerked me from my chair and tied my hands behind my back once more. Then they pushed me roughly towards the door.

"We've got a wounded man!" I shouted. "At least you can give him some attention."

Kabanov merely waved a hand and I was thrust so violently by one of the guards that I lost my balance and fell outside the doorway. I managed to avoid injury by rolling, but it was painful. Secured as I was, I couldn't get to my feet quickly. My guards stood grinning at my efforts. Then they hustled me back to the prison hut, snatched Lodge, and dragged him away.

"What happened?" Judith Milson demanded. The unsteadiness of her voice betrayed that she was near to panic.

I answered quietly: "A lot of questions."

"And when will we be released?"

"That's one I can't answer."

"But you can tell us something. You know much more than we do."

"Your ignorance is your best protection at the moment," I impressed on her. "It must be obvious you don't know what's going on. Once give them a different idea and you'll be in for a damned unpleasant time."

She gasped.

"And if you want to go on living, stick to the story that Keefe's on Okama."

Her eyes widened. Then she shivered. "I'm desperately afraid," she confessed. "I've never even thought myself a brave woman."

"No harm in appearing frightened," I told her. "That's your best weapon."

This silenced her and I was thankful, having more than enough to occupy my mind. Pat had said nothing; merely come across and perched beside me on a box, leaning against me slightly.

There were two major worries. The first concerned Kabanov's intentions. I'd learnt something of them, but not enough. When were we to be cold-bloodedly exterminated? It had to be under cover of night for Swale's boat to be towed out along the reef and capsized there, with a drowned body flung upon exposed coral where breakers were unlikely to wash it off again. If I was correct in my assumption that a small submarine or some other craft was hidden in the marine cave, the operation could be carried out whenever it suited Kabanov. Otherwise Kabanov would be compelled to wait until Jimmy Prak came across in the lugger. He might, in either case, prefer to make use of the lugger, because she was a safer boat to take near the dangerous reef.

The other serious worry was my fear that Jimmy Prak would put in an appearance before Keefe could get into action. Once Jimmy Prak talked with Kabanov the game was up. He'd know that Keefe wasn't on Okama with Swale. Kabanov would immediately post sentries everywhere. In addition, the rest of us, myself in particular, would be in for a grim time.

I stared moodily at the sunlight through the open door of the hut, and at the shadow of the guard as he passed and repassed. Each crossing was like the dropping of a grain of sand in a large hour-glass.

At last there were steps outside and Lodge was thrust into the hut. I estimated he'd not been with Kabanov for anywhere near so long as I had, which was a good sign. He staggered to a box and slumped on it. The two young terrorists closed in on Judith Milson. She gave a cry of fear.

"Keep your head," I said. "You'll be all right."

She didn't answer. They shoved her out every bit as roughly as they'd treated Lodge and me. I heard her cry out again.

"Damned swine," Lodge muttered.

"How did it go?" I asked him.

"That swarthy bastard fired a lot of questions. Mostly about you and Keefe."

"You didn't let on that Keefe's here?" I asked quietly. There was always a chance the guard outside knew English.

"You don't have to worry about that. I kept my wits about me. I've been questioned before. The Japs got me in the last war."

I expected him to start being inquisitive—naturally; but he didn't. He lowered his head in the familiar way, looking simply dejected. It was an indication he wanted to be left severely alone; but I wasn't giving in to it.

"What brought you here, Lodge?" I asked. "I suppose it was Judith Milson's idea?"

"I should have known better," he murmured. "She always causes trouble."

"She sent a message asking you to make some excuse for returning to Main Island and then to bring her across to join us," I suggested.

"You seem to know it all," he retorted morosely.

"Guesswork," I admitted.

"Well, she sent this letter by Swale, though Challie actually gave it to me." He added reluctantly: "There was an inducement."

"She promised to do something about her husband's report to the company?"

Lodge raised his head for a moment. "You're smart," he said grudgingly. "So bloody smart we're landed in your particular mess right up to our necks." He shuffled round on the box and turned his back to me.

Pat surprised me by saying: "It's no new experience for you to be in a tight corner, is it? How are you making out?"

"I could do with some luck."

"But you're not beaten yet?"

"No, but I'll be easier in mind when all this questioning's over."

"You don't have to worry about me. I know what to say."

"For God's sake don't let it appear you're keeping anything back. You'll be up against a man without scruples or mercy."

She caught her breath. "You mean he wouldn't hesitate to—to—a burning cigarette and that sort of thing."

"That sort of thing," I agreed soberly. I knew that a quiver of apprehension went through her, and added: "Interrogating me was the real business though, and I feel pretty confident I won that round. The questioning of you others is more or less routine, checking on my story where he can."

"But you're anxious about Mother?"

"Uneasy. However, if she comes back fairly soon and they don't pounce on me, it'll be a good sign."

"I'd be scared to death if you weren't here," she whispered, leaning closer.

I didn't answer. I was watching the broad bar of sunlight through the doorway, trying to calculate the passing of time. For time was the important element, everything depending on how long this would last and how long that would be delayed. I'd the fatalistic thought that somewhere ahead lay the climax, the moment of victory or defeat. We were voyagers, travelling towards a point of time, and there was no advancing or retarding it. The image of the hour-glass returned. An hour-glass to eternity, perhaps.

My thoughts were disturbed by a commotion outside and I looked up hopefully. Judith Milson's return would mean that her ordeal had been short, with the chances still favourable. And she it was, but I was immediately apprehensive because of her sobbing.

Instinctively I jumped up. A buffet from one of the guards slumped me heavily back on the box. Then Pat was seized and pushed to the open door. Anger seethed up in me but there was nothing I could do.

As soon as Pat had gone I turned my attention to Judith Milson.

"What happened?" I asked sharply.

"That big brute! He said I was slow with my answers. I couldn't help it. He got me confused. And he started to shout. Then—he—he slapped my face, *hard*!"

"What did you tell him about Keefe?" I demanded.

"I said he's on Okama because Pastor Swale's down with fever."

I breathed more freely. "Then it seems you did very well. I'm sorry he started to get tough."

"I hope he pays for it." Her voice was sultry.

"It's highly probable he will," I said.

Lodge interrupted harshly: "Yellow bastards. I've been in their hands once before." He mumbled something I couldn't catch, then said: "Give me a chance of getting my own back. Just give me a chance."

"Take it easy," I urged. "And we aren't in the hands of the Japs, you know."

"You don't know them!"

He had me worried. I guessed his temperature was soaring, and if it went much higher he'd be completely delirious —which would be a serious complication.

He wasn't too bad yet, though, and lapsed into broody silence.

"When are you going to explain all this?" Judith Milson asked.

"Not until I'm reasonably sure there'll be no more questioning. You've experienced the man getting a bit nasty. Imagine what he'd be like if he suspected you were withholding information."

She became as quiet as Lodge.

I watched the broad bar of sunlight again and tried to persuade myself all was well with Pat, fully aware of the foolishness of trying to reassure myself. This concern over her was nerve-fraying, worse in its effect on me than the responsibility for my part in our ultimate escape. It was an ordeal which didn't last long though. She came in, walking between the guards, her head held high. And some quality about her seemed to restrain them, for they refrained from manhandling her into the hut. She walked straight over to me and whispered: "All's well."

I felt extremely proud of her, and I think that was the moment when I first understood to the full the meaning of togetherness.

After this we were left for about an hour. When the guards returned, one kept us covered while the other freed our hands. We were permitted to drink water, and there was a bowl of rice with some unappetising mess of meat and vegetables. We had to eat with our hands and none of us took much. Lodge refused to touch it.

Afterwards our hands were once again secured and the guards brought four palliasses which they flung down in a corner of the hut, pulling aside some boxes to make space for them. Then they departed and there was only one sentry outside.

I felt the situation was encouraging. It seemed Kabanov was satisfied with my story, also that there was no intention of killing us immediately. Perhaps I was right in assuming he'd wait until Jimmy Prak arrived in Hooley's lugger.

"Are we to be tied up like this all night?" Judith Milson complained. "It's going to be damned uncomfortable—in more ways than one."

"They took my knife when they searched me," Lodge said. "There might have been a chance with that. We'll never untie these knots."

"Oh—that searching! It was an outrage!" Judith Milson exclaimed.

Evidently this had happened while I was making my way down the slope of the gully. I thought maliciously that it was probably the first time Judith Milson had taken no pleasure in a man's hands passing over her body.

But there were more urgent considerations. Lodge's fever seemed to be fluctuating considerably and this seemed to be one of the periods when he was most like his normal self. I needed his help and he'd be of little use when he was delirious. I rose from the box and went across to him.

"If you lie down and roll over with your back to me," I said, "you'll be able to get a grip on the heel of my left sandal."

He stared at me blankly. "What the devil for?"

"It's a special heel. Wrench it off and you'll find a razor blade—single-edged type, so you can hold it without cutting yourself."

"Ingenious," he muttered. "So that's why you've been so confident."

"That and other things. But don't waste time. There's a lot to do."

He obeyed. While he was getting down I instructed Pat to move so that she screened us as much as possible from the door should the sentry glance inside. The fast-fading light was an additional help.

I sat on the box Lodge had vacated, and when I felt his groping fingers on my left sandal I braced myself. There was a wrench which jerked at my ankle.

"It's off," he grunted. And a second or so later he said: "I've found the blade."

I dropped to the hut floor and shuffled back until our hands were touching. The ropes binding our wrists were thin but strong. They went around about half a dozen times and there were intermediate knottings. I kept my wrists as far apart as I could, straining against the rope. Lodge began to cut. It wasn't easy for him but he managed well. The blade only slipped once and he let go of it before it could bite deeply into my flesh. I felt a warm trickle, but it didn't seem serious. One of the coils snapped and I was able to widen the gap between my wrists slightly.

"My fingers are bloody stiff," he complained. "It's a cramping job."

"You're doing fine," I encouraged.

Again there was a snapping of rope and another freeing sensation, tantalising because so limited. But Lodge persisted and at last there was nothing securing me. I licked the small gash and rubbed the angry grooves where the rope had bitten into me.

I released Lodge first, because if we had the ill luck to be discovered and there was a chance of overpowering our guard before he gave the alarm, he would be more useful than the others.

Then I freed Pat, while Lodge did a similar service to Judith Milson, who said thankfully: "Well, that's something. But what happens next? I mean—we just can't walk out, can we?"

"Nothing happens yet," I said. I gathered up the bits of rope and hid them under one of the boxes. I continued: "The best thing will be to lie down. A rest's going to be valuable. Provided your hands aren't too much in evidence the guard won't notice anything wrong if he looks in. But should he come across make certain your hands still appear tied."

Lodge was the first to drop down. He did so with a deep sigh. "My God, I'm weary!"

I was the last, having been to the doorway to check there was nothing suspicion making in the appearance of the others. Then I joined them. Pat rolled near to me, so near I could feel the softness of her hair against my cheek. She said, very softly: "I don't think I'm afraid any longer. It's going to be all right, isn't it?"

"I hope so. There'll be some touch-and-go moments."

She was silent for a minute or so, then, the tip of her nose brushing my ear deliciously, she said: "I want you to tell me something."

"If I can."

"You know what all this is in aid of? You expected to find this gang here?"

"Hoped to find them here. It wasn't a certainty."

"And you knew there was desperate danger? That—that—you might not get away?"

"Yes. Why do you ask?"

She gave a contented sigh. "Just to satisfy myself. I understand now."

"Understand what?"

"You know what," she whispered. Her lips touched my cheek and moved over my skin until our mouths met. Then she pressed harder.

It was dark inside the hut. Now that my arms were free I no longer had to make guesses at the time. They'd not taken my watch and it had a luminous dial. I lay looking at the slowly moving minute hand, and wondered how near Keefe would be. There was noise in the little valley; the lively chattering of voices, occasional singing. I speculated on whether they were songs of indoctrination. With so much racket going on and everybody awake it might be well that Keefe would hold back. On the other hand, he might decide that the obvious preoccupation with the festivity—or whatever it was—could be turned to advantage.

I'd a more immediate worry. Lodge was on the fringe of delirium again, moving restlessly and talking incoherently about the Japs. He seemed to have the fixed idea that he was back in the P.O.W. camp. The lucid intervals were becoming rarer and it looked as though we were in for a lot of trouble with him. We might have to knock him senseless and carry him, which would be the very devil if we were faced with a fighting withdrawal.

Pat was actually sleeping, her body so close that I could feel the movement of her breasts as she breathed. At last, nearing the time arranged with Keefe, I roused her by sliding my hand over one of them and pressing gently.

"What is it?" she murmured drowsily.

"Time for action," I said.

She sat up. Then she bent and kissed me. "Be careful, darling. You frighten me. I don't know what desperate things you're planning."

"The stakes are worth them," I said. "Now listen carefully. I want you to awaken your mother. Make sure that she doesn't cry out—whatever happens. And you must try to soothe Lodge if necessary. A tall order, I'm afraid. There's more to it. You'll have to keep a tight grip."

"You can rely on me," she said.

I squeezed her hand. "It's going to be ugly. First I'll take a peep outside. Then, if all's favourable, I'm going to tackle the guard. Not pleasant to contemplate—but there's only one way of doing it. A quick way."

She shuddered slightly.

"He's a trained terrorist, remember. Dedicated to killing."

"I know. But it's still rather horrible."

"It's also his life or ours. They wouldn't let us go from here, you know."

"I'd guessed as much. I suspected it, and when they took me to that man who asked all the questions I was sure. There's no mercy in his make-up. He's a—a monster."

I kissed her. As I stood up she said quietly: "Come back safely. But if it goes wrong—remember I don't want to live if——"

I put a hand on her shoulder. "It won't go wrong," I promised, and wished I could be as confident as my voice sounded.

I went cautiously to the doorway. So far as I knew the guard had only looked in once. That had been a long time ago and he'd seemed satisfied that we were sleeping. Behind me I heard Pat talking quietly to her mother.

At the doorway I pressed tight against the side of the hut and peered carefully. I couldn't see the guard. Across the valley was the red glow of a fire. Someone threw more wood on it and the flames leapt, high and greedy. There was one standing figure, a man making a speech and waving his arms vigorously. All the others were squatting around. All except three, that is, and I guessed at once they were the men from the outpost who'd failed in their duty. They were dangling by their wrists from a stout branch of a tree, their bodies twitching awkwardly. I guessed they were strung up so that only the tips of their toes were touching the ground. I wondered how long the poor devils had been enduring this, and I guessed they'd had no sympathy from their fellows, only jeers.

The fire was too far away for the speaker's words to carry, too far to identify him. He wasn't Kabanov, of that I could be sure. Looking in the other direction I could see a light shining from a hut and felt certain this was the one where we'd been taken for questioning. So it was likely Kabanov was still there, perhaps patiently sifting all the information he'd obtained from us, searching for some discrepancy. I hoped he wouldn't find one.

I ventured out a little farther, looking for the sentry. He was near the corner of the hut and all his interest seemed concentrated on what was happening around the fire. The mere fact of being debarred from participating because of guard duty would make everything seem the more attractive.

I measured the distance to him, calculated it in cautious steps. My hand had stiffened, ready for the lethal unarmed combat blow, the fatal chop at the right spot on the neck. I wavered between acting at once and waiting, with the risk of increasing doubts and one hesitation leading to another. Then, unwittingly, he helped me. The orator had raised his voice, seeming to give emphasis to an important passage. The man on guard moved forward a step or two, craning his neck in an effort to catch the words. There would be no second opportunity such as this. I tensed and sprang. I was on him before he sensed danger, striking with all the force I could muster, and the jarring blow sickened me. I caught him as he fell and dragged him into the hut. It was all over within seconds, but sweat flooded my forehead and my heart was pounding.

Judith Milson gave a shuddering moan and covered her eyes. Pat was at my side.

"He—he's dead?"

I straightened up. "He's dead." I rushed out to grab the rifle and his cap. When I returned Pat was over the body, removing the bandolier.

"A bit ghoulish," she said, and her voice was shaky.

She was right. I didn't relish stripping the still-warm tunic from the man I'd killed. I goaded myself with the thought of urgency.

The tunic was a bad fit and wouldn't fasten; but it didn't matter at night. Pat helped with the belt and bandolier. I tugged the cap on to my head. Then I stepped into the open, with an anxious look towards the fire. The speaker was still hard at it and all was well. I gave a long sigh of relief. I needed to relax, but couldn't; there were still things to be done.

I called to Pat. "How's Lodge?"

"Much the same. Not moving."

"Up to you, then." A bayonet was dangling from the belt. I passed it to her. "Cut a slit at the back of the hut—big enough for us to get through."

She took the bayonet without a word, and her silence was in itself an indication that I could rely on her. My next act was to tie my handkerchief round my left wrist. This was a sign for Keefe that I'd succeeded in changing places with the sentry. He'd be able to see it before he was near enough to distinguish features.

I started to pace to and fro, alert for anyone approaching. I'd not merely Keefe in mind. There was the possibility of a change of guard. Or of the equivalent of an orderly officer making the rounds. In either of these events my impersonation couldn't survive anything more searching than a casual glance. I wasn't sanguine about the chances of effecting a second killing without raising the alarm.

Once more I was depressed by the realisation of how all hinged upon the element of time. How long before Keefe arrived? Would I be left undisturbed until then?

So far, all was satisfactory apart from Lodge's condition which was a serious threat to our hopes of success. There was more to it than the difficulties of getting a sick man to the boat. Had he been fit I could have entrusted him with the task of going on ahead, taking the two women with him, so that Keefe and I would have greater freedom if it came to a fighting withdrawal. And if we failed they'd still have a start and a chance of survival. But instead of being able to depend on Lodge, he was the weakest of us and likely to be our undoing.

Over at the fire the singing was renewed. I wondered how long the celebration or whatever it was would last. I looked anxiously towards the mountain peak, whose clouds obscured the moon. How much longer would there be of the more favourable near-darkness? There was no escaping this pressure of time.

Pat called softly to me. I mover nearer.

"Captain Lodge seems to feel better," she reported. "He's taken over from me and is working on the back of the hut."

This was unexpected. My doubts were confirmed when I asked: "How much better?" and she replied: "He's stronger, but still a bit queer in the head. I think he believes he's escaping from the Japs. He's muttering about taking Pincher and Chalky along with him and what lousy luck it is poor Snowy being dead, because he could have made a bid for it as well."

It sounded bad. I warned her to be prepared for a sudden collapse. And after this I stood near the doorway in case Lodge should become light-headed and try to wander into the open.

Some ten or fifteen minutes passed, still with no sign of the party round the fire breaking up, still with no indication that Keefe was near. And the light still burned in Kabanov's hut.

"Paul!" This time Pat's call was urgent.

"What is it?" I demanded.

"Captain Lodge! He's gone!"

I didn't wait for any more. I rushed to one corner of the hut and then another, looking about me in all directions. I couldn't see him. It was infuriating that he was somewhere near, that he couldn't have covered much ground yet, and that I daren't go in search because the lengthy absence of a sentry in front of our hut would certainly be noticed.

I returned to the doorway, fuming. I said to Pat: "What happened?"

"He finished the opening at the back of the hut. He turned to me and said he'd push through, just to make sure we could get out easily when the time came. I'm sorry, Paul! It sounded so reasonable that it didn't even occur to me to stop him."

"Of course it wouldn't. And then?"

"When he didn't come back I thought perhaps he'd gone to look upon a hedge—you know?—or had seen somebody and dropped flat until the danger was over. I called, quietly; then I risked peering out. And he'd gone."

I muttered a string of curses. Lodge had thrown everything in jeopardy. The only hope was that in this phantasy of escaping from the Japs, he might act with something of a madman's cunning. What would he do once he was clear, probably convinced he had Chalky and Pincher with him? Go into hiding? Strike deep into jungle, or up the slopes of the mountain? Or would some deep flicker of sanity guide him to the coast and the boat? If so, he'd sail without us, increasing our peril because we'd have to make for the natural jetty first and then be compelled to lose valuable time in skirting the treacherous stretch of sand until we came to where we'd concealed the boat in which Keefe and I had made our crossing.

"How serious is it?" Pat whispered.

"Pretty bloody serious," I said. There was no sense in hiding anything from her; she was capable of working out plenty for herself. I told her to return to the back of the hut and to keep watch through the slit, reporting to me immediately if she spotted Lodge.

Judith Milson asked: "Anything I can do? This waiting's driving me up the wall!" Her voice was sharp, betraying her nerves.

"You can keep a grip on yourself," I said. Then, full of uneasiness, I resumed my monotonous pacing outside the hut.

The next half-hour was one of the longest of my life, a drawn-out mental torture. Each anticipated minute was pregnant with disaster. So much could go wrong and the penalty of failure was all too certain. The three agonised figures suspended from the tree gave grim emphasis to this.

At last Pat called again, and as I came to the doorway there was Keefe's voice.

"Things a bit tight, old chap, eh?"

I could only whisper, from a dry throat: "Thank God you're here."

I couldn't see him. He was keeping well inside the hut. He said: "Spotted the bandage on your wrist. Didn't like the idea of crawling to you, so I made my way round to where your girl was keeping watch."

I didn't challenge the relationship. "She's told you about Lodge?"

"Yes. Tricky. No sign of him since?"

"Not a glimpse."

"Probably well on his way to the boat."

"And no chance he'll wait for us."

"Seen Kabanov over by the fire?" This was typical of Keefe. No crying over spilt milk. Get on with the job.

I answered: "No. Did you spot a hut with a light shining from it?"

"Yes. That's where he is?"

"I think so. We were taken there for questioning. It's likely there's a German officer-type with him."

"So! Chief Instructor, no doubt. Germans are always well up in the dirtier tricks of war. I'd thought of waiting until everything settles down, but this binge may go on all night."

"You've been a hell of a time getting here," I complained.

"Missed the cleft in the rock and had to climb—only discovered it from above. Then it wasn't easy scrambling down. Found myself the wrong end of the camp. I've practically worn my knees out with crawling."

"What's the plan now?" I asked.

He laughed softly. "Officially, I stroll over to Kabanov's quarters and ask him to leave the island with me. And nobody would be more annoyed than the people who gave me the instructions. Kabanov's the last man they want on their hands. I'll go out by the back of this hut and work round there while everybody's happy at the camp fire. I've a silencer fitted to my automatic, so if I'm slick I shouldn't raise merry hell. Then I'll get back here as fast as I can."

"And if there's a slip-up?"

"Sergius and his German pal won't have silencers fitted to their guns. If you hear shooting it's *sauve-qui-peut*, old chap. But I'll have got Kabanov, so clear out as fast as you can. There's no guard on the cleft through the rock ridge. I'll keep up a diversion as long as possible. Don't get the fool idea of trying to help me, because the odds will be impossible. You'll have enough trouble of your own, anyway."

There was no disputing this, so I said nothing.

He went on: "I'll keep your gun. Then if things go wrong I'll be able to put up more resistance."

"Don't shoot Kabanov with the wrong one," I cautioned.

He laughed softly, and sounded carefree. I liked him more at this moment. He was still, I suspected, acting his

209

favourite rôle; but it was a pretty solid performance. And perhaps he'd succeed. He'd pulled off the fantastic more than once in the past.

I moved just into the hut. In the darkness our hands gripped for a second, a silent wishing of luck. As I stepped outside again I heard Judith Milson whispering to him; but she didn't delay him, because there was quickly a slight scuffling and Pat reported: "He's gone."

I said: "I want you both at the back of the hut, ready to dash for it the instant I give the word. Make for the rocks as fast as you can and work along them until you come to the narrow cleft."

"You'll be with us?" she asked sharply.

"Covering the withdrawal," I assured her.

More logs had been cast on the fire, and by the increased light I saw the movement of the long grass as Keefe crept on the long diagonal which would take him to Kabanov's quarters. I traced the line, noting how dangerously near to the fire he'd pass. I guessed he wouldn't make a detour unless it was essential.

I watched his progress until the grass movement was imperceptible. I could no longer hear the dry-paper rustle of it either.

My grip was tight on the rifle. Some of the hazards were behind us now; but I knew that the coming moments were those which would determine everything. The glimmering hope was that the very daring of Keefe's plan would bring success. A lesser man might have waited, and ended by being caught in the betraying light of dawn; but Keefe had selected as his weapons audacity and speed.

There was singing at the camp fire again, and anxiety focused my attention on the figures clustered there, while at the same time I tried to judge Keefe's position in relation to them. And because my gaze was more on Keefe's side of the fire I didn't spot Lodge immediately. When I did it was too late. He must have kept low, crawling painstakingly through the grass, or I should have seen him earlier; but by the time his movements attracted my attention he was rising to his feet. My heart leapt to my throat. He started to run straight for the fire. He was carrying some object, clutching it to him.

There was nothing I could do about Lodge, but Keefe was still this side of the fire, and as soon as the terrorists were aroused he was certain to be spotted. I had to go in and help.

As I raced forward there were shouts and a surge of rising figures. I had a glimpse of Keefe's head and shoulders, then looked at Lodge. He hadn't slackened speed or wavered. My own rush was checked by a flashing consciousness of utter powerlessness. In contrast to my body, my mind was working fast. This, I realised, was the moment in time that I'd dreaded, the moment when the intricate patternings of events in our several lives were to come together in a climax.

There was a sharp burst of firing but Lodge didn't go down. He swerved and then twisted his body in readiness for throwing. I had a flash of foreknowledge, abandoned all caution and shouted to Keefe: "Down! For God's sake—down!" I dropped flat myself as Lodge staggered and flung his burden straight at the fire.

I had a confused impression of more shots and shrill cries of alarm, and then the valley seemed to split open in a fireball flash and an explosion which rumbled and rolled away to the jungle and the rock ridge. There was a great gust rushing over me, bending the grass low. Then a fractional silence and immediately after it a hellish babel of agony and torment. Shaking, I struggled to my feet and stared in petrified horror. There was not one fire now but several, for there were patches of fiercely burning grass. And the merciless light from them showed deathly still figures, and figures bent and writhing, and a few staggering blindly as if groping for safety. The tree of punishment, where the three men had been suspended, was afire, and all that remained of them was a solitary arm, dangling and swaying like a khaki stocking from a clothes-line.

Keefe was safe, scrambling to his feet. And in the same moment I saw the German and Kabanov rushing out from their hut. Keefe fired and the German pitched forward. I charged on as Kabanov started shooting. And Keefe was too slow. Perhaps he was dazed from the blast of the explosion. I saw him slump down slowly. Then I was near enough and my finger tightened on the trigger and released a burst of angry, chattering bullets. Kabanov reeled, spun like a top, and fell.

I reached Keefe's side. He was face downwards and I turned him over gently. There were flames near us and by their light I saw his familiar, fascinating smile. I lowered my head, thinking he was going to speak; but he didn't. The smile stiffened and became a horrible, set grin.

I let Keefe slip to the ground. He'd dropped both automatics and I scooped them up, thrusting them into the pockets of my tunic. Then I went over to Kabanov and made sure he was dead. As I turned, two men came running between the fires. I sent a burst at them. One fell, the other turned and raced away.

Then I, too, took to my heels. There seemed to be fire everywhere in the valley. The night breeze was spreading it fast, so that the flames jumped swiftly in the dry grass. Already two huts were burning.

The one in which we'd been imprisoned and the other near by were the most distant and still safe. As I approached, and the ghastly cries of the dying were left behind, growing fainter, I saw Pat coming to meet me. Judith Milson was leaning limply against the doorway of the hut.

Pat was fighting hard for self-control. She gulped as she tried to speak, then managed to say: "It—it's all over?"

I checked that one of the automatics was loaded and handed it to her. "Take this. We're getting out."

Judith Milson cried: "John! Where's John Keefe?" Her voice was cracked, shrill.

"Died bravely," I said.

There was a moaning deep in her throat and I thought she was going to pass out; but Pat took her firmly by the arm. As we passed the next hut I had a sudden idea and paused. I was right. A gash was cut in it and the bayonet lay in the grass. I pushed inside. The door was open and there was sufficient light for me to see that this was a well-filled store. I searched swiftly and soon discovered a stack of boxes which I judged were similar to that which Lodge had flung into the fire. I carried one to the light and checked the stencilled marking. It was explosive. These, no doubt, were sabotage boxes ready for the use of Kabanov's students when they graduated from his training school. I took the one and also a length of tow. Then I rejoined Pat and her mother.

I wished I could start a fire near the hut, but then I saw it wouldn't be necessary. There was already a flame patch relentlessly advancing.

Pat relieved me of the box temporarily, leaving me free to deal with any attackers, though I felt the risk was slight for the time being. There was too much to occupy the shaken minds of the survivors and no Kabanov to restore order.

The three of us had reached the great ridge of rock and were safely down the narrow cleft when we heard a rumbling explosion from the valley. I hoped it would be assumed we'd perished in it.

Then, in the contrasting death-like silence, we started the arduous journey to the coast.

By the time we dragged ourselves slowly along the rock jetty to Swale's boat we were all near exhaustion. Oddly, Judith Milson had borne up well. Throughout the whole of our flight she'd not spoken a word. She was in a kind of

213

trance. Immediately she was in the boat I told her to lie down and she obeyed, listlessly, without argument.

I unwedged the anchor and then struggled with the recalcitrant engine. At last it came into spluttering, resentful life. We slid smoothly from the rock and anxiety began to lift from me.

"We're safe now?" Pat asked.

Safer, but not entirely safe. There were still two dangers. One, that we might encounter the lugger in our crossing back to Okama, I could do nothing about. The other I'd anticipated and hoped to encounter. I was thinking of organised pursuit and the craft, of whatever type it was, lying in the marine cavern. If many sailors were among the survivors we'd have no chance in a sea chase. Our clumsy, slow-moving, unarmed boat would be an easy prey.

So, in answer to Pat, I said: "There's one more task. Afterwards, we should be all right."

"What can I do?"

"Matches are essential. Are there any in the boat?" I knew that if there weren't I'd have to use up more time in going to the other cave, the smaller one where Keefe and I had concealed our boat. There were matches in it. Those I'd had on my person had been taken when I was searched.

Pat was sure there were some and she quicky found them.

"Good. There's nothing more for the moment."

We passed along the stretch of the quicksands and came to the rock-strewn waters in the region of the great cavern. I had to cut back the speed and proceed with extreme caution, all nerves about hazarding the boat. What made the tension worse was the noisiness of the engine. The big rocks seemed to act as sounding boards and we might have been a dozen boats. Then the big cave yawned black in front of us and I was tempted to go right in and try to solve the mystery. But it was too risky. There might be a boom or other obstruction placed as a precaution against curious voyagers. There could even be somebody aboard whatever craft they used, especially if, as I suspected, it was a submarine.

I cut out the engine and we bobbed and grated alongside the entrance. I worked quickly, fixing my explosive and its tow fuse. There was a rock overhang, a long fault which seemed ideal for my purpose. When I was ready, I climbed up to it and Pat handed me the box, standing in the boat and reaching as high as she could. I managed to get a firm grasp and hauled up the small but heavy box. I placed it in position and laid the tow so that it could burn sheltered from the breeze.

Below me, Pat, who was keeping watch, called softly: "Hurry! I think I saw a light over by the sand."

My fingers were quivering with stress as I struck the match. It seemed a long time before the tow ignited properly, but as soon as I dared I dropped down into the boat.

"I'm sure it was a light," Pat said urgently. "Looked to me like a torch."

I bent over the engine. This time, warmed up, it didn't give trouble. As we moved out along the narrow, deep channel, I turned my head. Pat was right. I saw the flicker of *three* torches. It was pursuit, sure enough, and men were picking their way along some path behind the sands, I supposed.

At any moment they might see us. Perhaps we were out of range, but I wasn't taking any unnecessary risks. I ordered Pat to keep down, and crouched as low as I could myself. There was a welcome movement of the boat as we cleared the rocks and were exposed to the slight swell of the open sea. I altered course and then coaxed the engine into giving us her best speed.

There was no shooting and we saw no more lights. We were right out by the reef, with Okama lying directly ahead, when the last explosion of the night took place. It was followed by prolonged rumbling, as if half the cliff was falling.

Judith Milson sat up with a cry of fear. "What was that?"

"The end of the Dea-Dinda," I said.

She made no reply to this and lay back. I thought she was dozing, but a few minutes later she jerked up again and cried out in anguish: "Why did he have to die? Why?"

Pat went to her. "Try to rest, Mother," she said gently. "Don't think about it now."

The engine took us to safety, well beyond the gap in the reef, and then packed up after a brief attack of spluttering. Pat held a lamp, while I attempted to get the damned thing going again. I succeeded eventually, but we were not able to make more than half speed and it was dawn when we reached the harbour, passed the anchored lugger, and arrived at the landing stage. One man stood watching us come in. I recognised a powerfully built body immediately. It was Sergeant Ilala.

And it was Sergeant Ilala, I learned later, who had probably saved us from absolute failure by preventing Jimmy Prak from sailing, undoubtedly for La Caverne, early the previous night. It had come about because the papers which had been stolen from us were discovered in the bushes near Milson's bungalow on Main Island. The news was no surprise; we'd expected they'd be dumped after scrutiny. It was possible Jimmy Prak had planted them on the occasion when I'd watched him near the bungalow, and this would explain why he'd not told Hooley where he'd been. While Hooley certainly had suspicions about Jimmy Prak's activities, it was obvious he was never given gratuitous information.

Sergeant Ilala saw it as his duty to return the papers to their rightful owners without delay. Milson's launch was serviceable again and the sergeant sought permission to use it for a quick run to Okama and back, fully expecting a long wrangle. But Milson seemed preoccupied with other matters, and instead of raising objections gave brusque permission and detailed two members of the now idle crew of the schooner to make the trip.

When the sergeant came to Okama he was met with the news that Challie's body had been discovered. He sent the launch back and settled down to this fresh investigation. He recognised the knife as partner to the one which had been thrown at me, and by the end of the day had unearthed the information that Challie and Jimmy Prak both possessed knives of this pattern. While Hooley was drinking with Chang Yu, Jimmy Prak, on his way to the lugger, was arrested for Challie's murder.

I couldn't leave it at that. I had to explain Challie's death, just as I was forced to tell with reservations a great deal more. The magnitude of events had destroyed secrecy. I'd some misgivings at the start, but Sergeant Ilala justified my high opinion of him. He had limitations, but they were offset by a very shrewd native intelligence.

When I stopped talking he stroked his chin with a massive hand and said: "There has been funny business going on for some time, sir. But there was never enough in the whispering for me to do anything. This Challie and Jimmy Prak very bad men. But I cannot arrest a man because I think him bad. And now that I know how Challie was killed I have to let Jimmy Prak go—which is a sad thing."

"It might be worth holding him a bit longer," I said, and told him our suspicions about the robberies from the store on Main Island.

He cheered up considerably. "Perhaps that is why Mr. Milson looks worried. He may have discovered what is going on. And now I know why I was told a silly story about somebody stealing from the lugger and Mr. Hooley's bungalow. It was to get me out of the way for when such things were happening." A gleam came into his eyes which promised plenty of trouble for Hooley, Jimmy Prak, and a few other people.

. This talk with Sergeant Ilala, which took place at Chang Yu's hotel, lasted a long time. At the end I was satisfied with the way it had gone and very pleased that the sergeant, for all his tough appearance, had a broad streak of kindness. He would want to question Pat and her mother; but he was perfectly willing to postpone this until they'd recovered somewhat from their ordeal. There would be a lot of business ahead, he warned me. He would have to take statements and everything must be referred to the assistant district officer, Mr. Trubshaw. I assured him he would have his statements and he departed happily, especially as he could continue to hold Jimmy Prak, who was at present under guard in a village hut.

"I will tell him," he announced, "that other charges will be brought against him. He is going to be most unhappy—which is what should happen to bad men."

I was unutterably tired after all this, and rested for a while. I thought of seeing Swale, who was making good progress though still confined to his room; but I decided to leave it until the next day.

I'd fixed up accommodation in the Annexe for Pat and her mother. Judith Milson didn't emerge from her room. Food was taken to her, but she ate very little. Pat, looking wonderfully refreshed, though her eyes were still shadowed with tragedy, joined me for dinner. It was a rather silent meal, both of us feeling a constraint. We talked later, sitting on the verandah, and I filled in her knowledge by telling her things I'd previously kept back from her.

"So that's it," I finished. "Victory, I suppose, but at a cost which emphasises the narrowness of the margin between it and defeat. Although the odds were so heavy against us, things should have gone better. It was poor old Lodge who altered everything. It started, I suppose, with the burning of the schooner, which seemed absolutely unrelated to the

affairs of Keefe and myself. That resulted in Lodge being
with us. And then, because of the letter your mother sent
him, he brought you to La Caverne—and from the moment
of his arrival there events were forced on us."

She was silent for a few minutes. Then she said: "I
wonder why he did it. Killing himself and so many others,
I mean. He must have known it was suicidal. Or was he
completely out of his mind?"

"We can never know the truth," I said. "But what I think
is this. . . . When he slipped away from our hut he imagined
himself back in the Jap P.O.W. camp. He was about to
escape and he was going to take two of his friends—Chalky
and Pincher—with him. He must have thought they were
in the next hut. But they weren't, and when he looked out
towards the fire he believed he was seeing the hated Japs
celebrating. He also saw those poor devils suspended from
the branch of the tree. He jumped to the conclusion they
were Pincher and Chalky and some other fellow, and that
they'd been tortured. Can you imagine his blind rage? He'd
already discovered the boxes of explosive and he had the
mad urge to destroy all the damned Japs, to blow them to
hell. I doubt if he even considered his own survival. And
it's quite a thought, assuming I'm right, that if Kabanov
hadn't inflicted a cruel punishment on the three sentries
who'd failed in their duty it would never have happened."

"But because it did, John Keefe had to die."

"Yes. He should have been all right when the German
and Kabanov came at him, but his reactions were a bit slow.
I think he was dazed by the blast."

There was a long pause. At last Pat said: "He wouldn't
have been serious with Mother? I mean, he was amusing
himself, wasn't he? He'd have left her?"

"He'd have left her," I said gently.

"But she'll never believe that. She'll keep him in her
heart as the hero who died, and she'll secretly cherish the
idea that he died in trying to save her."

"And what will she do?"

"Go back to Main Island. Go on living the same frustrated life, enduring a husband she no longer loves—whom she never did love properly, anyway."

"How much does he suspect?"

"Everything, I think. He knows she's unfaithful. He said as much. There was another of those rows when she announced that Captain Lodge had returned to take us to Okama."

"I wonder he allowed it."

"She was ready for him. You see, she was keeping something back for use at the right moment. A while ago she'd taken it into her head to collect something from the store instead of asking Kim Lee to bring it to her. He wasn't around, so she looked for herself and made the discovery that stacks of stuff was missing. She came away quickly and said nothing.

"Well, she cut Dad's anger clean off by telling him he was being robbed and was too inefficient to realise it. He stared at her with his mouth open. She accused Kim Lee and said there must be some cooking of the books going on. His face was awful—grey-white. He rushed out of the bungalow without another word. I think he locked himself in his office. We packed, and went down to the jetty to board Pastor Swale's boat and we saw nothing more of Dad."

I whistled softly. "So there's been hell to pay on Main Island."

"I imagine so."

This time the pause was longer. Then Pat said quietly: "And what do you do now?"

"There's plenty of trouble ahead. Official statements and clearing everything up."

"I suppose so," she said flatly.

"But more immediately I want a talk with Swale. I believe he's sufficiently recovered to see visitors. I wasn't equal to it to-day." I hesitated, then added: "I'm not sure I like the chap a lot, but it doesn't do to be fussy when there's only one pastor available."

I heard her catch her breath. Her chair scraped slightly as she jumped up. But I was quick, too. I caught her and as I drew her close to me I could tell she was trembling. Then, through her lips, the trembling passed to me and when she said softly: "To-morrow seems so far away," I couldn't reply. I wasn't aware of physical movement, but we were at the door of my room and the verandah behind us was empty except for the unoccupied chairs and the shadows of the palms. Or was it completely empty? Perhaps it was only the night breeze, or some larger wave rushing against the reef, but I could have sworn I heard Keefe's muffled laughter.

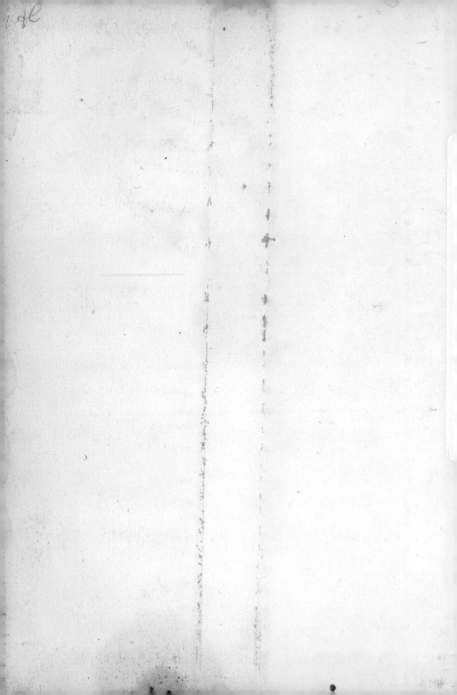